"His most harrowing medical horror story."
—The New York Times

Basis for the NBC-TV film *Virus*

OUTBREAK

Murder and intrigue reach epidemic proportions when a devastating plague sweeps the country. Dr. Marissa Blumenthal of the Atlanta Centers for Disease Control investigates—and soon discovers the medical world's deadliest secret . . .

"Horrifying, timely, unsettling . . . Cook is a master."
—Charleston Evening Post

DR. ROBIN COOK, a graduate of Columbia Medical School, finished his postgraduate medical training at Harvard. He is the author of numerous bestselling novels.

continued . . .

More praise for

OUTBREAK

"JUST WHEN YOU THOUGHT IT WAS SAFE TO GO BACK INTO THE HOSPITAL, ROBIN COOK STRIKES AGAIN." —*Richmond Times-Dispatch*

"CHILLING SUSPENSE . . . AS GOOD AS, OR EVEN BETTER THAN, HIS BOOK *COMA* . . . Will keep the reader on the edge of his easy chair." —*The Sunday Oklahoman*

"A FAST READ." —*New York Daily News*

"A CONTAGIOUS SUCCESS . . . DIFFICULT TO PUT DOWN . . . Cook, who is also a surgeon, has a writing style that is as clean, quick, and precise as the sweep of his scalpel . . . TRULY ENJOYABLE . . . CATCH IT."

—The Associated Press

"READERS WILL ENJOY THIS FAST-PACED NOVEL about a subject everyone seems concerned about today: a fast-spreading disease for which there is no cure."

—*The Wichita Falls Times*

"ROBIN COOK'S FLAIR FOR SPOOKY MEDICAL SITUATIONS IS HERE IN FULL FORCE." —*Kirkus Reviews*

"*OUTBREAK* MANAGES TO GRIP . . . The things that Robin Cook did well in *Coma* are all at work [here]."

—*The Washington Post*

"STARTS OFF WITH A BANG, THE ACTION NEVER FLAGS." —*Marlborough Enterprise/Hudson Daily Sun*

"HIS MOST TIMELY NOVEL OF MEDICAL HORROR SINCE *COMA*." —*Mystery News*

"INTRIGUING . . . A HIGHLY IMAGINATIVE TALE."

—*The Indianapolis News*

"ONE OF HIS BEST . . . A medical thriller that seems only a step away from current realities. Cook's knowledge of medicine and his dynamic style make his works exciting and fast-paced . . . Read *Outbreak* and enjoy. Caution: You could become addicted to Cook's easy reading style."

—*Times Herald-Record*

"FASCINATING . . . HORRIFYING . . . There are enough merciless fiends, chilly moments and hairbreadth escapes to please Cook's fans." —*San Diego Tribune*

"A SUSPENSE CHILLER OF GREAT DELIGHT."

—*The Nashville Banner*

"KEEPS YOU FLIPPING THE PAGES." —*The Desert Sun*

TITLES BY ROBIN COOK

Death Benefit
Cure
Intervention
Foreign Body
Critical
Crisis
Marker
Seizure
Shock
Abduction
Vector
Toxin
Invasion
Chromosome 6
Contagion
Acceptable Risk
Fatal Cure
Terminal
Blindsight
Vital Signs
Harmful Intent
Mutation
Mortal Fear
Outbreak
Mindbend
Godplayer
Fever
Brain
Sphinx
Coma
The Year of the Intern

ROBIN COOK

OUTBREAK

BERKLEY BOOKS, NEW YORK

THE BERKLEY PUBLISHING GROUP
Published by the Penguin Group
Penguin Group (USA) Inc.
375 Hudson Street, New York, New York 10014, USA
Penguin Group (Canada), 90 Eglinton Avenue East, Suite 700, Toronto, Ontario M4P 2Y3, Canada
(a division of Pearson Penguin Canada Inc.)
Penguin Books Ltd., 80 Strand, London WC2R 0RL, England
Penguin Group Ireland, 25 St. Stephen's Green, Dublin 2, Ireland (a division of Penguin Books Ltd.)
Penguin Group (Australia), 250 Camberwell Road, Camberwell, Victoria 3124, Australia
(a division of Pearson Australia Group Pty. Ltd.)
Penguin Books India Pvt. Ltd., 11 Community Centre, Panchsheel Park, New Delhi—110 017, India
Penguin Group (NZ), 67 Apollo Drive, Rosedale, North Shore 0632, New Zealand
(a division of Pearson New Zealand Ltd.)
Penguin Books (South Africa) (Pty.) Ltd., 24 Sturdee Avenue, Rosebank, Johannesburg 2196,
South Africa

Penguin Books Ltd., Registered Offices: 80 Strand, London WC2R 0RL, England

OUTBREAK

A Berkley Book / published by arrangement with G. P. Putnam's Sons

PRINTING HISTORY
G. P. Putnam's Sons edition / January 1987
Berkley edition / February 1988

For information, address: The Berkley Publishing Group,
a division of Penguin Group (USA) Inc.,
375 Hudson Street, New York, New York 10014.

ISBN: 978-0-425-10687-7

BERKLEY®
Berkley Books are published by The Berkley Publishing Group,
a division of Penguin Group (USA) Inc.,
375 Hudson Street, New York, New York 10014.
BERKLEY® is a registered trademark of Penguin Group (USA) Inc.
The "B" design is a trademark of Penguin Group (USA) Inc.

PRINTED IN THE UNITED STATES OF AMERICA

55 54 53 52 51 50

For my mother, Audrey, who ultimately is responsible for all this.

Prologue

Zaire, Africa
September 7, 1976

A TWENTY-ONE-YEAR-OLD Yale biology student by the name of John Nordyke woke up at dawn at the edge of a village north of Bumba, Zaire. Rolling over in his sweat-drenched sleeping bag, he stared out through the mesh flap of his nylon mountain tent, hearing the sounds of the tropical rain forest mixed with the noises of the awakening village. A slight breeze brought the warm, pungent odor of cow dung permeated with the acrid aroma of cooking fires. High above him he caught glimpses of monkeys skittering through the lush vegetation that shielded the sky from his view.

He had slept fitfully, and as he pulled himself upright, he was unsteady and weak. He felt distinctly worse than he had the night before, when he'd been hit by chills and fever an hour or so after dinner. He guessed he had malaria even though he'd been careful to take his chloroquine phosphate as prophylaxis against it. The problem was that it had been impossible to avoid the clouds of mosquitoes that emanated each evening from the hidden pools in the swampy jungle.

With a hesitant gait, he made his way into the village and inquired about the nearest clinic. An itinerant priest told him that there was a Belgian mission hospital in Yambuku, a small town located a few kilometers to the east. Sick and frightened, John quickly broke camp, stuffed his tent and sleeping bag into his backpack and set out for Yambuku.

John had taken a six-month leave from college to photograph African animals, such as the highland gorilla, which were threatened by extinction. It had been his boyhood dream to emulate the famous nineteenth-century explorers who had originally opened the Dark Continent.

Yambuku was scarcely larger than the village he'd just left, and the mission hospital did not inspire confidence. It was no more than a meager collection of cinder-block buildings, all in dire need of repair. The roofs were either rusting corrugated metal or thatched like the native huts, and there seemed no signs of electricity.

After checking in with a nun, swathed in traditional attire, who spoke only French, John was sent to wait among a throng of natives in all states of debility and disease. Looking at the other patients, he wondered if he wasn't likely to catch something worse than what he already had. Finally he was seen by a harried Belgian doctor who could speak a little English, though not much. The examination was rapid, and as John had already surmised, the diagnosis was a "touch" of malaria. The doctor ordered an injection of chloroquine and advised John to return if he didn't feel better within the next day or so.

The examination over, John was sent into the treatment room to wait in line for his injection. It was at that point that he noticed the lack of aseptic technique. The nurse did not have disposable needles but merely rotated one of three syringes. John was certain that their short stay in the sterilizing solution was not nearly long enough to render them germ-free. Besides, the nurse fished them out of the fluid with her fingers. When it became his turn, he was tempted to say something, but his French was not fluent enough, and he knew he needed the medicine.

During the next few days, John was glad that he'd been silent since he soon was feeling better. He stayed in the Yambuku area, occupying himself by photographing the Budza tribesmen. They were avid hunters and eager to demonstrate their prowess to the blond foreigner. By the third day John was preparing to recommence his journey up the Zaire River, following Henry Stanley's footsteps, when his health took a rapid turn for the worse. The first thing he noticed was a violent headache, followed in rapid succession by chills, fever, nausea and diarrhea. Hoping it would pass, he took to his tent and shivered through the night, dreaming of home with clean sheets and a bathroom down the hall. By morning he felt weak and dehydrated, having vomited several times in the darkness. With great difficulty, he got his things together and made his way slowly to the mission hospital. When he arrived in the compound, he vomited bright red blood and collapsed on the clinic floor.

An hour later he woke in a room occupied by two other patients, both suffering from drug-resistant malaria.

The doctor, the same man who'd examined John on

his previous visit, was alarmed by the severity of John's condition and noted some curious additional symptoms: a strange rash over his chest and small surface hemorrhages in his eyes. Although the doctor's diagnosis was still malaria, he was troubled. It was not a typical case. As an added precaution, he decided to include a course of chloramphenicol in case the boy had typhoid fever.

September 16, 1976

Dr. Lugasa, District Health Commissioner for the Bumba region, glanced out the open window of his office at the expanse of the Zaire River as it shimmered in the morning sunlight. He wished it was still called the Congo with all the mystery and excitement that name invoked. Then, forcing his mind back to work, he looked again at the letter he'd just received from the Yambuku Mission Hospital concerning the deaths of an American male, one John Nordyke, and of a visiting farmer from a plantation near the Ebola River. The mission doctor claimed that their deaths had been caused by an unknown infection that spread rapidly; two patients housed with the American, four members of the planter's household who'd been caring for the farmer, and ten of the clinic's outpatients had come down with severe cases of the same illness.

Dr. Lugasa knew that he had two choices. First, he could do nothing, which was undoubtedly the wisest choice. God knew what kind of rampant endemic diseases there were out there in the bush. His second option was to fill out the bewildering array of official forms reporting the incident to Kinshasa where someone like himself, but higher on the bureaucratic ladder, would probably decide it was prudent to do nothing. Of course Dr. Lugasa knew that if he elected to fill out the forms, he would then be obligated to journey up to Yambuku, an idea that was particularly odious to him at that particularly damp, hot time of year.

With a twinge of guilt, Dr. Lugasa let the onionskin letter slip into the wastebasket.

September 23, 1976

A week later Dr. Lugasa was nervously shifting his weight from one foot to the other as he watched the aged DC-3 aircraft land at the Bumba airport. First out was Dr. Bouchard, Dr. Lugasa's superior from Kinshasa. The day before, Dr. Lugasa had telephoned Dr. Bouchard to inform him that he'd just received word that a serious outbreak of an unknown disease was in progress in the area around the Yambuku Mission Hospital. It was affecting not only the local inhabitants, but the hospital staff as well. He had not mentioned the letter he'd received some seven days before.

The two doctors greeted each other on the tarmac and then climbed into Dr. Lugasa's Toyota Corolla. Dr. Bouchard asked if there was any more news from Yambuku. Dr. Lugasa cleared his throat, still upset about what he'd learned that morning from the wireless. Apparently eleven of the medical staff of seventeen were already dead, along with one hundred and fourteen villagers. The hospital was closed since there was no one well enough to run it.

Dr. Bouchard decided that the entire Bumba region had to be quarantined. He quickly made the necessary calls to Kinshasa and then told the reluctant Dr. Lugasa to arrange transportation for the next morning so they could visit Yambuku and assess the situation firsthand.

September 24, 1976

The following day when the two doctors pulled into the deserted courtyard of the Yambuku Mission Hospital they were greeted by an eerie stillness. A rat scampered along the balustrade of an empty porch, and a putrid odor assaulted their senses. Holding cotton handkerchiefs over their noses, they reluctantly got out of the Land Rover and gingerly looked into the nearest building. It contained two corpses, both beginning to decay in the heat. It wasn't until they'd peered into the third building that they found someone still alive, a nurse delirious with fever. The doctors went into the deserted operating room and put on gloves, gowns and masks in a belated attempt to protect themselves. Still fearful for their own health, they tended to the sick nurse and then searched for more of the staff. Among nearly thirty dead, they found four other patients barely clinging to life.

Dr. Bouchard radioed Kinshasa and requested emergency aid from the Zairean Air Force to airlift several patients from the mission hospital back to the capital. But by the time the infectious disease department at the university hospital was consulted about how to isolate the patients during transport, only the nurse still lived. Isolation techniques would have to be excellent, Bouchard pointed out, because they were obviously dealing with a highly contagious and very deadly disease.

September 30, 1976

The Belgian nurse airlifted to Kinshasa died at 3:00 A.M. despite six days of massive supportive therapy. No diagnosis was made, but after the autopsy, samples of her blood, liver, spleen and brain were sent to the Institut de Médicine Tropical in Antwerp, Belgium; to the Centers for Disease Control in Atlanta, U.S.A.; and to the Microbiological Research Establishment in Porton Down, England. In the Yambuku area there were now two hundred ninety-four known cases of the illness, with a fatality rate of approximately ninety percent.

October 13, 1976

The Yambuku virus was isolated almost simultaneously at the three international laboratories. It was noted to be structurally similar to the Marburg virus, first seen in 1967 in a fatal outbreak in laboratory workers handling green monkeys from Uganda. The new virus, considerably more virulent than Marburg, was named Ebola after the Ebola River north of Bumba. It was thought to be the most deadly microorganism seen since the bubonic plague.

November 16, 1976

Two months after the initial outbreak, the unknown disease in Yambuku was considered successfully contained since no new cases had been reported in the area for several weeks.

December 3, 1976

The quarantine of the Bumba region was lifted and air service reinstated. The Ebola virus had evidently returned to its original source. Where that source was remained a complete mystery. An international team of professionals, including Dr. Cyrill Dubchek of the Centers for Disease Control who had played a big role in localizing the Lassa Fever virus, had scoured the area, searching for a reservoir for the Ebola virus within mammals, birds, and insects. The virologists had no success whatsoever. Not even a clue.

Los Angeles, California
January 14
Present Day

Dr. Rudolph Richter, a tall, dignified ophthalmologist originally from West Germany, and cofounder of the Richter Clinic in Los Angeles, adjusted his glasses and looked over the advertising proofs laid out on the circular table in the clinic's conference room. To his right was his brother and partner, William, a business-school graduate, who was examining the proofs with equal attention. The material was for the next quarter's drive for new prepaid subscribers to the clinic's health-care plan. It was aimed at young people, who as a group were relatively healthy. That was where the real money was in the prepaid health-care business, William had been quick to point out.

Rudolph liked the proofs. It was the first good thing that had happened to him that day. It was a day that had begun badly with a fender-bender on the entrance to the San Diego freeway, resulting in a nasty dent in his new BMW. Then there was the emergency surgery that had backed up the clinic. Then there was the tragic AIDS patient with some weird complication who'd coughed in his face while he tried to examine the man's retinas. And on top of everything else, he'd been bitten by one of the monkeys used in his ocular herpes project. What a day!

Rudolph picked up an ad scheduled for the L.A. *Times Sunday Magazine*. It was perfect. He nodded at William, who motioned for the ad man to continue. The next part of the presentation was a slick thirty-second TV spot slotted for the evening news. It portrayed carefree bikini-clad girls on a Malibu beach, playing volley ball with some handsome young men. It reminded Rudolph of an expensive Pepsi ad, though it extolled the concept of prepaid health maintenance as delivered by an organization like the Richter Clinic in contrast to conventional fee-for-service medicine.

Along with Rudolph and William were a handful of other staff doctors, including Dr. Navarre, Chief of Medicine. They were all directors of the clinic and held small amounts of stock.

William cleared his throat and asked if there were any questions from the staff. There were none. After the advertising people had departed, the group voiced unanimous approval of what had been presented. Then, after a brief discussion about the construction of a new satellite clinic to deal with the increase in subscribers from the Newport Beach area, the meeting was adjourned.

Dr. Richter returned to his office and cheerfully tossed the advertising proofs into his briefcase. It was a sumptuous room, considering the relatively low professional salary he drew as a physician in the group. But his salary was just incidental remuneration compared to the profits from his percentage of the outstanding stock. Both the Richter Clinic and Dr. Rudolph Richter were in sound financial shape.

After catching up on his calls, Dr. Richter made rounds on his own postoperative inpatients: two retinal detachments with difficult medical histories. Both were doing well. On his way back to his office, he thought about how little surgery he was doing as the sole ophthalmologist of the clinic. It was disturbing, but with all the ophthalmologists in town, he was lucky to have what he did. He was thankful that his brother had talked him into the clinic idea eight years ago.

Changing his white coat for a blue blazer and picking up his briefcase, Dr. Richter left the clinic. It was after 9:00 P.M., and the two-tiered parking garage was almost empty. During the day it was always full, and William was already talking about the need to expand it, not only for the spaces but for the depreciation; issues like that Rudolph didn't truly understand, nor did he want to.

Musing about the economics of the clinic, Dr. Richter

was unaware of two men who had been waiting in the shadows of the garage. He remained unaware even after they fell in step behind him. The men were dressed in dark business suits. The taller of the two had an arm that seemed permanently frozen into a flexed position. In his hand was a fat briefcase that he held high due to the immobility of the elbow joint.

Nearing his car, Dr. Richter sensed the footsteps behind him as they quickened in pace. An uncomfortable sensation gripped his throat. He swallowed hard and cast a nervous glance over his shoulder. He caught sight of the two men, who seemed to be coming directly toward him. As they passed beneath an overhead light, Dr. Richter could appreciate that they were carefully dressed, with fresh shirts and silk ties. That made him feel a little better. Even so, he moved more quickly, rounding the back end of his car. Fumbling for the keys, he unlocked the driver's-side door, tossed in his briefcase, and slid into the welcome smell of coach leather. He started to close the door, when a hand stopped him. Dr. Richter reluctantly raised his eyes to what turned out to be the calm, blank face of one of the men who had followed him. The suggestion of a smile crossed the man's countenance as Dr. Richter looked at him inquiringly.

Dr. Richter tried again to pull his door shut, but the man held it firmly from the outside.

"Could you tell me the time, doctor?" asked the man politely.

"Certainly," said Richter, glad to have a safe explanation for the man's presence. He glanced at his watch, but before he had a chance to speak, he felt himself rudely pulled from the car. He made a half-hearted effort to struggle, but he was quickly overwhelmed and stunned by an open-handed blow to the side of his face that knocked him to the ground. Hands roughly searched for his wallet, and he heard fabric tear. One of the men said "businessman," in what sounded like a disparaging tone, while the other said, "Get the briefcase." Dr. Richter felt his watch yanked from his wrist.

It was over as quickly as it had begun. Dr. Richter heard footsteps recede and a car door slam, then the screech of tires on the smooth concrete. For a few moments he lay without moving, glad to be alive. He found his glasses and put them on, noting that the left lens was cracked. As a surgeon, his primary concern was for his hands; they were the first thing he checked, even before he picked himself up off the ground. Getting to his feet, he began to examine the rest of himself. His white shirt and his tie were smeared with grease. A button was missing from the front of his blazer, and in its place was a small horseshoe-shaped tear. His pants were torn from the right front pocket all the way down to his knee.

"God, what a day!" he voiced to himself, thinking that being mugged made the morning's fender-bender seem trivial by comparison. After a moment's hesitation, he recovered his keys and returned to the clinic, going back to his office. He called security, then debated whether to call the L.A. police. The idea of bad publicity for the clinic made him hesitate, and really, what would the police have done? While he argued with himself, he called his wife to explain that he'd be a little later than expected. Then he went into the lavatory to examine his face in the mirror. There was an abrasion over the right cheekbone that was sprinkled with bits of parking-garage grit. As he gingerly blotted it with antiseptic, he tried to estimate how much he had contributed to the muggers' welfare. He guessed he'd had about a hundred dollars in his wallet as well as all his credit cards and identification, including his California medical license. But it was the watch that he most hated to lose; it had been a gift from his wife. Well, he could replace it, he thought, as he heard a knock on his outer door.

The security man was fawningly apologetic, saying that such a problem had never happened before, and that he wished he'd been in the area. He told Dr. Richter that he'd been through the garage only a half-hour before, on his normal rounds. Dr. Richter assured the man that he was not to blame and that his, Richter's, only concern was that steps be taken to make certain that such an incident did not reoccur. The doctor then explained his reasons for not calling the police.

The following day, Dr. Richter did not feel well but he attributed the symptoms to shock and the fact that he'd slept poorly. By five-thirty, though, he felt ill enough to consider canceling a rendezvous he had with his mistress, a secretary in the medical records department. In the end, he went to her apartment but left early to get some rest, only to spend the night tossing restlessly in his bed.

The next day, Dr. Richter was really ill. When he stood up from the slit lamp, he was light-headed and dizzy. He tried not to think about the monkey bite or being coughed on by the AIDS patient. He was well aware that AIDS was not transmitted by such casual contact: it was the undiagnosed superinfection that worried him. By three-thirty he had a chill and the beginnings of a headache of migraine intensity. Thinking he had developed a fever, he canceled the rest of the afternoon's appointments and left the clinic. By then he was quite certain he had the flu. When he arrived home, his wife took one look at his pale face and red-rimmed eyes, and sent him to bed. By eight o'clock, his headache was so bad that he took a Percodan. By nine, he had violent stomach cramps and diarrhea. His wife wanted to call Dr. Navarre, but Dr. Richter told her that she was being an alarmist and that he'd be fine. He took some Dalmane and fell asleep. At four o'clock he woke up and dragged himself into the bathroom, where he vomited blood. His terrified wife left him long enough to call an ambulance to take him to the clinic. He did not complain. He didn't have the strength to complain. He knew that he was sicker than he'd ever been in his life.

1

January 20

SOMETHING DISTURBED MARISSA Blumenthal. Whether the stimulus came from within her own mind, or from some minor external change, she did not know. Nonetheless her concentration was broken. As she raised her eyes from the book in her lap she realized that the light outside the window had changed from its pale wintery white to inky blackness. She glanced at her watch. No wonder. It was nearly seven.

"Holy Toledo," muttered Marissa, using one of her expressions left over from childhood. She stood up quickly and felt momentarily dizzy. She had been sprawled out on two low slung vinyl-covered chairs in a corner of the library of the Centers for Disease Control (CDC) in Atlanta for more hours than she cared to think about. She had made a date for that evening and had planned on being home by six-thirty to get ready.

Hefting Fields' ponderous *Virology* textbook, she made her way over to the reserve shelf, stretching her cramped leg muscles en route. She'd run that morning, but had only put in two miles, not her usual four.

"Need help getting that monster on the shelf?" teased

Mrs. Campbell, the motherly librarian, buttoning her omnipresent gray cardigan. It was none too warm in the library.

As in all good humor, there was some basis in truth for Mrs. Campbell's whispered comment. The virology textbook weighed ten pounds—one-tenth as much as Marissa's hundred-pound frame. She was only five feet tall, although when people asked, she said she was five-two, though that was only in heels. To return the book, she had to swing it back and then almost toss it into place.

"The kind of help I need with this book," said Marissa, "is to get the contents into my brain."

Mrs. Campbell laughed in her subdued fashion. She was a warm, friendly person, like most everyone at CDC. As far as Marissa was concerned, the organization had more the feeling of an academic institution than a federal agency, which it had officially become in 1973. There was a pervading atmosphere of dedication and commitment. Although the secretaries and maintenance personnel left at four-thirty, the professional staff invariably stayed on, often working into the wee hours of the morning. People believed in what they were doing.

Marissa walked out of the library, which was hopelessly inadequate in terms of space. Half the Center's books and periodicals were stored haphazardly in rooms all over the complex. In that sense the CDC was very much a federally regulated health agency, forced to scrounge for funding in an atmosphere of budget cutting. Marissa noted it also *looked* like a federal agency. The hall was painted a drab, institutional green, and the floor was covered in a gray vinyl that had been worn thin down the middle. By the elevator was the inevitable photograph of a smiling Ronald Reagan. Just beneath the picture someone had irreverently tacked up an index card that said: "If you don't like this year's appropriation, just wait until next year!"

Marissa took the stairs up one flight. Her office—it was generous to call it that; it was more cubbyhole than office—was on the floor above the library. It was a windowless storage area that might have been a broom closet at one time. The walls were painted cinder block, and there was just enough room for a metal desk, file cabinet, light and swivel chair. But she was lucky to have it. Competition for space at the Center was intense.

Yet despite the handicaps, Marissa was well aware that the CDC worked. It had delivered phenomenal medical service over the years, not only in the U.S., but in foreign countries as well. She remembered vividly how the Center had solved the Legionnaires Disease mystery a number of years back. There had been hundreds of such cases since the organization had been started in 1942 as the Office of Malaria Control to wipe out that disease in the American South. In 1946 it had been renamed the Communicable Disease Center, with separate labs set up for bacteria, fungi, parasites, viruses and rickettsiae. The following year a lab was added for zoonoses, diseases that are animal ailments but that can be transmitted to man, like plague, rabies and anthrax. In 1970 the organization was renamed again, this time the Centers for Disease Control.

As Marissa arranged some articles in her government-issue briefcase, she thought about the past successes of the CDC, knowing that its history had been one of the prime reasons for her considering coming to the Center. After completing a pediatric residency in Boston, she had applied and had been accepted into the Epidemiology Intelligence Service (EIS) for a two-year hitch as an Epidemiology Intelligence Service Officer. It was like being a medical detective. Only three and a half weeks previously, just before Christmas, she'd completed her introductory course, which supposedly trained her for her new role. The course was in public-health administration, biostatistics and epidemiology—the study and control of health and disease in a given population.

A wry smile appeared on Marissa's face as she pulled on her dark blue overcoat. She'd taken the introductory course, all right, but as had happened so often in her medical training, she felt totally ill-equipped to handle a real emergency. It was going to be an enormous leap from the classroom to the field if and when she was sent out on an assignment. Knowing how to relate to cases of a specific disease in a coherent narrative that would reveal cause, transmission and host factors was a far cry from deciding how to control a real outbreak involving real people and a real disease. Actually, it wasn't a question of "if," it was only a question of "when."

Picking up her briefcase, Marissa turned off the light and headed back down the hall to the elevators. She'd taken the introductory epidemiology course with forty-eight other men and women, most of whom, like herself, were trained physicians. There were a few microbiologists, a few nurses, even one dentist. She wondered if they all shared her current crisis of confidence. In medicine, people generally didn't talk about such things; it was contrary to the "image."

At the completion of the training, she'd been assigned to the Department of Virology, Special Pathogens Branch, her first choice among the positions available. She had been granted her request because she'd ranked number one in the class. Although Marissa had little background in virology, which was the reason she'd been spending so much time in the library, she'd asked to be assigned to the department because the current epidemic of AIDS had catapulted virology into the forefront of research. Previously it had always played second fiddle to bacteriology. Now virology was where the "action" was, and Marissa wanted to be a part of it.

At the elevators, Marissa said hello to the small group of people who were waiting. She'd met some of them, mostly those from the Department of Virology, whose administrative office was just down the hall from her cubicle. Others were strangers, but everyone acknowledged her. She might have been experiencing a crisis of confidence in her professional competence, but at least she felt welcome.

On the main floor Marissa stood in line to sign out, a requirement after 5:00 P.M., then headed to the parking area. Although it was winter, it was nothing like what she'd endured in Boston for the previous four years, and she didn't bother to button her coat. Her sporty red Honda Prelude was as she'd left it that morning: dusty, dirty and neglected. It still had Massachusetts license plates; replacing them was one of the many errands that Marissa had not yet found time to do.

It was a short drive from the CDC to Marissa's rented house. The area around the Center was dominated by Emory University, which had donated the land to the CDC in the early '40s. A number of pleasant residential neighborhoods surrounded the university, running the gamut from lower middle class to conspicuously rich. It was in one of the former neighborhoods, in the Druid Hills section, that Marissa had found a house to rent. It was owned by a couple who'd been transferred to Mali, Africa, to work on an extended birth-control project.

Marissa turned onto Peachtree Place. It seemed to her that everything in Atlanta was named "peachtree." She passed her house on the left. It was a small two-story wood-frame building, reasonably maintained except for the grounds. The architectural style was indeterminant, except for two Ionic columns on the front porch. The windows all had fake shutters, each with a heart-shaped area cut out in the center. Marissa had used the term "cute" to describe it to her parents.

She turned left at the next street and then left again. The property on which the house sat went all the way through the block, and in order for Marissa to get to the garage, she had to approach from the rear. There was a circular drive in front of the house, but it didn't connect with the rear driveway and the garage. Apparently in the past the two driveways had been connected, but someone had built a tennis court, and that had ended the connection. Now, the tennis court was so overgrown with weeds it was barely discernible.

Knowing that she was going out that evening, Marissa did not put her car in the garage, but just swung around and backed it up. As she ran up the back steps, she heard the cocker spaniel, given to her by one of her pediatric colleagues, barking welcome.

Marissa had never planned on having a dog, but six months previously a long-term romantic relationship that she had assumed was leading to marriage had suddenly ended. The man, Roger Shulman, a neurosurgical resident at Mass. General, had shocked Marissa with the news that he had accepted a fellowship at UCLA and that he wanted to go by himself. Up until that time, they had agreed that Marissa would go wherever Roger went to finish his training, and indeed Marissa had applied for pediatric positions in San Francisco and Houston. Roger had never even mentioned UCLA.

As the baby in the family, with three older brothers and a cold and dominating neurosurgeon for a father, Marissa had never had much self-confidence. She took the breakup with Roger very badly and had been barely able to drag herself out of bed each morning to get to the hospital. In the midst of her resultant depression, her friend Nancy had presented her with the dog. At first Marissa had been irritated, but Taffy—the puppy had worn the cloyingly sweet name on a large bow tied around its neck—soon won Marissa's heart, and, as Nancy had judged, it helped Marissa to focus on something besides her hurt. Now Marissa was crazy about the dog, enjoying having "life" in her home, an object to receive and return her love. Coming to the CDC, Marissa's only worry had been what to do with Taffy when she was sent out in the field. The issue weighed heavily on her until the Judsons, her neighbors on the right, fell in love with the dog and offered—no, demanded—to take Taffy any time Marissa had to go out of town. It was like a godsend.

Opening the door, Marissa had to fend off Taffy's excited jumps until she could turn off the alarm. When the owners had first explained the system to Marissa, she'd listened with only half an ear. But now she was glad she had it. Even though the suburbs were much safer than the city, she felt much more isolated at night than she had in Boston. She even appreciated the "panic button" that she carried in her coat pocket and which she could use to set off the alarm from the driveway if she saw unexpected lights or movement inside the house.

While Marissa looked over her mail, she let Taffy expend some of her pent-up energy racing in large circles around the blue spruce in the front yard. Without fail, the Judsons let the dog out around noon; still from then until Marissa got home in the evening was a long time for an eight-month-old puppy to be cooped up in the kitchen.

Unfortunately, Marissa had to cut Taffy's exuberant exercise short. It was already after seven, and she was expected at dinner at eight. Ralph Hempston, a successful ophthalmologist, had taken her out several times, and though she still had not gotten over Roger, she enjoyed Ralph's sophisticated company and the fact that he seemed content to take her to dinner, the theater, a concert without pressuring her to go to bed. In fact, tonight was the first time he'd invited her to his house, and he'd made it clear it was to be a large party, not just the two of them.

He seemed content to let the relationship grow at its own pace, and Marissa was grateful, even if she suspected the reason might be the twenty-two-year difference in their ages; she was thirty-one and he was fifty-three.

Oddly enough the only other man Marissa was dating in Atlanta was four years younger than she. Tad Schockley, a microbiologist Ph.D. who worked in the same department she ultimately had been assigned to, had been smitten by her the moment he'd spied her in the cafeteria during her first week at the Center. He was the exact opposite of Ralph Hempston: socially painfully shy, even when he'd only asked her to a movie. They'd gone out a half dozen times, and thankfully he, like Ralph, had not been pushy in a physical sense.

Showering quickly, Marissa then dried herself off and put on makeup almost automatically. Racing against time, she went through her closet, rapidly dismissing various combinations. She was no fashion plate but liked to look her best. She settled on a silk skirt and a sweater she'd gotten for Christmas. The sweater came down to mid-thigh, and she thought that it made her look taller. Slipping on a pair of black pumps, she eyed herself in the full-length mirror.

Except for her height, Marissa was reasonably happy with her looks. Her features were small but delicate, and her father had actually used the term "exquisite" years ago when she'd asked him if he thought she was pretty. Her eyes were dark brown and thickly lashed, and her thick, wavy hair was the color of expensive sherry. She wore it as she had since she was sixteen: shoulder length, and pulled back from her forehead with a tortoiseshell barrette.

It was only a five-minute drive to Ralph's, but the neighborhood changed significantly for the better. The houses grew larger and were set back on well-manicured lawns. Ralph's house was situated on a large piece of property, with the driveway curving gracefully up from the street. The drive was lined with azaleas and rhododendrons that in the spring had to be seen to be believed, according to Ralph.

The house itself was a three-story Victorian affair with an octagonal tower dominating the right front corner. A large porch, defined by complicated gingerbread trim, started at the tower, extended along the front of the house and swept around the left side. Above the double-doored front entrance and resting on the roof of the porch was a circular balcony roofed with a cone that complemented the one on top of the tower.

The scene looked festive enough. Every window in the house blazed with light. Marissa drove around to the left, following Ralph's instructions. She thought that she was a little late, but there were no other cars.

As she passed the house, she glanced up at the fire escape coming down from the third floor. She'd noticed it one night when Ralph had stopped to pick up his forgotten beeper. He'd explained that the previous owner had made servants' quarters up there, and the city building department had forced him to add the fire escape. The black iron stood out grotesquely against the white wood.

Marissa parked in front of the garage, whose complicated trim matched that of the house. She knocked on the back door, which was in a modern wing that could not be seen from the front. No one seemed to hear her. Looking through the window, she could see a lot of activity in the kitchen. Deciding against trying the door to see if it was unlocked, she walked around to the front of the house and rang the bell. Ralph opened the door immediately and greeted her with a big hug.

"Thanks for coming over early," he said, helping her off with her coat.

"Early? I thought I was late."

"No, not at all," said Ralph. "The guests aren't supposed to be here until eight-thirty." He hung her coat in the hall closet.

Marissa was surprised to see that Ralph was dressed in a tuxedo. Although she'd acknowledged how handsome he looked, she was disconcerted.

"I hope I'm dressed appropriately," she said. "You didn't mention that this was a formal affair."

"You look stunning, as always. I just like an excuse to wear my tux. Come, let me show you around."

Marissa followed, thinking again that Ralph looked the quintessential physician: strong, sympathetic features and hair graying in just the right places. The two walked into the parlor, Ralph leading the way. The decor was attractive but somewhat sterile. A maid in a black uniform was putting out hors d'oeuvres. "We'll begin in here. The drinks will be made at the bar in the living room," Ralph said.

He opened a pair of sliding-panel doors, and they stepped into the living room. A bar was to the left. A young man in a red vest was busily polishing the glassware. Beyond the living room, through an arch, was the formal dining room. Marissa could see that the table was laid for at least a dozen people.

She followed Ralph through the dining room and out into the new wing, which contained a family room and a large modern kitchen. The dinner party was being catered, and three or four people were busy with the preparations.

After being reassured that everything was under control, Ralph lead Marissa back to the parlor and explained that he'd asked her to come over early in hopes that she'd act as hostess. A little surprised—after all, she'd only been out with Ralph five or six times—Marissa agreed.

The doorbell rang. The first guests had arrived.

Unfortunately, Marissa had never been good at keeping track of people's names, but she remembered a Dr. and Mrs. Hayward because of his astonishingly silver hair. Then there was a Dr. and Mrs. Jackson, she sporting a diamond the size of a golf ball. The only other names Marissa recalled afterward were Dr. and Dr. Sandberg, both psychiatrists.

Making an attempt at small talk, Marissa was awed by the furs and jewels. These people were not small-town practitioners.

When almost everyone was standing in the living room with a drink in hand, the doorbell sounded again. Ralph was not in sight, so Marissa opened the door. To her utter surprise she recognized Dr. Cyrill Dubchek, her boss at the Special Pathogens Branch of the Department of Virology.

"Hello, Dr. Blumenthal," said Dubchek comfortably, taking Marissa's presence in stride.

Marissa was visibly flustered. She'd not expected anyone from the CDC. Dubchek handed his coat to the maid, revealing a dark blue Italian-tailored suit. He was a striking man with coal black, intelligent eyes and an olive complexion. His features were sharp and aristocratic. Running a hand through his hair, which was brushed straight back from his forehead, he smiled. "We meet again."

Marissa weakly returned the smile and nodded toward the living room. "The bar is in there."

"Where's Ralph?" asked Dubchek, glancing into the crowded living room.

"Probably in the kitchen," said Marissa.

Dubchek nodded, and moved off as the doorbell rang again. This time Marissa was even more flabbergasted. Standing before her was Tad Schockley!

"Marissa!" said Tad, genuinely surprised.

Marissa recovered and allowed Tad to enter. While she took his coat, she asked, "How do you know Dr. Hempston?"

"Just from meetings. I was surprised when I got an invitation in the mail." Tad smiled. "But who am I to turn down a free meal, on my salary?"

"Did you know that Dubchek was coming?" asked Marissa. Her tone was almost accusing.

Tad shook his head. "But what difference does it make?" He looked into the dining room and then up the main staircase. "Beautiful house. Wow!"

Marissa grinned in spite of herself. Tad, with his short sandy hair and fresh complexion, looked too young to be a Ph.D. He was dressed in a corduroy jacket, a woven tie and gray flannels so worn, they might as well have been jeans.

"Hey," he said. "How do you know Dr. Hempston?"

"He's just a friend," said Marissa evasively, gesturing for Tad to head into the living room for a drink.

Once all the guests had arrived, Marissa felt free to move away from the front door. At the bar, she got herself a glass of white wine and tried to mingle. Just before the group was summoned into the dining room, she found herself in a conversation with Dr. Sandberg and Dr. and Mrs. Jackson.

"Welcome to Atlanta, young lady," said Dr. Sandberg.

"Thank you," said Marissa, trying not to gawk at Mrs. Jackson's ring.

"How is it you happened to come to the CDC?" asked Dr. Jackson. His voice was deep and resonant. He not only looked like Charlton Heston; he actually sounded as if he could play Ben Hur.

Looking into the man's deep blue eyes, she wondered how to answer his seemingly sincere question. She certainly wasn't going to mention anything about her former lover's flight to L.A. and her need for a change. That wasn't the kind of commitment people expected at the CDC. "I've always had an interest in public health." That was a little white lie. "I've always been fascinated by stories of medical detective work." She smiled. At least that was the truth. "I guess I got tired of looking up runny noses and into draining ears."

"Trained in pediatrics," said Dr. Sandberg. It was a statement, not a question.

"Children's Hospital in Boston," said Marissa. She always felt a little ill at ease talking with psychiatrists. She couldn't help but wonder if they could analyze her motives better than she could herself. She knew that part of the reason she had gone into medicine was to enable her to compete with her brothers in their relationships with their father.

"How do you feel about clinical medicine?" asked Dr. Jackson. "Were you ever interested in practicing?"

"Well, certainly," replied Marissa.

"How?" continued Dr. Jackson, unknowingly making Marissa feel progressively uneasy. "Did you see yourself solo, in a group, or in a clinic?"

"Dinner is served," called Ralph over the din of conversation.

Marissa felt relieved as Dr. Jackson and Dr. Sandberg turned to find their wives. For a moment she had felt as if she were being interrogated.

In the dining room Marissa discovered that Ralph had seated himself at one end of the table and had placed her at the other. To her immediate right was Dr. Jackson, who thankfully forgot about his questions concerning clinical medicine. To her left was the silver-haired Dr. Hayward.

As the meal progressed, it became even clearer that Marissa was dining with the cream of Atlanta's medical community. These were not just doctors; they were the most successful private practitioners in the city. The only exceptions to this were Cyrill Dubchek, Tad and herself.

After several glasses of good wine, Marissa was more talkative than normal. She felt a twinge of embarrassment when she realized that the entire table was listening to her description of her childhood in Virginia. She told herself to shut up and smile, and she was pleased when the conversation switched to the sorry state of American medicine and how prepaid health-care groups were eroding the foundations of private practice. Remembering the furs and jewels, Marissa didn't feel that those present were suffering too much.

"How about the CDC?" asked Dr. Hayward, looking across at Cyrill. "Have you been experiencing budgetary constraints?"

Cyrill laughed cynically, his smile forming deep creases in his cheeks. "Every year we have to do battle with the Office of Management and Budget as well as the House Appropriations Committee. We've lost five hundred positions due to budgetary cuts."

Dr. Jackson cleared his throat: "What if there were a

serious outbreak of influenza like the pandemic of 1917–1918. Assuming your department would be involved, do you have the manpower for such an eventuality?"

Cyrill shrugged. "It depends on a lot of variables. If the strain doesn't mutate its surface antigens and we can grow it readily in tissue culture, we could develop a vaccine quite quickly. How quickly, I'm not sure. Tad?"

"A month or so," said Tad, "if we were lucky. More time to produce enough to make a significant difference."

"Reminds me of the swine flu fiasco a few years ago," interjected Dr. Hayward.

"That wasn't the CDC's fault," said Cyrill defensively. "There was no doubt about the strain that appeared at Fort Dix. Why it didn't spread is anybody's guess."

Marissa felt a hand on her shoulder. Turning, she found herself looking at one of the black-dressed waitresses.

"Dr. Blumenthal?" whispered the girl.

"Yes."

"There is a phone call for you."

Marissa glanced down the table at Ralph, but he was busy talking with Mrs. Jackson. She excused herself and followed the girl to the kitchen. Then it dawned on her, and she felt a stirring of fear, like the first time she had been called at night as an intern: It had to be the CDC. After all, she was on call and she'd dutifully left Ralph's number. No one else knew she was there.

"Dr. Blumenthal?" asked the CDC operator, when Marissa picked up the phone.

The call was switched to the duty officer. "Congratulations," he said jovially. "There has been an epidemic aid request. We had a call from the California State Epidemiologist, who would like CDC help on a problem in L.A. It's an outbreak of unknown but apparently serious illness in a hospital called the Richter Clinic. We've gone ahead and made a reservation for you on Delta's flight to the coast that leaves at 1:10 A.M. We've arranged hotel accommodations at a place called the Tropic Motel. Sounds divine. Anyway, good luck!"

Replacing the receiver, Marissa left her hand on the phone for a moment while she caught her breath. She didn't feel prepared at all. Those poor, unsuspecting people in California had called the CDC expecting to get an epidemiologic expert, and instead, they were going to get her, Marissa Blumenthal. All five feet of her. She made her way back to the dining room to excuse herself and say good-bye.

2

January 21

BY THE TIME MARISSA had gotten her suitcase from the baggage carousel, waited for the rent-a-car van, gotten the rent-a-car (the first one wouldn't start), and had somehow managed to find the Tropic Motel, the sky had begun to lighten.

As she signed in, she couldn't help thinking of Roger. But she wouldn't call. She'd promised herself that much several times on the flight.

The motel was depressing, but it didn't matter. Marissa didn't think she'd be spending much time there. She washed her hands and face, combed her hair and replaced her barrette. With no other plausible reason for delay, she returned to the rent-a-car and set out for the Richter Clinic. The palms of her hands were damp against the steering wheel.

The clinic was conveniently situated on a wide thoroughfare. There were few cars at that time of morning. Marissa pulled into a parking garage, took a ticket and found a spot near the entrance. The entire structure was modern, including the garage, the clinic, and what Marissa guessed was the hospital, which appeared to be seven stories tall. Getting out of the car, she stretched, then lifted out her briefcase. In it were her class notes from the epidemiology portion of the introductory course—as if that would be any help—a note pad, pencils, a small textbook on diagnostic virology, an extra lipstick and a pack of chewing gum. What a joke.

Once inside, Marissa noted the familiar hospital odor of disinfectant—a smell that somehow calmed her and made her feel instantly at home. There was an information booth, but it was empty. She asked a maintenance man mopping the floor how to get to the hospital wing, and he pointed to a red stripe on the floor. Marissa followed it to the emergency room. There was little activity there, with few patients in the waiting room and only two nurses behind the main desk. Marissa sought out the on-call doctor and explained who she was.

"Oh, great!" said the ER doctor enthusiastically. "Are we glad you're here! Dr. Navarre has been waiting all night for you. Let me get him."

Marissa absentmindedly played with some paper clips. When she looked up, she realized the two nurses were staring at her. She smiled and they smiled back.

"Can I get you some coffee?" asked the taller of the two.

"That would be nice," said Marissa. In addition to her basic anxiety, she was feeling the effects of only two hours of fitful sleep on the flight from Atlanta.

Sipping the hot liquid, Marissa recalled the Berton Roueche medical detective stories in *The New Yorker*. She wished that she could be involved in a case like the one solved by John Snow, the father of modern epidemiology: A London cholera epidemic was aborted when Snow deductively isolated the problem to a particular London water pump. The real beauty of Snow's work was that he did it before the germ theory of disease was accepted. Wouldn't it be wonderful to be involved in such a clear-cut situation?

The door to the on-call room opened, and a handsome, black-haired man appeared. Blinking in the bright ER light, he came directly toward Marissa. The corners of his mouth pulled up in a big smile. "Dr. Blumenthal, we are so glad to see you. You have no idea."

As they shook hands, Dr. Navarre gazed down at Marissa. Standing next to her, he was momentarily taken aback by her diminutive size and youthful appearance. To be polite, he inquired about her flight and asked if she was hungry.

"I think it would be best to get right down to business," said Marissa.

Dr. Navarre readily agreed. As he led Marissa to the hospital conference room, he introduced himself as chief of the department of medicine. This news didn't help Marissa's confidence. She recognized that Dr. Navarre undoubtedly knew a hundred times more than she about infectious disease.

Motioning for Marissa to sit at the round conference table, Dr. Navarre picked up the phone and dialed. While the call was going through, he explained that Dr. Spenser Cox, the State Epidemiologist was extremely eager to talk to Marissa the moment she arrived.

Wonderful, thought Marissa, forcing a weak smile.

Dr. Cox sounded equally as happy as Dr. Navarre that Marissa was there. He explained to her that unfortunately he was currently embroiled in a problem in the

San Francisco Bay area involving an outbreak of hepatitis B that they thought could be related to AIDS.

"I assume," continued Dr. Cox, "that Dr. Navarre has told you that the problem at the Richter Clinic currently involves only seven patients."

"He hasn't told me anything yet," said Marissa.

"I'm sure he is just about to," said Dr. Cox. "Up here, we have almost five hundred cases of hepatitis B, so you can understand why I can't come down there immediately."

"Of course," said Marissa.

"Good luck," said Dr. Cox. "By the way, how long have you been with the CDC?"

"Not that long," admitted Marissa.

There was a short pause. "Well, keep me informed," said Dr. Cox.

Marissa handed the receiver back to Dr. Navarre, who hung up. "Let me bring you up to date," he said, switching to a standard medical monotone as he pulled some three-by-five cards from his pocket. "We have seven cases of an undiagnosed, but obviously severe, febrile illness characterized by prostration and multi-system involvement. The first patient to be hospitalized happens to be one of the cofounders of the clinic, Dr. Richter himself. The next, a woman from the medical records department." Dr. Navarre began placing his three-by-five cards on the table. Each one represented a patient. He organized them in the order in which the cases had presented themselves.

Discreetly snapping open her briefcase without allowing Dr. Navarre to see what it contained, Marissa extracted her note pad and a pencil. Her mind raced back to the courses she'd recently completed, remembering that she needed to break the information down into understandable categories. First the illness: Was it really something new? Did a problem really exist? That was the province of the simple 2 × 2 table and some rudimentary statistics. Marissa knew she had to characterize the illness even if she couldn't make a specific diagnosis. The next step would be to determine host factors of the victims, such as age, sex, health, eating habits, hobbies, etc., then to determine time, place and circumstances in which each patient displayed initial symptoms, in order to learn what elements of commonality existed. Then there would be the question of transmission of the illness, which might lead to the infectious agent. Finally, the host or reservoir would have to be irradicated. It sounded so easy, but Marissa knew it would be a difficult problem, even for someone as experienced as Dubchek.

Marissa wiped her moist hand on her skirt, then picked up her pencil once more. "So," she said, staring at the blank page. "Since no diagnosis has been made, what's being considered?"

"Everything," said Dr. Navarre.

"Influenza?" asked Marissa, hoping she wasn't sounding overly simplistic.

"Not likely," said Dr. Navarre. "The patients have respiratory symptoms but they do not predominate. Besides, serological testing has been negative for influenza virus in all seven patients. We don't know what they have, but it is not influenza."

"Any ideas?" asked Marissa.

"Mostly negatives," said Dr. Navarre. "Everything we've tested has been negative: blood cultures, urine cultures, sputum cultures, stool cultures, even cerebrospinal fluid cultures. We thought about malaria and actually treated for it, though the blood smears were negative for the parasites. We even treated for typhoid, with either tetracycline or chloramphenicol, despite the negative cultures. But, just like with the antimalarials, there was no effect whatsoever. The patients are all going downhill no matter what we do."

"You must have some kind of differential diagnosis," said Marissa.

"Of course," responded Dr. Navarre. "We've had a number of infectious disease consults. The consensus is that it is a viral problem, although leptospirosis is still a weak contender." Dr. Navarre searched through his index cards, then held one up. "Ah, here are the current differential diagnoses: leptospirosis, as I mentioned; yellow fever; dengue; mononucleosis; or, just to cover the bases, some other enteroviral, arboviral or adenoviral infection. Needless to say, we've made about as much progress in the diagnostic realm as the therapeutic."

"How long has Dr. Richter been hospitalized?" asked Marissa.

"This is his fifth day. I think you should see the patients to have an idea of what we are dealing with." Dr. Navarre stood up without waiting for Marissa's response. She found she had to trot to keep up with him. They went through swinging doors and entered the hospital proper. Nervous as she was, Marissa could not help being impressed by the luxurious carpeting and almost hotellike decor.

She got on the elevator behind Dr. Navarre, who introduced her to an anesthesiologist. Marissa returned the man's greeting, but her thoughts were elsewhere. She was certain that her seeing the patients at that moment was not going to accomplish anything except to make her feel "exposed." This issue had not occurred to her while taking the introductory course back in Atlanta. Suddenly it seemed like a big problem. Yet what could she say?

They arrived at the nurses' station on the fifth floor. Dr. Navarre took the time to introduce Marissa to the night staff, who were making their initial preparations to change shifts.

"All seven patients are on this floor," said Dr. Navarre. "It has some of our most experienced personnel. The two in critical condition are in separate cubicles in the medical intensive-care unit just across the hall. The rest are in private rooms. Here are the charts." With an open palm, he thumped a pile stacked on the corner of the counter top. "I assume you'd like to see Dr. Richter first." Dr. Navarre handed Richter's chart to Marissa.

The first thing she looked at was the "vital-sign" sheet. Beginning his fifth hospital day, she noticed that the doctor's blood pressure was falling and his temperature was rising. Not a good omen. Rapidly she perused the chart. She knew that she'd have to go over it carefully later. But even a cursory glance convinced her that the workup had been superb, better than she could have done herself. The laboratory work had been exhaustive. Again she wondered what in God's name she was doing there pretending to be an authority.

Going back to the beginning of the chart, Marissa read the section entitled "history of the present illness." Something jumped out at her right away. Six weeks previous to the onset of symptoms Dr. Richter had attended an ophthalmological convention in Nairobi, Kenya.

She read on, her interest piqued. One week prior to his illness, Dr. Richter had attended an eyelid surgery conference in San Diego. Two days prior to admission he'd been bitten by a Cercopitheceus aethiops, whatever the hell that was. She showed it to Dr. Navarre.

"It's a type of monkey," said Dr. Navarre. "Dr. Richter always has a few of them on hand for his ocular herpes research."

Marissa nodded. She glanced again at the laboratory values and noted that the patient had a low white count, a low ESR and low thrombocytes. Other lab values indicated liver and kidney malfunction. Even the EKG showed mild abnormalities. This guy was virulently sick.

Marissa laid the chart down on the counter.

"Ready?" questioned Dr. Navarre.

Although Marissa nodded that she was, she would have preferred to put off confronting the patients. She had no delusions of grandeur that she would uncover some heretofore missed, but significant, physical sign, and thereby solve the mystery. Her seeing the patients at that point was pure theater and, unfortunately, risky business. She followed Dr. Navarre reluctantly.

They entered the intensive-care unit, with its familiar backdrop of complicated electronic machinery. The patients were immobile victims, secured with tangles of wires and plastic tubing. There was the smell of alcohol, the sound of respirators and cardiac monitors. There was also the usual high level of nursing activity.

"We've isolated Dr. Richter in this side room," said

Dr. Navarre, stopping at the closed doorway. To the left of the door was a window, and inside the room Marissa could make out the patient. Like the others in the unit, he was stretched out beneath a canopy of intravenous bottles. Behind him was a cathode-ray tube with a continuous EKG tracing flashing across its screen.

"I think you'd better put on a mask and gown," said Dr. Navarre. "We're observing isolation precautions on all the patients for obvious reasons."

"By all means," said Marissa, trying not to sound too eager. If she had her way, she'd climb into a plastic bubble. She slipped on the gown and helped herself to a hat, mask, booties, and even rubber gloves. Dr. Navarre did likewise.

Unaware she was doing it, Marissa breathed shallowly as she looked down at the patient, who, in irreverent vernacular, looked as if he was about to "check out." His color was ashen, his eyes sunken, his skin slack. There was a bruise over his right cheekbone; his lips were dry, and dried blood was caked on his front teeth.

As Marissa stared down at the stricken man, she didn't know what to do; yet she self-consciously felt obliged to do something, with Dr. Navarre hanging over her, watching her every move. "How do you feel?" asked Marissa. She knew it was a stupid, self-evident question the moment it escaped from her lips. Nonetheless Richter's eyes fluttered open. Marissa noticed some hemorrhages in the whites.

"Not good," admitted Dr. Richter, his voice a hoarse whisper.

"Is it true you were in Africa a month ago?" she

asked. She had to lean over to hear the man, and her heart went out to him.

"Six weeks ago," said Dr. Richter.

"Did you come in contact with any animals?" asked Marissa.

"No," managed Dr. Richter after a pause. "I saw a lot but didn't handle any."

"Did you attend anyone who was ill?"

Dr. Richter shook his head. Speaking was obviously difficult for him.

Marissa straightened up and pointed to the abrasion under the patient's right eye. "Any idea what this is?" she asked Dr. Navarre.

Dr. Navarre nodded. "He was mugged two days before he got sick. He hit his cheek on the pavement."

"Poor guy," said Marissa, wincing at Dr. Richter's misfortune. Then, after a moment, she added, "I think I've seen enough for now."

Just inside the door leading back to the ICU proper, there was a large frame holding a plastic bag. Both Marissa and Dr. Navarre peeled off their isolation apparel and returned to the fifth-floor nurses' station. Compulsively, Marissa washed her hands in the sink.

"What about the monkey that bit Dr. Richter?" she asked.

"We have him quarantined," said Dr. Navarre. "We've also cultured him in every way possible. He appears to be healthy."

They seemed to have thought of everything. Marissa picked up Dr. Richter's chart to see if his conjunctival hemorrhages had been noted. They had.

Marissa took a deep breath and looked over at Dr.

Navarre, who was watching her expectantly. "Well," she said vaguely, "I've got a lot of work to do with these charts." Suddenly she remembered reading about a category of disease called "viral hemorrhagic fever." They were extremely rare, but deadly, and a number of them came from Africa. Hoping to add something to the tentative diagnoses already listed by the clinic doctors, she mentioned the possibility.

"VHF was already brought up," said Dr. Navarre. "That was one of the reasons we called the CDC so quickly."

So much for that "zebra" diagnosis, thought Marissa, referring to a medical maxim that when you hear hoofbeats, think of horses, not zebras.

To her great relief, Dr. Navarre was paged for an emergency. "I'm terribly sorry," he said, "but I'm needed in the ER. Is there anything I can do before I go?"

"Well, I think it would be better to improve the isolation of the patients. You've already moved them to the same general area of the hospital. But I think you should place them in a completely isolated wing and begin complete barrier nursing, at least until we have some idea as to the communicability of the disease."

Dr. Navarre stared at Marissa. For a moment she wondered what he was thinking. Then he said, "You're absolutely right."

Marissa took the seven charts into a small room behind the nurses' station. Opening each, she learned that, besides Dr. Richter, there were four women and two men who presumably had the same illness. Somehow, they all had to have had direct contact with each other or been exposed to the same source of contamination. Marissa kept reminding herself that her method of attack on a field assignment, particularly her first, was to gather as much information as she could and then relay it to Atlanta. Going back to Dr. Richter's chart, Marissa read everything, including the nurses' notes. On a separate sheet in her notebook, she listed every bit of information that could possibly have significance, including the fact that the man had presented with an episode of hematemesis, vomiting blood. That certainly didn't sound like influenza. The whole time she was working her mind kept returning to the fact that Dr. Richter had been in Africa six weeks previously. That had to be significant even though a month's incubation was unlikely, given the symptomology, unless he had malaria, which apparently he did not. Of course there were viral diseases like AIDS with longer incubation periods, but AIDS was not an acute viral infectious disease. The incubation period for such a disease was usually about a week, give or take a few days. Marissa painstakingly went through all the charts amassing diverse data on age, sex, life-style, occupation and living environment, and recording her findings on a separate page in her notebook for each of the patients. Rather quickly, she realized that she was dealing with a diverse group of people. In addition to Dr. Richter, there was a secretary, a woman who worked in medical records at the Richter Clinic; two housewives; a plumber; an insurance salesman and a real estate broker. Opportunity for commonality seemed remote with a group this diverse, yet all of them must have been exposed to the same source.

Reading the charts also gave Marissa a better clinical

picture of the illness she was dealing with. Apparently it began rather suddenly, with severe headaches, muscle pain and high fever. Then the patients experienced some combination of abdominal pain, diarrhea, vomiting, sore throat, cough and chest pain. A shiver went down Marissa's spine as she thought about having been exposed to the disease.

Marissa rubbed her eyes. They felt gritty from lack of sleep. It was time to visit the rest of the patients whether she wanted to or not. There were a lot of gaps, particularly in activities of each patient in the days directly preceding their illness.

She started with the medical secretary, who was located in a room next to Dr. Richter's in the ICU, and then worked her way through to the last patient to be admitted. Before seeing each case, she carefully dressed in full protective clothing. All the patients were seriously ill, and none felt much like talking. Still, Marissa went through her list of questions, concentrating on whether each patient was acquainted with any of the other people who were ill. The answer was always no, except that each one knew Dr. Richter, and all were members of the Richter Clinic health plan! The answer was so obvious she was surprised that no one seemed to have spotted it. Dr. Richter might have spread the disease himself since he might even have been in contact with the medical secretary. She asked the ward clerk to call for all the patients' clinic outpatient records.

While she was waiting, Dr. Navarre called. "I'm afraid we have another case," he said. "He's one of the lab techs here at the clinic. He's in the emergency room. Do you want to come down?"

"Is he isolated?" asked Marissa.

"As well as we can do it down here," said Dr. Navarre. "We're preparing an isolation wing upstairs on the fifth floor. We will move all the cases there the moment it is ready."

"The sooner the better," said Marissa. "For the time being, I recommend that all nonessential lab work be postponed."

"That's okay by me," said Dr. Navarre. "What about this boy down here? Do you want to see him?"

"I'm on my way," said Marissa.

En route to the ER, Marissa could not shake the feeling that they were on the brink of a major epidemic. Concerning the lab tech, there were two equally disturbing possibilities: the first was that the fellow had contracted the illness in the same fashion as the others, i.e., from some active source of deadly virus in the Richter Clinic; the second, more probable in Marissa's estimation, was that the lab tech had been exposed to the agent from handling infected material from the existing cases.

The ER personnel had placed the new patient in one of the psychiatric cubicles. There was a Do Not Enter sign on the door. Marissa read the technician's chart. He was a twenty-four-year-old male by the name of Alan Moyers. His temperature was 103.4. After donning protective gown, mask, hat, gloves and booties, Marissa entered the tiny room. The patient stared at her with glazed eyes.

"I understand you're not feeling too well," said Marissa.

"I feel like I've been run over by a truck," said Alan. "I've never felt this bad, even when I had the flu last year."

"What was the first thing you noticed?"

"The headache," said Alan. He tapped his fingers against the sides of his forehead. "Right here is where I feel the pain. It's awful. Can you give me something for it?"

"What about chills?"

"Yeah, after the headache began, I started to get them."

"Has anything abnormal happened to you in the lab in the last week or so?"

"Like what?" asked Alan, closing his eyes. "I did win the pool on the last Lakers game."

"I'm more interested in something professional. Were you bitten by any animals?"

"Nope. I never handle any animals. What's wrong with me?"

"How about Dr. Richter? Do you know him?"

"Sure. Everybody knows Dr. Richter. Oh, I remember something. I stuck myself with a vacu-container needle. That never happened to me before."

"Do you remember the patient's name on the vacu-container?"

"No. All I remember is that the guy didn't have AIDS. I was worried about that, so I looked up his diagnosis."

"What was it?"

"Didn't say. But it always says AIDS if it is AIDS. I don't have AIDS, do I?"

"No, Alan, you don't have AIDS," said Marissa.

"Thank God," said Alan. "For a moment there, I was scared."

Marissa went out to find Dr. Navarre, but he was occupied with a cardiac arrest that had just been brought in by ambulance. Marissa asked the nurse to tell him that she was going back to the fifth floor. Returning to the elevators, Marissa began organizing her thoughts to call Dr. Dubchek.

"Excuse me."

Marissa felt a tap on her arm and turned to face a stocky man with a beard and wire-rimmed glasses. "Are you Dr. Blumenthal from the CDC?" asked the man.

Nonplussed at being recognized, Marissa nodded. The man stood blocking her entrance to the elevator. "I'm Clarence Herns, with the L.A. *Times*. My wife works the night shift up in the medical ICU. She told me that you were here to see Dr. Richter. What is it the man has?"

"At this point, no one knows," said Marissa.

"Is it serious?"

"I imagine your wife can answer that as well as I."

"She says the man is dying and that there are six other similar cases, including a secretary from medical records. Sounds to me like the beginnings of an epidemic."

"I'm not sure that 'epidemic' is the right word. There does seem to be one more case today, but that's the only one for two days. I hope it will be the last, but no one knows."

"Sounds scary," said the reporter.

"I agree," said Marissa. "But I can't talk any longer. I'm in a hurry."

Dodging the insistent Mr. Herns, Marissa boarded the next elevator and returned to the cubicle behind the fifth-floor nurses' station and put through a collect call to Dr. Dubchek. It was quarter-to-three in Atlanta, and she got Dubchek immediately.

"So, how's your first field assignment?" he asked.

"It's a bit overwhelming," said Marissa. Then, as succinctly as she could, she described the seven cases she'd seen, admitting that she had not learned anything that the Richter Clinic doctors didn't already know.

"That shouldn't bother you," said Dubchek. "You have to keep in mind that an epidemiologist looks at data differently than a clinician, so the same data can mean different things. The clinician is looking at each case in particular, whereas you are looking at the whole picture. Tell me about the illness."

Marissa described the clinical syndrome, referring frequently to her note pad. She sensed that Dubchek was particularly interested in the fact that two of the patients had vomited blood, that another had passed bloody diarrhea and that three had conjunctival hemorrhages in their eyes. When Marissa said that Dr. Richter had been to an ophthalmology meeting in Africa, Dubchek exclaimed, "My God, do you know what you are describing?"

"Not exactly," said Marissa. It was an old medical-school ploy: try to stay on neutral ground rather than make a fool of yourself.

"Viral hemorrhagic fever," said Dubchek, ". . . and if it came from Africa, it would be Lassa Fever. Unless it was Marburg or Ebola. Jesus Christ!"

"But Richter's visit was over six weeks ago."

"Darn," said Dubchek, almost angrily. "The longest incubation period for that kind of fulminating illness is about two weeks. Even for quarantine purposes, twenty days is considered adequate."

"The doctor was also bitten by a monkey two days before he became ill," offered Marissa.

"And that's too short an incubation period. It should be five or six days. Where's the monkey now?"

"Quarantined," said Marissa.

"Good. Don't let anything happen to that animal, particularly if it dies. We've got to test it for virus. If the animal is involved, we have to consider the Marburg virus. In any case, the illness certainly sounds like a viral hemorrhagic fever, and until proven otherwise, we'd better consider it as such. We've worried about something like this happening for some time; the problem is that there's no vaccine and no treatment."

"What about the mortality rate?" asked Marissa.

"High. Tell me, does Dr. Richter have a skin rash?"

Marissa couldn't remember. "I'll check."

"The first thing I want you to do is draw bloods, obtain urine samples, and do throat swabs for viral culture on all seven cases, and have them rushed to the CDC. Use Delta's small-package service. That will be the fastest way. I want you personally to draw the blood, and for Christ's sake be careful. From the monkey, too, if you can. Pack the samples in dry ice before shipping them."

"I've just seen what might be another case," said Marissa. "One of the clinic's lab techs."

"Include him, too. It sounds increasingly serious. Make sure that all the patients are totally isolated with complete barrier nursing. And tell whoever is in charge not to do any lab work until I get there."

"I have," said Marissa. "You're coming yourself?"

"You bet I am," said Dubchek. "This could be a national emergency. But it is going to take some time to prepare the Vickers Mobile Lab. Meanwhile, start setting up a quarantine for contacts, and try to get in touch with the people who sponsored that eye meeting in Africa and see if any of the other doctors who went are ill. And one other thing: don't say anything to the press. With all the publicity about AIDS, I don't think the public could deal with the threat of another fatal viral disease. There could be widespread panic. And Marissa, I want you to wear full protective clothing, including goggles, when you see the patients. The pathology department should have them if no one else does. I'll be there as soon as possible."

Hanging up, Marissa experienced a rush of anxiety. She wondered if she'd already exposed herself to the virus. Then she worried about having already talked to Clarence Herns from the L.A. *Times*. Well, what was done was done. She was glad that Dubchek was coming. She knew she'd been in over her head from the moment she'd arrived in L.A.

After putting in a call for Dr. Navarre, Marissa had one of the nurses help her get the materials ready to draw blood from the patients. She needed vacu-containers with anticoagulants, plastic bags, and sodium hypochlorite to decontaminate the outside of the bags. She also needed urine containers and throat swabs. Then she phoned the micro lab and asked to have containers of viral transport media sent up, along with shipment containers and dry ice. When Dr. Navarre called, she related what Dubchek had said about complete barrier nursing and about no lab tests until he'd arrived with a special facility. She also mentioned that they had better get together to talk about systematically quarantining all contacts. Dr. Navarre agreed, shocked to hear that Dubchek thought they might be dealing with viral hemorrhagic fever.

Following Dubchek's advice, Marissa got goggles from pathology. She'd never thought about catching an illness through her eyes, but she was aware that their surface was a mucous membrane and was obviously as available to viral assault as her nasal mucosa. When she was fully attired in hood, goggles, mask, gown, gloves and booties, she went to Dr. Richter's cubicle to begin her sampling.

Before she started, she examined him for a skin rash. His arms were clear, but he did have a curious red area about the size of a quarter on his right thigh. Lifting up his hospital gown, Marissa noted a fine, but definite, maculopapular eruption covering most of his trunk. She was impressed that Dubchek had anticipated it.

She drew the blood first, then filled the urine container from the catheter bag. After each was sealed, she washed its exterior with sodium hypochlorite, then put it in a second bag. After the exterior of the second bag was washed in the disinfectant, she allowed it to be removed from the room.

Disposing of the hood, mask, gown, gloves and booties, and then donning new ones, Marissa went on to the next patient, the medical secretary, whose name was Helen Townsend. Marissa repeated the same procedures she'd done on Dr. Richter, including looking for skin eruptions. Helen also had a faint rash on her trunk, but no red circle on her thigh or elsewhere. She seemed less ill than Richter, but none of the patients appeared well enough to question Marissa much as she went about her sampling. Only Alan Moyers could muster the strength to offer some objections. At first he refused to allow Marissa to draw blood unless she told him what his diagnosis was. He was terrified. When Marissa told him the truth, that she did not know what he had and that that was why she needed the samples, he finally gave in.

As for the monkey, Marissa didn't even attempt to get a blood sample. The animal keeper was out for the day, and she had no intention of trying to handle the animal alone. The monkey looked healthy enough, but was not friendly. He threw feces at Marissa through the mesh of his cage.

Once Marissa completed the packing, making certain that all the screw caps were tightly in place so that carbon dioxide from the dry ice could not penetrate the samples, she personally rode out to the airport and sent the boxes on their way to Atlanta. Luckily she got them on a convenient nonstop.

Back at the Richter Clinic, Marissa made a detour to the small clinic library. There were a few standard texts there that included sections on viral diseases. She quickly scanned the entries for Lassa Fever, Marburg and Ebola virus. Then she understood Dubchek's excited reaction on the telephone. These were the most deadly viruses known to man.

Arriving back on the fifth floor, Marissa found that all eight patients had been isolated in a separate wing. She also found that the clinic outpatient records she'd ordered had arrived. After putting in a call for Dr. Navarre, Marissa sat down and began to study the charts.

The first belonged to Harold Stevens, the real estate broker. She started from the back and immediately discovered that the last outpatient entry was a visit to Dr.

Richter: Harold Stevens had chronic open-angle glaucoma and saw Dr. Richter on a regular basis. His last checkup had been on January 15, four days before he was admitted to the hospital.

With a sense of growing certainty Marissa looked at the last entry on each chart. There it was. Each patient had seen Dr. Richter on either the fifteenth or the sixteenth of January. All except Helen Townsend, the secretary from medical records, and Alan, the lab tech. The last entry in Ms. Townsend's outpatient file recorded a visit to an OB-GYN man for cystitis. Alan had seen an orthopod the previous year for a sprained ankle he'd suffered in a hospital basketball league. Except for the medical secretary and the lab tech, there was the strong suggestion that Dr. Richter was the source of the illness. The fact that he'd seen five of the patients just before he developed symptoms had to be significant.

Marissa could explain the lab tech getting the illness by his sticking himself with a contaminated needle, but she couldn't immediately explain Helen Townsend. Marissa had to assume that Helen had seen Dr. Richter sometime earlier in the week. She had come down with the illness just forty-eight hours after the doctor. Maybe he had spent a lot of time in medical records earlier that week.

Marissa's musings were interrupted by the ward clerk, who said that Dr. Navarre had called to ask if Marissa would kindly come down to the hospital conference room.

Returning to the room where she'd started the day reminded Marissa of how long she'd been working. She felt bone weary as Dr. Navarre closed the door and introduced the other person who was present. He was William Richter, Dr. Richter's brother.

"I wanted to thank you personally for being here," said William. Although he was impeccably dressed in a pin-striped suit, his haggard face was mute testimony to his lack of sleep. "Dr. Navarre has told me your tentative diagnosis. I want to assure you that we will support your effort to contain this illness to the limits of our resources. But we are also concerned about the negative impact the situation could have on our clinic. I hope that you agree that no publicity would be the best publicity."

Marissa felt mildly outraged, when so many lives were at stake, but Dubchek himself had said essentially the same thing.

"I understand your concern," she said, uncomfortably aware that she had already spoken to a reporter. "But I think we have to initiate further quarantine measures." Marissa went on to explain that they would have to separate the possible contacts into primary and secondary contacts. Primary contacts would be those people who had spoken with or touched one of the current eight patients. Secondary contacts would be anyone who had had contact with a primary contact.

"My God," said Dr. Navarre. "We're talking about thousands of people."

"I'm afraid so," said Marissa. "We're going to need all the manpower the clinic can spare. We'll also tap the resources of the State Health Department."

"We'll provide the manpower," said Mr. Richter. "I'd prefer to keep this 'in-house.' But shouldn't we wait until we actually have a diagnosis?"

"If we wait, it may be too late," said Marissa. "We can always call off the quarantine if it is unnecessary."

"There's no way we'll keep this from the press," moaned Mr. Richter.

"To be truthful," said Marissa, "I think the press can play a positive role by helping us reach all the contacts. Primary contacts must be instructed to stay as isolated as possible for a week and to take their temperatures twice a day. If they run a fever of 101° or over, they'll have to come to the clinic. Secondary contacts can go about their business but should still take their temperatures once a day.

Marissa stood up and stretched. "When Dr. Dubchek arrives he may have some suggestions. But I believe what I've outlined is standard CDC procedure. I'll leave its implementation up to the Richter Clinic. My job is to try to find out where the virus originated."

Leaving two stunned men in her wake, Marissa left the conference room. Passing from the hospital to the clinic building, she approached the clinic information booth, asking directions to Dr. Richter's office. It was on the second floor, and Marissa went directly up.

The door was closed but unlocked. Marissa knocked and entered. Dr. Richter's receptionist was dutifully behind her desk. Apparently she hadn't expected company, because she quickly stubbed out a cigarette and put the ashtray in one of the desk drawers.

"Can I help you?" she asked. She was fiftyish with silver-gray, tightly permed hair. Her name tag said Miss Cavanagh. Reading glasses perched on the very end of her nose, their temple pieces connected by a gold chain that went around her neck.

Marissa explained who she was, adding, "It's important that I try to determine how Dr. Richter contracted his illness. To do that, I want to reconstruct his schedule for a week or two prior to his getting sick. Could you do that for me? I'm going to ask his wife to do the same."

"I suppose I could," said Miss Cavanagh.

"Did anything out of the ordinary happen that you can recall?"

"Like what?" asked Miss Cavanagh, with a blank face.

"Like his being bitten by a monkey or getting mugged in the parking garage!" Marissa's voice had a sharp edge to it.

"Those things did happen," said Miss Cavanagh.

"I realize that," said Marissa. "How about anything else odd or different."

"I can't think of anything at the moment. Wait, he did dent his car."

"Okay, that's the idea," encouraged Marissa. "Keep thinking. And by the way, did you make the arrangements for his African medical meeting?"

"Yes."

"How about the San Diego meeting?"

"That too."

"I would like to have the phone numbers of the sponsoring organizations. If you could look them up for me, I'd appreciate it. Also I'd like to have a list of all the patients Dr. Richter saw during the two weeks before his illness. And finally: do you know Helen Townsend?"

Miss Cavanagh took her glasses off her nose and let them hang on their chain. She sighed disapprovingly.

"Does Helen Townsend have the same illness as Dr. Richter?"

"We believe she does," said Marissa, watching Miss Cavanagh's face. The receptionist knew something about Helen Townsend, but she seemed reluctant to speak, toying with the keys of her typewriter. "Was Helen Townsend a patient of Dr. Richter's?" Marissa prodded.

Miss Cavanagh looked up. "No, she was his mistress. I warned him about her. And there: she gave him some disease. He should have listened to me."

"Do you know if he saw her just before he got sick?"

"Yes, the day before."

Marissa stared at the woman. Helen Townsend didn't give Dr. Richter the disease; it was the other way around. But she didn't say anything. It all fit into place. She could now relate all the known cases to Dr. Richter. Epidemiologically, that was extremely important. It meant that Dr. Richter was an index case and that he, and only he, had been exposed to the unknown reservoir of the virus. Now it was even more important for her to reconstruct the man's schedule in minute detail.

Marissa asked Miss Cavanagh to start working on an outline of Dr. Richter's schedule for the last two weeks. She told the woman that she'd be back, but if needed, she could be paged through the hospital operator.

"Can I ask you a question?" said Miss Cavanagh timidly.

"Of course," said Marissa, with a hand on the door.

"Is there a chance I might get ill?"

Marissa had been suppressing the thought because she didn't want to frighten the woman, but she could not lie.

After all, the secretary would have to be considered a primary contact.

"It's possible," said Marissa. "We will be asking you to restrict some of your activities during the next week or so, and I'd advise you to check your temperature twice a day. Personally, however, I think you will be fine since you haven't experienced any symptoms so far."

Back at the hospital, Marissa fought off her own fears and her developing fatigue. She had too much to do. She had to go over the clinic charts in detail. She hoped to find a reason why some of Dr. Richter's patients had gotten the disease and others hadn't. Also Marissa wanted to call Dr. Richter's wife. Between the wife and the secretary, she hoped she could construct a reasonably complete diary of the man's activities during the two weeks before he became ill.

Returning to the fifth floor, Marissa ran into Dr. Navarre. He looked as tired as Marissa felt. "Dr. Richter's condition is deteriorating," he said. "He's bleeding from everywhere: injection sites, gums, GI tract. He's on the brink of kidney failure, and his blood pressure is way down. The interferon we gave him had no effect whatsoever, and none of us knows what else to try."

"What about Helen Townsend?" asked Marissa.

"She's worse, too," said Dr. Navarre. "She's also starting to bleed." He sat down heavily.

Marissa hesitated for a minute and then reached for the phone. She placed another collect call to Atlanta, hoping Dubchek was already on his way. Unfortunately, he wasn't. He came on the line.

"Things are pretty bad here," reported Marissa. "Two patients are experiencing significant hemorrhagic symptoms. Clinically, it is looking more and more like viral hemorrhagic fever, and no one knows what to do for these people."

"There's little that can be done," said Dubchek. "They can try heparinization. Otherwise, supportive therapy—that's about it. When we make a specific diagnosis we may be able to use hyperimmune serum, if it is available. On that track, we've already got your samples, and Tad has begun processing them."

"When will you be coming?" asked Marissa.

"Shortly," said Dubchek. "We've got the Vickers Mobile Isolation Lab all packed."

Marissa woke up with a start. Thankfully, no one had come into the little room behind the nurses' station. She looked at her watch. It was ten-fifteen at night. She'd only been asleep for five or ten minutes.

Getting to her feet, she felt dizzy. Her head ached and she had the beginnings of a sore throat. She prayed that her symptoms were a product of exhaustion and not the beginnings of viral hemorrhagic fever.

It had been a busy evening. Four more cases had presented themselves in the ER, all complaining of severe headache, high fever and vomiting. One already had hemorrhagic signs. The patients were all family members of the previous victims, underlining the need for strict quarantine. The virus was already into the third generation. Marissa had prepared viral samples and had them shipped to Atlanta by an overnight carrier.

Recognizing that she was at the limit of her strength,

Marissa decided to go back to her motel. She was just leaving when the floor nurse said Dr. Richter's wife was able to see her. Realizing it would be cruel to put her off, Marissa met her in the visitors' lounge. Anna Richter, a well-dressed, attractive woman in her late thirties, did her best to fill in her husband's schedule over the past two weeks, but she was desperately upset, not just alarmed about her husband but fearful for their two young children as well. Marissa was reluctant to press her for too much detail. Mrs. Richter promised to provide a more complete chronology the next day. Marissa walked her to the doctor's BMW. Then she found her own car and drove to the Tropic Motel where she fell directly into bed.

3

January 22

ARRIVING AT THE CLINIC the next morning, Marissa was surprised to see a number of TV trucks pulled up to the hospital entrance, with their transmission antennae raised against the morning sky. When she tried to enter through the parking garage, she was stopped by a policeman and had to show her CDC identification.

"Quarantine," the policeman explained, and told her to enter the clinic through the main hospital entrance where the TV trucks were located.

Marissa obeyed, wondering what had been happening during the six-plus hours she'd been away. TV cables snaked their way along the floor to the conference room, and she was amazed at the level of activity in the main corridor. Spotting Dr. Navarre, she asked him what was going on.

"Your people have scheduled a news conference," he explained. His face was haggard and unshaven, and it seemed obvious he had not been to bed. He took a newspaper from under his arm and showed it to Marissa: A NEW AIDS EPIDEMIC, shouted the headline. The article was illustrated with a photo of Marissa talking with Clarence Herns.

"Dr. Dubchek felt that such a misconception could not be allowed to continue," said Dr. Navarre.

Marissa groaned. "The reporter approached me right after I'd arrived. I really didn't tell him anything."

"It doesn't matter," said Dr. Navarre, patting her gently on the shoulder. "Dr. Richter died during the night, and with the four new cases, there was no way this could have been kept from the media."

"When did Dr. Dubchek arrive?" asked Marissa, getting out of the way of a camera crew headed into the conference room.

"A little after midnight," said Dr. Navarre.

"Why the police?" asked Marissa, noticing a second uniformed officer standing by the doors leading to the hospital.

"After Dr. Richter died, patients started signing themselves out of the hospital, until the State Commissioner of Health issued an order placing the whole building under quarantine."

Marissa excused herself and made her way through a throng of press and TV people outside the conference room. She was glad Dubchek had arrived to take charge but wondered why he hadn't gotten in touch with her. When she entered the room, Dubchek was just about to start speaking.

He handled himself well. His calm no-nonsense manner quieted the room immediately. He began by introducing himself and the other doctors from the CDC. There was Dr. Mark Vreeland, Chief of Medical Epidemiology; Dr. Pierce Abbott, Director of the Department of Virology; Dr. Clark Layne, Director of the Hospital Infectious Disease Program; and Dr. Paul

Eckenstein, Director of the Center for Infectious Disease.

Dubchek then went on to downplay the incident, saying that the problem was not "A New AIDS Epidemic" by any stretch of the imagination. He said that the California State Epidemiologist had requested help from the CDC to look into a few cases of unexplained illness thought to be of viral origin.

Looking at reporters eager for copy, Marissa could tell they were not buying Dubchek's calm assessment. The idea of a new, unknown and frightening viral illness made for exciting news.

Dubchek continued by saying that there had only been a total of sixteen cases and that he thought the problem was under control. He pointed to Dr. Layne and announced that he would be overseeing the quarantine efforts and added that experience proved this kind of illness could be controlled by strict hospital isolation.

At this, Clarence Herns jumped up, asking, "Did Dr. Richter bring this virus back from his African conference?"

"We don't know," said Dubchek. "It is a possibility, but doubtful. The incubation period would be too long, since Dr. Richter returned from Africa over a month ago. The incubation period for this kind of illness is usually about a week."

Another reporter got to her feet: "If the incubation period for AIDS can be five years, how can you limit it here to less than a month?"

"That's exactly the point," said Dubchek, his patience wearing thin. "The AIDS virus is totally different from our current problem. It is essential that the media understand this point and communicate it to the public."

"Have you isolated the new virus?" asked another reporter.

"Not yet," admitted Dubchek. "But we do not expect to have any difficulty. Again, that's because it is a very different virus from AIDS. It should only take a week or so to culture it."

"If the virus has not been isolated," continued the same reporter, "how can you say that it is different from the AIDS virus?"

Dubchek stared at the man. Marissa could sense the doctor's frustration. Calmly he said, "Over the years we've come to realize that totally different clinical syndromes are caused by totally different microorganisms. Now that is all for today, but we will keep you informed. Thank you for coming at this early hour."

The conference room erupted as each reporter tried to get one more question answered. Dubchek ignored them as he and the other doctors made their exit. Marissa tried to push through the crowd but couldn't. Outside the conference room the uniformed policeman kept the reporters from entering the hospital proper. After showing her CDC identity card, Marissa was allowed to pass. She caught up to Dubchek at the elevators.

"There you are!" said Dubchek, his dark eyes lighting up. His voice was friendly as he introduced Marissa to the other men.

"I didn't know so many of you were coming," she said as they boarded the elevator.

"We didn't have much choice," said Dr. Layne.

Dr. Abbott nodded. "Despite Cyrill's comments at the news conference, this outbreak is extraordinarily serious. An appearance of African viral hemorrhagic fever in the developed world has been a nightmare we've lived with since the illness first surfaced.

"If it proves to be African viral hemorrhagic fever," added Dr. Eckenstein.

"I'm convinced," said Dr. Vreeland. "And I think the monkey will turn out to be the culprit."

"I didn't get samples from the monkey," admitted Marissa quickly.

"That's okay," said Dubchek. "We sacrificed the animal last night and sent specimens back to the Center. Liver and spleen sections will be far better than blood."

They arrived on the fifth floor, where two technicians from the CDC were busy running samples in the Vickers Mobile Isolation Lab.

"I'm sorry about that L.A. *Times* article," said Marissa when she could speak to Dubchek alone. "The reporter approached me when I first entered the hospital."

"No matter," said Dubchek. "Just don't let it happen again." He smiled and winked.

Marissa had no idea what the wink meant, nor the smile, for that matter. "Why didn't you call me when you arrived?" she asked.

"I knew you'd be exhausted," explained Dubchek. "There really wasn't any need. We spent most of the night getting the lab set up, autopsying the monkey, and just getting oriented. We also improved the isolation situation by having fans installed. Nonetheless, you are to be congratulated. I think you did a fine job getting this affair underway."

"For the moment, I'm buried in administrative detail," continued Dubchek, "but I do want to hear what you've learned. Maybe you and I could have dinner tonight. I've gotten you a room at the hotel where we are staying. I'm sure it's better than the Tropic Motel."

"There's nothing wrong with the Tropic," said Marissa. She felt an odd twinge of discomfort, as if her intuition were trying to tell her something.

Marissa went back to her small room behind the nurses' station and began to catch up on her own paperwork. First she phoned the sponsoring organizations for the two medical meetings Dr. Richter had attended. She told them that she needed to know if any of the other attendees had become ill with a viral disease. Then, gritting her teeth at the cruelty of her next call, she dialed Dr. Richter's home number and asked if she could pick up the diary Mrs. Richter had promised her the night before.

The neighbor who answered the phone seemed appalled by her request, but, after checking with the widow, told Marissa to come over in half an hour.

Marissa drove up to the beautifully landscaped house and nervously rang the bell. The same neighbor answered and rather angrily directed Marissa to the living room. Anna Richter appeared a few minutes later. She seemed to have aged ten years overnight. Her face was pale, and her hair, which had been so carefully curled the night before, hung about her face in lank strands.

The neighbor helped her to a chair, and Marissa was amazed to see that she was anxiously folding and unfolding some lined papers that seemed to contain the requested list of her husband's activities over the last weeks. Knowing what a strain the woman must have been under, Marissa didn't know what to say, but Anna simply handed her the sheets saying, "I couldn't sleep last night anyway, and maybe this will help some other poor family." Her eyes filled with tears. "He was such a good man . . . a good father . . . my poor children."

Despite knowing of his affair with Helen Townsend, Marissa decided that Dr. Richter must have been a pretty good husband. Anna's grief seemed real, and Marissa left her as soon as she politely could.

The notes that she read before starting the car were surprisingly detailed. Put together with a further interview with Miss Cavanagh and the doctor's appointment book, Marissa felt they would give her as good a picture of Richter's last few weeks as anyone could get.

Back at the hospital, Marissa made a separate sheet of paper for each day of January and listed Richter's activities. One fact she discovered was that he had complained to Miss Cavanagh about an AIDS patient named Meterko who was suffering from an undiagnosed retinal disorder. It sounded like something Marissa should look into.

In the afternoon, the phone in Marissa's cubicle rang. Picking it up, she was startled to hear Tad Schockley's voice. The connection was so good that for a moment she thought he was there in L.A.

"Nope," said Tad, responding to her question. "I'm still here in Atlanta. But I need to speak to Dubchek. The hospital operator seemed to think that you might know where he was."

"If he's not in the CDC room, then I guess he's gone to his hotel. Apparently they were up all last night."

"Well, I'll try the hotel, but in case I don't get him, could you give him a message?"

"Of course," said Marissa.

"It's not good news."

Straightening up, Marissa pressed the phone to her ear. "Is it personal?"

"No," said Tad with a short laugh. "It's about the virus you people are dealing with. The samples you sent were great, especially Dr. Richter's. His blood was loaded with virus—more than a billion per milliliter. All I had to do was spin it down, fix it and look at it with the electron microscope."

"Could you tell what it was?" asked Marissa.

"Absolutely," said Tad excitedly. "There are only two viruses that look like this, and it tested positive with indirect fluorescene antibody for Ebola. Dr. Richter has Ebola Hemorrhagic Fever."

"Had," said Marissa, mildly offended by Tad's callous enthusiasm.

"Did the man die?" asked Tad.

"Last night," said Marissa.

"It's not surprising. The illness has a ninety percent plus fatality rate."

"My God!" exclaimed Marissa. "That must make it the deadliest virus known."

"Some people might give rabies that dubious honor," said Tad. "But personally I think it is Ebola. One of the problems is that almost nothing is known about this illness because there has been so little experience. Except for a couple of outbreaks in Africa, it's an unknown entity. You're going to have your work cut out for you trying to explain how it popped up in Los Angeles."

"Maybe not," said Marissa. "Dr. Richter had been bitten just prior to his illness by a monkey that had come from Africa. Dr. Vreeland is pretty sure the monkey was the source."

"He's probably right," agreed Tad. "Monkeys were responsible for an outbreak of hemorrhagic fever in '67. The virus was named Marburg after the town in Germany where it occurred. The virus looks a lot like Ebola."

"We'll soon know," said Marissa. "Now it's up to you. Hepatic and splenic sections from the monkey are on the way. I'd appreciate it if you'd check them right away and let me know."

"My pleasure," said Tad. "Meanwhile, I'm going to start work on the Ebola virus and see how easily I can culture it. I want to figure out what strain it is. Let Dubchek and the others know they're dealing with Ebola. If nothing else, it will make them super careful. I'll talk with you soon. Take care."

Leaving the cubicle, Marissa stepped across the hall and peered into the CDC room. It was deserted. Going into the neighboring room, she asked the technicians where everyone was. They told her that some of the doctors were down in pathology, since two more of the patients had died, and some were in the ER admitting several new cases. Dr. Dubchek had gone back to the hotel. Marissa told the technicians that they were dealing with Ebola. She left it to them to pass the bad news to the others. Then she went back to her paperwork.

The Beverly Hilton was just as Dubchek had described. It was certainly nicer than the seedy Tropic Motel, and it was closer to the Richter Clinic. But it still seemed like unnecessary effort to Marissa as she plodded after the bellman down the eighth-floor corridor to her room. The bellman turned on all the lights while she waited at the door. She gave him a dollar, and he left.

She'd never unpacked at the Tropic, so the move wasn't difficult. Yet she wouldn't have made it if Dubchek hadn't insisted. He'd called her that afternoon, several hours after she'd talked with Tad. She'd been afraid to call him, thinking that she'd awaken him. As soon as he was on the line, she told him Tad's news about the outbreak being Ebola Hemorrhagic Fever, but he took it in stride, almost as if he'd expected it. He then had given her directions to the hotel and told her that she merely had to pick up the key for 805, since she was already registered. And he had told her that they'd eat at seven-thirty, if that was all right with her, and that she should just come to his room, which was conveniently located a few doors from hers. He said he'd order up so they could go over her notes while they ate.

As she eyed the bed, Marissa's exhaustion cried for attention, but it was already after seven. Getting her cosmetics bag from her suitcase, she went into the bathroom. After washing, brushing out her hair and touching up her makeup, Marissa was ready. From her briefcase, she removed the sheets of information concerning Dr. Richter's activities before he'd become ill. Clutching them to her, she walked down to Dubchek's door and knocked.

He answered her knock and, smiling, motioned for her to come in. He was on the phone, apparently talking to Tad. Marissa sat down and tried to follow the conversation. It seemed the samples from the monkey had arrived and they had tested clear.

"You mean the electron microscopy showed no virus at all?" said Dubchek.

There was a long silence as Tad relayed the details of the outcomes of the various tests. Looking at her watch,

Marissa calculated that it was almost eleven in Atlanta. Tad was certainly putting in overtime. She watched Dubchek, realizing the man had a disturbing effect on her. She recalled how unnerved she'd been when he'd turned up at Ralph's dinner party and was upset to find herself inexplicably attracted to him now. From time to time he looked up, and her glance was trapped by an unexpected glint in his dark eyes. He'd removed his jacket and tie, and a *V* of tanned skin was visible at the base of his neck.

Finally he hung up the phone and walked over to her, gazing down at her. "You're certainly the best-looking thing I've seen today. And I gather your friend Tad would agree. He seemed very concerned that you don't put yourself at risk."

"Certainly I'm in no more danger than anyone else involved in this," she said, vaguely annoyed at the turn the conversation was taking.

Dubchek grinned. "I guess Tad doesn't feel the rest of the staff is as cute."

Trying to turn the talk to professional matters, Marissa asked about the monkey's liver and spleen sections.

"Clean so far," said Dubchek, with a wave of his hand. "But that was only by electron microscopy. Tad has also planted the usual viral cultures. We'll know more in a week."

"In the meantime," said Marissa, "we'd better look elsewhere."

"I suppose so," said Dubchek. He seemed distracted. He ran a hand over his eyes as he sat down across from her.

Leaning forward, Marissa handed over her notes. "I thought that you might be interested in looking at these." Dubchek accepted the papers and glanced through them while Marissa talked.

In a chronological fashion, Marissa described what she'd been doing since her arrival in L.A. She made a convincing argument that Dr. Richter was the index case and that he was the source of the Ebola, spreading the disease to some of his patients. She explained his relationship to Helen Townsend and then described the two medical meetings that Dr. Richter had attended. The sponsoring organizations were sending complete lists of the attendees, with their addresses and phone numbers, she added.

Throughout her monologue Dubchek nodded to indicate that he was listening, but somehow he seemed distracted, concentrating more on her face than on what she was saying. With so little feedback, Marissa trailed off and stopped speaking, wondering if she were making some fundamental professional error. After a sigh, Dubchek smiled. "Good job," he said simply. "It's hard to believe that this is your first field assignment." He stood up at the sound of a knock on the door. "Thank goodness. That must be dinner. I'm starved."

The meal itself was mediocre; the meat and vegetables Dubchek had ordered were lukewarm. Marissa wondered why they couldn't have gone down to the dining room. She'd thought that he'd intended to talk business, but as they ate, the conversation ranged from Ralph's dinner party and how she came to know him, to the CDC and whether or not she was enjoying her assignment. Toward the end of the meal Dubchek suddenly said, "I wanted to tell you that I am a widower."

"I'm sorry to hear that," said Marissa sincerely, wondering why the man was bothering to inform her about his personal life.

"I just thought you should know," he added, as if reading her mind. "My wife died two years ago in an auto accident."

Marissa nodded, once again uncertain how to reply.

"What about you?" asked Dubchek. "Are you seeing anyone?"

Marissa paused, toying with the handle of her coffee cup. She had no intention of discussing her breakup with Roger. "No, not at the moment," she managed to tell him. She wondered if Dubchek knew that she had been dating Tad. It had not been a secret, but it wasn't public knowledge either. Neither of them had told people at the lab. Suddenly Marissa felt even more uncomfortable. Her policy of not mixing her personal and professional lives was being violated, she felt. Looking over at Dubchek, she couldn't help but acknowledge that she found him attractive. Perhaps that was why he made her feel so uncomfortable. But there was no way she was interested in a more personal relationship with him, if that was what this was leading up to. All at once she wanted to get out of his room and return to her work.

Dubchek pushed back his chair and stood up. "If we're going back to the clinic maybe we should be on our way."

That sounded good to Marissa. She stood up and went over to the coffee table to pick up her papers. As she straightened up, she realized that Dubchek had come up behind her. Before she could react, he put his hands on her shoulders and turned her around. The action so surprised her that she stood frozen. For a brief moment their lips met. Then she pulled away, her papers dropping to the floor.

"I'm sorry," he said. "I wasn't planning that at all, but ever since you arrived at CDC I've been tempted to do that. God knows I don't believe in dating anyone I work with, but it's the first time since my wife died that I've really been interested in a woman. You don't look like her at all—Jane was tall and blond—but you have that same enthusiasm for your work. She was a musician, and when she played well, she had the same excited expression I've seen you get."

Marissa was silent. She knew she was being mean, that Dubchek certainly had not been harassing her, but she felt embarrassed and awkward and was unwilling to say something to ease over the incident.

"Marissa," he said gently, "I'm telling you that I'd like to take you out when we get back to Atlanta, but if you're involved with Ralph or just don't want to . . ." his voice trailed off.

Marissa bent down and gathered up her notes. "If we're going back to the hospital, we'd better go now," she said curtly.

He stiffly followed her out the door to the elevator. Later, sitting silently in her rent-a-car, Marissa berated herself. Cyrill was the most attractive man she'd met since Roger. Why had she behaved so unreasonably?

4

February 27

ALMOST FIVE WEEKS LATER, as the taxi bringing her home from the airport turned onto Peachtree Place, Marissa was wondering if she would be able to reestablish a pleasant, professional relationship with Dubchek now that they were both back in Atlanta. He had left a few days after their exchange at the Beverly Hilton, and the few meetings they'd had at the Richter Clinic had been curt and awkward.

Watching the lighted windows as the cab drove down her street, seeing the warm family scenes inside, she was overcome with a wave of loneliness.

After paying the driver and turning off the alarm, Marissa hustled over to the Judsons' and retrieved Taffy and five weeks' worth of mail. The dog was ecstatic to see her, and the Judsons couldn't have been nicer. Rather than making Marissa feel guilty about being gone for so long, they acted truly sad to see Taffy leave.

Back in her own house, Marissa turned up the heat to a comfortable level. Having a puppy there made all the difference in the world. The dog wouldn't leave her side and demanded almost constant attention.

Thinking about supper, she opened the refrigerator only to discover that some food had gone bad. She shut the door, deciding to tackle the job of cleaning it out the next day. She dined on Fig Newtons and Coke as she leafed through her mail. Aside from a card from one of her brothers and a letter from her parents, it was mostly pharmaceutical junk.

Marissa was startled when the phone rang, but when she picked up the receiver, she was pleased to hear Tad's voice welcoming her home to Atlanta. "How about going out for a drink?" he asked. "I can pop over and pick you up."

Marissa's first response was to say that she was exhausted after her trip, but then she remembered on her last call from L.A. he'd told her he had finished his current AIDS project and was hard at work on what he called Marissa's Ebola virus. Suddenly feeling less tired, she asked how those tests were going.

"Fine!" said Tad. "The stuff grows like wildfire in the Vero 98 tissue cultures. The morphology portion of the study is already complete, and I've started the protein analysis."

"I'm really interested in seeing what you're doing," said Marissa.

"I'll be happy to show you what I can," said Tad. "Unfortunately, a majority of the work is done inside the maximum containment lab."

"I'd assumed as much," said Marissa. She knew that the only way such a deadly virus could be handled was in a facility that did just what its name suggested—contained the microorganisms. As far as Marissa knew, there were only four such facilities in the world—one at the CDC, one in England, one in Belgium and one in the Soviet Union. She didn't know if the Pasteur Institute in Paris had one or not. For safety reasons entry was restricted to a few authorized individuals. At that time, Marissa was not one of them. Yet, having witnessed Ebola's devastating potential, she told Tad that she was really eager to see his studies.

"You don't have clearance," said Tad, surprised by what seemed to him her naiveté.

"I know," said Marissa, "but what could be so terrible about showing me what you're doing with the Ebola in the lab right now and then going out for a drink. After all, it's late. No one will know if you take me now."

There was a pause. "But entry is restricted," said Tad plaintively.

Marissa was fully aware that she was being manipulative, but there was certainly no danger to anyone if she were to go in with Tad. "Who's to know?" she asked coaxingly. "Besides, I *am* part of the team."

"I guess so," Tad agreed reluctantly.

It was obvious that he was wavering. The fact that Marissa would only see him if he took her into the lab seemed to force his decision. He told her that he'd pick her up in half an hour and that she wasn't to breathe a word to anyone else.

Marissa readily agreed.

"I'm not so sure about this," admitted Tad, as he and Marissa drove toward the CDC.

"Relax," said Marissa. "I'm an EIS officer assigned to Special Pathogens for goodness sakes." Purposefully, Marissa pretended to be a little irritated.

"But we could ask for your clearance tomorrow," suggested Tad.

Marissa turned toward her friend. "Are you chickening out?" she demanded. It was true that Dubchek was due back from a trip to Washington the next day and that a formal request could be made. But Marissa had her doubts about what his response would be. She felt that Dubchek had been unreasonably cold over the last few weeks, even if her own stupidity had been the cause. Why she hadn't had the nerve to apologize or even say she'd like to see him one evening, she didn't know. But with every day that passed, the coolness between them, particularly on his side, increased.

Tad pulled into the parking lot, and they walked in silence to the main entrance. Marissa mused about men's egos and how much trouble they caused.

They signed in under the watchful eyes of the security guard and dutifully displayed their CDC identity cards. Under the heading "Destination," Marissa wrote "office." They waited for the elevator and went up three floors. After walking the length of the main building, they went through an outside door to a wire-enclosed catwalk that connected the main building to the virology labs. All the buildings of the Center were connected on most floors by similar walkways.

"Security is tight for the maximum containment lab," said Tad as he opened the door to the virology building. "We store every pathological virus known to man."

"All of them?" asked Marissa, obviously awed.

"Just about," said Tad like a proud father.

"What about Ebola?" she asked.

"We have Ebola samples from every one of the previous outbreaks. We've got Marburg; smallpox, which otherwise is extinct; polio; yellow fever; dengue; AIDS. You name it; we've got it."

"God!" exclaimed Marissa. "A menagerie of horrors."

"I guess you could say that."

"How are they stored?" she asked.

"Frozen with liquid nitrogen."

"Are they infective?" asked Marissa.

"Just have to thaw them out."

They were walking down an ordinary hall past a myriad of small, dark offices. Marissa had previously been in this portion of the building when she'd come to Dubchek's office.

Tad stopped in front of a walk-in freezer like the kind seen in a butcher shop.

"You might find this interesting," he said, as he pulled open the heavy door. A light was on inside.

Timidly Marissa stepped over the threshold into the cold, moist air. Tad was behind her. She felt a thrill of fear as the door swung shut and latched with a click.

The interior of the freezer was lined with shelves holding tiny vials, hundreds of thousands of them. "What is this?" asked Marissa.

"Frozen sera," said Tad, picking up one of the vials, which had a number and a date written on it. "Samples from patients all over the world with every known viral disease and a lot of unknown ones. They're here for immunological study and obviously are not infective."

Marissa was still glad when they returned to the hallway.

About fifty feet beyond the walk-in freezer the hall

turned sharply to the right, and as they rounded the corner, they were confronted by a massive steel door. Just above the doorknob was a grid of push buttons similar to Marissa's alarm system. Below that was a slot like the opening for a credit card at an automatic bank teller. Tad showed Marissa a card that he had around his neck on a leather thong. He inserted it into the slot.

"The computer is recording the entry," he said. Then he tapped out his code number on the push button plate: 43-23-39. "Good measurements," he quipped.

"Thank you," said Marissa, laughing. Tad joined in. Since the virology building had been deserted, he seemed more relaxed. After a short delay, there was a mechanical click as the bolt released. Tad pulled open the door. Marissa felt as if she had entered another world. Instead of the drab, cluttered hallway in the outer part of the building, she found herself surrounded by a recently constructed complex of color-coded pipes, gauges and other futuristic paraphernalia. The lighting was dim until Tad opened a cabinet door, exposing a row of circuit breakers. He threw them in order. The first turned on the lights in the room in which they were standing. It was almost two stories tall and was filled with all sorts of equipment. There was a slight odor of phenolic disinfectant, a smell that reminded Marissa of the autopsy room at her medical school.

The next circuit breaker lit up a row of portholelike windows that lined the sides of a ten-foot-high cylinder that protruded into the room. At the end of the cylinder was an oval door like the watertight hatch on a submarine.

The final circuit breaker caused a whirring noise as

some kind of large electrical machinery went into gear. "Compressors," said Tad in response to Marissa's questioning look. He didn't elaborate. Instead, with a sweep of his hand he said: "This is the control and staging area for the maximum containment lab. From here we can monitor all the fans and filters. Even the gamma-ray generators. Notice all the green lights. That means that everything is working as it is supposed to be. At least hopefully!"

"What do you mean, 'hopefully'?" asked Marissa, somewhat alarmed. Then she saw Tad's smile and knew he was teasing her. Still, she suddenly wasn't one hundred percent sure she wanted to go through with the visit. It had seemed like such a good idea when she'd been in the safety of her home. Now, surrounded by all this alien equipment and knowing what kinds of viruses were inside, she wasn't so certain. But Tad didn't give her time to change her mind. He opened the airtight door and motioned for Marissa to go inside. Marissa had to duck her head slightly while stepping over the six-inch-high threshold. Tad followed her, then closed and bolted the door. A feeling of claustrophobia almost overwhelmed her, especially when she had to swallow to clear her ears due to the pressure change.

The cylinder was lined with the portholelike windows Marissa had seen from the outer room. Along both sides were benches and upright lockers. At the far end were shelves and another oval airtight door.

"Surprise!" said Tad as he tossed Marissa some cotton suits. "No street clothes allowed."

After a moment's hesitation during which time Marissa vainly glanced around for a modicum of privacy, she began unbuttoning her blouse. As embarrassed as she was to be stripping down to her underwear in front of Tad, he seemed more self-conscious than she. He made a big production of facing away from her while she changed.

They then went through a second door. "Each room that we enter as we go into the lab is more negative in terms of pressure than the last. That ensures that the only movement of air will be into the lab, not out."

The second room was about the size of the first but with no windows. The smell of the phenolic disinfectant was more pronounced. A number of large, blue plastic suits hung on pegs. Tad searched until he found one he thought would fit Marissa. She took it from his outstretched hand. It was like a space suit without a backpack or a heavy bubble helmet. Like a space suit, it covered the entire body, complete with gloves and booties. The part that covered the head was faced with clear plastic. The suit sealed with a zipper that ran from the pubic area to the base of the throat. Issuing from the back, like a long tail, was an air hose.

Tad pointed out green piping that ran along the sides of the room at chest height, saying that the entire lab was laced with such pipes. At frequent intervals were rectangular lime green manifolds with adapters to take the air hoses from the suits. Tad explained that the suits were filled with clean, positive-pressure air so that the air in the lab itself was never breathed. He rehearsed with Marissa the process of attaching and detaching the air hose until he was convinced she felt secure.

"Okay, time to suit up," said Tad, as he showed Marissa how to start working her way into the bulky garment. The process was complicated, particularly getting her head inside the closed hood. As she looked out through the clear plastic face mask, it fogged immediately.

Tad told her to attach her air hose, and instantly Marissa felt the fresh air cool her body and clear the face piece. Tad zipped up the front of her suit and with practiced moves, climbed into his own. He inflated his suit, then detached his air hose, and carrying it in his hand, moved down to the far door. Marissa did the same. She had to waddle to walk.

To the right of the door was a panel. "Interior lights for the lab," explained Tad as he threw the switches. His voice was muffled by the suit; it was difficult for her to understand, especially with the hiss of the incoming air in the background. They went through another airtight door, which Tad closed behind them.

The next room was half again smaller than the first two, with walls and piping all covered with a white chalky substance. The floor was covered with a plastic grate.

They attached their air hoses for a moment. Then they moved through a final door into the lab itself. Marissa followed close behind Tad, moving her air hose and connecting it where he did.

Marissa was confronted by a large rectangular room with a central island of lab benches surmounted by protective exhaust hoods. The walls were lined with all sorts of equipment—centrifuges, incubators, various microscopes, computer terminals, and a host of things Marissa did not recognize. To the left there was also a bolted insulated door.

Tad took Marissa directly to one of the incubators and opened up the glass doors. The tissue culture tubes were fitted into a slowly revolving tray. Tad lifted out one and handed it to Marissa. "Here's your Ebola," he said.

In addition to the small amount of fluid the tube contained, it was coated (on one side) with a thin film—a layer of living cells infected with the virus. Inside the cells, the virus was forcing its own replication. As innocent as the contents looked, Marissa understood that there was probably enough infectious virus to kill everyone in Atlanta, perhaps the United States. Marissa shuddered, gripping the glass tube more tightly.

Taking the tube, Tad walked over to one of the microscopes. He positioned the airtight specimen, adjusted the focus, then stepped back so Marissa could look.

"See those darkened clumps in the cytoplasm?" he asked.

Marissa nodded. Even through the plastic face mask, it was easy to see the inclusion bodies Tad described, as well as the irregular cell nuclei.

"That's the first sign of infestation," said Tad. "I just planted these cultures. That virus is unbelievably potent."

After Marissa straightened up from the microscope, Tad returned the tube to the incubator. Then he began to explain his complicated research, pointing out some of the sophisticated equipment he was using and detailing his various experiments. Marissa had trouble concentrating. She hadn't come to the lab that night to discuss Tad's work, but she couldn't tell him that.

Finally he led her down a passageway to a maze of animal cages that reached almost to the ceiling. There were monkeys, rabbits, guinea pigs, rats and mice. Marissa could see hundreds of eyes staring at her: some listless, some with fevered hatred. In a far section of the room, Tad pulled out a tray of what he called Swiss ice mice. He was going to show them to Marissa, but he stopped. "My word!" he said. "I just inoculated these guys this afternoon, and most have already died." He looked at Marissa. "Your Ebola is really deadly—as bad as the Zaire '76 strain."

Marissa reluctantly glanced in at the dead mice. "Is there some way to compare the various strains?"

"Absolutely," said Tad, removing the dead mice. They went back to the main lab where Tad searched for a tray for the tiny corpses. He spoke while he moved, responding to Marissa's question. She found it hard to understand him when he wasn't standing directly in front of her. The plastic suit gave his voice a hollow quality, like Darth Vader's. "Now that I've started to characterize your Ebola," he said, "it will be easy to compare it with the previous strains. In fact I've begun with these mice, but the results will have to wait for a statistical evaluation."

Once he had the mice arranged on a dissecting tray, Tad stopped in front of the bolted insulated door. "I don't think you want to come in here." Without waiting for a response, he opened the door and went inside with the dead mice. A mist drifted out as the door swung back against his air hose.

Marissa eyed the small opening, steeling herself to follow, but before she could act, Tad reappeared, hastily shutting the door behind him. "You know, I'm also planning to compare the structural polypeptides and viral

RNA of your virus against the previous Ebola strains," he said.

"That's enough!" laughed Marissa. "You're making me feel dumb. I've got to get back to my virology textbook before making sense of all this. Why don't we call it a night and get that drink you promised me?"

"You're on," said Tad eagerly.

There was one surprise on the way out. When they had returned to the room with chalky walls, they were drenched by a shower of phenolic disinfectant. Looking at Marissa's shocked face, Tad grinned. "Now you know what a toilet bowl feels like."

When they were changing into their street clothes, Marissa asked what was in the room where he'd taken the dead mice.

"Just a large freezer," he said, waving off the question.

Over the next four days, Marissa readjusted to life in Atlanta, enjoying her home and her dog. On the day after her return, she'd tackled all the difficult jobs, like cleaning out the rotten vegetables from the refrigerator and catching up on her overdue bills. At work, she threw herself into the study of viral hemorrhagic fever, Ebola in particular. Making use of the CDC library, she obtained detailed material about the previous outbreaks of Ebola: Zaire '76, Sudan '76, Zaire '77 and Sudan '79. During each outbreak, the virus appeared out of nowhere and then disappeared. A great deal of effort was expended trying to determine what organism served as the reservoir for the virus. Over two hundred separate species of animals and insects were studied as potential hosts. All were negative. The only positive finding was some antibodies in an occasional domestic guinea pig.

Marissa found the description of the first Zairean outbreak particularly interesting. Transmission of the illness had been linked to a health-care facility called the Yambuku Mission Hospital. She wondered what possible points of similarity existed between the Yambuku Mission and the Richter Clinic, or for that matter, between Yambuku and Los Angeles. There couldn't be very many.

She was sitting at a back table in the library, reading again from Fields' *Virology*. She was studying up on tissue cultures as an aid to further practical work in the main virology lab. Tad had been helpful in setting her up with some relatively harmless viruses so that she could familiarize herself with the latest virology equipment.

Marissa checked her watch. It was a little after two. At three-fifteen she had an appointment with Dr. Dubchek. The day before, she'd given his secretary a formal request for permission to use the maximum containment lab, outlining the experimental work she wanted to do on the communicability of the Ebola virus. Marissa was not particularly sanguine about Dubchek's response. He'd all but ignored her since her return from Los Angeles.

A shadow fell across her page, and Marissa automatically glanced up. "Well! Well! She is still alive!" said a familiar voice.

"Ralph," whispered Marissa, shocked both by his unexpected presence in the CDC library and the loudness of his voice. A number of heads turned toward them.

"There were rumors she was alive but I had to see for

myself," continued Ralph, oblivious of Mrs. Campbell's glare.

Marissa motioned for Ralph to be silent, then took his hand and led him into the hallway where they could talk. She felt a surge of affection as she looked up at his welcoming smile.

"It's good to see you," said Marissa, giving him a hug. She felt a twinge of guilt for not having contacted him since returning to Atlanta. They'd talked on the phone about once a week during her stay in L.A.

As if reading her mind, Ralph said, "Why haven't you called me? Dubchek told me you've been back for four days."

"I was going to call tonight," she said lamely, upset that Ralph was getting information about her from Dubchek.

They went down to the CDC cafeteria for coffee. At that time of the afternoon the room was almost deserted, and they sat by the window overlooking the courtyard. Ralph said he was en route between the hospital and his office and that he had wanted to catch her before the evening. "How about dinner?" he asked, leaning forward and putting a hand on Marissa's. "I'm dying to hear the details of your triumph over Ebola in L.A."

"I'm not sure that twenty-one deaths can be considered a triumph," said Marissa. "Worse still from an epidemiologic point of view, we failed. We never found out where the virus came from. There's got to be some kind of reservoir. Just imagine the media reaction if the CDC had been unable to trace the Legionnaires bacteria to the air-conditioning system."

"I think you are being hard on yourself," said Ralph.

"But we have no idea if and when Ebola will appear again," said Marissa. "Unfortunately, I have a feeling it will. And it is so unbelievably deadly." Marissa could remember too well its devastating course.

"They couldn't figure out where Ebola came from in Africa either," said Ralph, still trying to make her feel better.

Marissa was impressed that Ralph was aware of the fact and told him so.

"TV," he explained. "Watching the nightly news these days gives one a medical education." He squeezed Marissa's hand. "The reason you should consider your time in L.A. successful is because you were able to contain what could have been an epidemic of horrible proportions."

Marissa smiled. She realized that Ralph was trying to make her feel good and she appreciated the effort. "Thank you," she said. "You're right. The outbreak could have been much worse, and for a time we thought that it would be. Thank God it responded to the quarantine. It's a good thing, because it carried better than a ninety-four percent fatality rate, with only two apparent survivors. Even the Richter Clinic seems to have become a victim. It now has as bad a reputation because of Ebola as the San Francisco bathhouses have because of AIDS."

Marissa glanced at the clock over the steam table. It was after three. "I have a meeting in a few minutes," she apologized. "You are a dear for stopping by, and dinner tonight sounds wonderful."

"Dinner it will be," said Ralph, picking up the tray with their empty cups.

Marissa hurried up three flights of stairs and crossed to the virology building. It didn't appear nearly as threatening in the daylight as it had at night. Turning toward Dubchek's office, Marissa knew that just around the bend in the hallway was the steel door that led to the maximum containment lab. It was seventeen after three when she stood in front of Dubchek's secretary.

It was silly for her to have rushed. As she sat across from the secretary, flipping through *Virology Times* with its virus-of-the-month centerfold, Marissa realized that of course Dubchek would keep her waiting. She glanced at her watch again: twenty of four. Beyond the door she could hear Dubchek on the telephone. And from the telephone console on the secretary's desk, she could see the little lights blink when he'd hang up and make another call. It was five of four when the door opened and Dubchek motioned for Marissa to come into his office.

The room was small, and cluttered with reprinted articles stacked on the desk, on the file cabinet and on the floor. Dubchek was in his shirt-sleeves, his tie tucked out of the way between the second and third button of his shirt. There was no apology or explanation of why she'd been kept waiting. In fact there was a suggestion of a grin on his face that particularly galled Marissa.

"I trust that you received my letter," she said, studiously keeping her voice businesslike.

"I did indeed," said Dubchek.

"And . . . ?" said Marissa after a pause.

"A few day's lab experience is not enough to work in the maximum containment lab," said Dubcheck.

"What do you suggest?" asked Marissa.

"Exactly what you are presently doing," said Dubchek. "Continue working with less-pathogenic viruses until you gain sufficient experience."

"How will I know when I've had enough experience?" Marissa realized that Cyrill had a point, but she wondered if his answer would have been different had they been dating. It bothered her even more that she didn't have the nerve to withdraw her earlier rebuff. He was a handsome man, one who attracted her far more than Ralph, whom she was happy enough to see for dinner.

"I believe *I* will know when you have had adequate experience," said Dubchek interrupting her thoughts, ". . . or Tad Schockley will."

Marissa felt cheered. If it were up to Tad, she was certain that she would eventually get the necessary authorization.

"Meanwhile," said Dubchek, stepping around his desk and sitting down, "I've got something more important to talk with you about. I've just been on the phone with a number of people, including the Missouri State Epidemiologist. They have a single case of a severe viral illness in St. Louis that they think might be Ebola. I want you to leave immediately, assess the situation clinically, send Tad samples and report back. Here's your flight reservation." He handed Marissa a sheet of paper. On it was written Delta, flight 1083, departure 5:34 P.M., arrival 6:06 P.M.

Marissa was stunned. With rush-hour traffic, it was going to be a near thing. She knew that as an EIS officer she should always have a bag packed, but she didn't, and there was Taffy to think of, too.

"We'll have the mobile lab ready if it is needed,"

Cyrill was saying, "but let's hope it's not." He extended his hand to wish her good luck, but Marissa was so preoccupied with the thought of possibly facing the deadly Ebola virus in less than four hours, that she walked out without noticing. She felt dazed. She'd gone in hoping for permission to use the maximum containment lab and was leaving with orders to fly to St. Louis! Glancing at her watch, she broke into a run. It was going to be close.

5

March 3

IT WAS ONLY AS the plane taxied onto the runway that Marissa remembered her date with Ralph. Well, she should touch down in time to catch him as soon as he got home. Her one small consolation was that she felt more comfortable professionally than she had en route to L.A. At least she had some idea of what would be demanded of her. Personally, however, knowing this time how deadly the virus could be, if indeed it was Ebola, Marissa was more frightened at the thought of her own exposure. Although she hadn't mentioned it to anyone, she still worried about contracting the disease from the first outbreak. Each day that passed without the appearance of suspicious symptoms had been a relief. But the fear had never completely disappeared.

The other thought that troubled Marissa was the idea of another Ebola case appearing so quickly. If it was Ebola, how did it get to St. Louis? Was it a separate outbreak from L.A. or merely an extension of that one? Could a contact have brought it from L.A., or could there be an "Ebola Mary" like the infamous "Typhoid Mary"? There were many questions, none of which made Marissa cheerful.

"Will you want dinner tonight?" asked a cabin attendant, breaking Marissa's train of thought.

"Sure," said Marissa dropping her tray table. She'd better eat, whether she was hungry or not. She knew that once she got to St. Louis she might not get the time.

As Marissa climbed out of the taxi that had taken her from the St. Louis airport to the Greater St. Louis Community Health Plan Hospital, she was thankful for the elaborate concrete porte cochere. It was pouring outside. Even with the overhead protection, she pulled up the lapels of her coat to avoid wind-driven rain as she ran for the revolving door. She was carrying her suitcase as well as her briefcase, since she'd not taken the time to stop in her hotel.

The hospital appeared an impressive affair even on a dark, rainy night. It was constructed in a modern style, with travertine-marble facing, and fronted by a three-stories-tall replica of the Gateway Arch. The interior was mostly blond oak and bright red carpeting. A pert receptionist directed Marissa to the administration offices, located through a pair of swinging doors.

"Dr. Blumenthal!" cried a diminutive oriental man, jumping up from his desk. She took a step backward as the man relieved her of her suitcase and enthusiastically pumped her freed hand. "I'm Dr. Harold Taboso," he said. "I'm the medical director here. And this is Dr. Peter Austin, the Missouri State Epidemiologist. We've been waiting for you."

Marissa shook hands with Dr. Austin, a tall, thin man with a ruddy complexion.

"We are thankful that you could come so quickly,"

said Dr. Taboso. "Can we get you something to eat or drink?"

Marissa shook her head, thanking him for his hospitality. "I ate on the plane," she explained. "Besides, I'd like to get directly to business."

"Of course, of course," said Dr. Taboso. For a moment he looked confused. Dr. Austin took advantage of his silence to take over.

"We're well aware of what happened in L.A. and we're concerned that we might be dealing with the same problem here. As you know, we admitted one suspicious case this morning, and two more have arrived while you were en route."

Marissa bit her lip. She had been hoping that this would turn out to be a false alarm, but with two more potential cases, it was difficult to sustain such optimism. She sank into the chair that Dr. Taboso proffered and said, "You'd better tell me what you have learned so far."

"Not much, I'm afraid," said Dr. Austin. "There has been little time. The first case was admitted around 4:00 A.M. Dr. Taboso deserves credit for sounding the alarm as soon as he did. The patient was immediately isolated, hopefully minimizing contacts here at the hospital."

Marissa glanced at Dr. Taboso. He smiled nervously, accepting the compliment.

"That was fortunate," said Marissa. "Was any lab work done?"

"Of course," said Dr. Taboso.

"That could be a problem," said Marissa.

"We understand," said Dr. Austin. "But it was ordered immediately on admittance, before we had any suspicion of the diagnosis. The moment my office was alerted we called the CDC."

"Have you been able to make any association with the L.A. outbreak? Did any of the patients come from L.A.?"

"No," said Dr. Austin. "We have inquired about such a possibility, but there has been no connection that we could find."

"Well," said Marissa, reluctantly getting to her feet. "Let's see the patients. I assume that you have full protective gear available."

"Of course," said Dr. Taboso as they filed out of the room.

They crossed the hospital lobby to the elevators. Riding up in the car, Marissa asked, "Have any of the patients been to Africa recently?"

The other two doctors looked at each other. Dr. Taboso spoke: "I don't believe so."

Marissa had not expected a positive answer. That would have been too easy. She watched the floor indicator. The elevator stopped on eight.

As they walked down the corridor, Marissa realized that none of the rooms they were passing were occupied. When she looked closer, she realized that most weren't even fully furnished. And the walls of the hall had only been primed, not painted.

Dr. Taboso noticed Marissa's expression. "Sorry," he said. "I should have explained. When the hospital was built, too many beds were planned. Consequently, the eighth floor was never completed. But we decided to use it for this emergency. Good for isolation, don't you agree?"

They arrived at the nurses' station, which seemed complete except for the cabinetry. Marissa took the first patient's chart. She sat down at the desk and opened the metal cover, noting the man's name: Zabriski. The vital-sign page showed the familiar complex of high fever and low blood pressure. The next page contained the patient's history. As Marissa's eyes ran down the sheet, she caught the man's full name: Dr. Carl M. Zabriski. Raising her eyes to Dr. Taboso, she asked incredulously, "Is the patient a physician?"

"I'm afraid so," answered Taboso. "He's an ophthalmologist here at the hospital."

Turning to Dr. Austin, she asked, "Did you know the index case in L.A. was also a doctor? In fact he was an ophthalmologist!"

"I was aware of the coincidence," said Dr. Austin, frowning.

"Does Dr. Zabriski do any research with monkeys?" asked Marissa.

"Not that I know of," answered Dr. Taboso. "Certainly not here at the hospital."

"No other physicians were involved in the L.A. outbreak that I can recall," said Dr. Austin.

"No," said Marissa. "Just the index case. There were three lab techs and one nurse, but no other doctors."

Redirecting her attention to the chart, Marissa went through it rapidly. The history was not nearly as complete as that done on Dr. Richter at the Richter Clinic. There were no references to recent travel or animal contact. But the lab workup was impressive, and although not all the tests were back, those that were suggested severe liver and kidney involvement. So far everything was consistent with Ebola Hemorrhagic Fever.

After Marissa finished with the chart, she got together the materials necessary for drawing and packing viral samples. When all was ready, she went down the hall with one of the nurses to the isolation area. There she donned hood, mask, gloves, goggles and booties.

Inside Zabriski's room, two other women were similarly attired. One was a nurse, the other a doctor.

"How is the patient doing?" asked Marissa as she moved alongside the bed. It was a rhetorical question. The patient's condition was apparent. The first thing Marissa noticed was the rash over the man's trunk. The second thing was signs of hemorrhage; a nasogastric tube snaked out of the man's nostril and was filled with bright red blood. Dr. Zabriski was conscious, but just barely. He certainly couldn't answer any questions.

A short conversation with the attending physician confirmed Marissa's impressions. The patient had been deteriorating throughout the day, particularly during the last hour, when they began to see a progressive fall in the blood pressure.

Marissa had seen enough. Clinically, the patient resembled Dr. Richter to a horrifying degree. Until proven otherwise, it had to be assumed that Dr. Zabriski and the other two subsequent admissions had Ebola Hemorrhagic Fever.

The nurse helped Marissa obtain a nasal swab as well as blood and urine samples. Marissa handled them as she'd done in L.A., double bagging the material and disinfecting the outsides of the bags with sodium hypochlorite. After removing her protective clothing and washing her hands, she returned to the nurses' station to call Dubchek.

The phone conversation was short and to the point. Marissa said that it was her clinical impression that they were dealing with another Ebola outbreak.

"What about isolation?"

"They've done a good job in that regard," reported Marissa.

"We'll be there as soon as possible," said Dubchek. "Probably tonight. Meanwhile, I want you to stop all further lab work and supervise a thorough disinfection. Also have them set up the same kind of quarantine of contacts that we used in L.A."

Marissa was about to reply when she realized that Dubchek had hung up. She sighed as she replaced the receiver; such a wonderful working relationship!

"Well," said Marissa to Drs. Taboso and Austin, "let's get to work."

They quickly set the quarantine measures in motion, arranging for the sterilization of the lab and assuring Marissa that her samples would be sent overnight to the CDC.

As they left to attend to their tasks, Marissa asked for the charts on the other two patients. The nurse, whose name was Pat, handed them to her, saying, "I don't know if Dr. Taboso mentioned this, but Mrs. Zabriski is downstairs."

"Is she a patient?" asked Marissa with alarm.

"Oh, no," said Pat. "She's just insisting on staying at the hospital. She wanted to be up here, but Dr. Taboso didn't think it was a good idea. He told her to stay in the first-floor lounge."

Marissa put down the two new charts, debating what she should do next. She decided to see Mrs. Zabriski, since she had very few details with regard to the doctor's recent schedule. Besides, she had to stop by the lab to check the sterilization. Asking directions from Pat, Marissa rode down to the second floor on the elevator. En route she looked at the faces of the people next to her and guessed what their responses would be when they heard that there had been an Ebola outbreak in the hospital. When the doors opened on the second floor, she was the only one who got off.

Marissa expected to find the evening shift in the lab and was surprised to see that the director, a pathologist by the name of Dr. Arthur Rand, was still in his office, even though it was after 8:00 P.M. He was a pompous older man, dressed in a plaid vest complete with a gold fob protruding from one of the pockets. He was unimpressed that Marissa had been sent by the CDC, and his facial expression did not change when Marissa said it was her clinical opinion that there was an outbreak of Ebola in his hospital.

"I was aware that was in the differential diagnosis."

"The CDC has requested that no more lab tests be done on the involved patients." Marissa could tell that the man was not going to make it easy for her. "We'll be bringing in an isolation lab sometime tonight."

"I suggest you communicate this to Dr. Taboso," said Dr. Rand.

"I have," said Marissa. "It's also our opinion that the lab here should be disinfected. In the outbreak in L.A. three cases were traced to the lab. I'd be willing to help, if you'd like."

"I believe that we can handle our own cleanup," said Dr. Rand with a look that seemed to say, *Do you think I was born yesterday?*

"I'm available if you need me," said Marissa as she turned and left. She'd done what she could.

On the first floor she made her way to a pleasant lounge with its own connecting chapel. She was unsure how she would recognize Mrs. Zabriski, but it turned out she was the only person in the room.

"Mrs. Zabriski," said Marissa softly. The woman raised her head. She was in her late forties or early fifties, with gray-streaked hair. Her eyes were red rimmed; it was obvious she had been crying.

"I'm Doctor Blumenthal," said Marissa gently. "I'm sorry to bother you, but I need to ask you some questions."

Panic clouded the woman's eyes. "Is Carl dead?"

"No," said Marissa.

"He's going to die, isn't he?"

"Mrs. Zabriski," said Marissa, wanting to avoid such a sensitive issue, especially since she believed the woman's intuition was correct. Marissa sat down next to her. "I'm not one of your husband's doctors. I'm here to help find out what kind of illness he has and how he got it. Has he done any traveling over the last—" Marissa was going to say three weeks, but remembering Dr. Richter's trip to Africa, she said instead, "—the last two months?"

"Yes," Mrs. Zabriski said wearily. "He went to a medical meeting in San Diego last month, and about a week ago he went to Boston."

"San Diego" made Marissa sit up straighter. "Was that an eyelid surgery conference in San Diego?"

"I believe so," said Mrs. Zabriski. "But Judith, Carl's secretary, would know for sure."

Marissa's mind whirled. Zabriski had attended the same meeting as Dr. Richter! Another coincidence? The only problem was that the conference in question had been about six weeks previous, about the same interval of time as from Dr. Richter's African trip to the appearance of his symptoms. "Do you know what hotel your husband stayed in while he was in San Diego?" asked Marissa. "Could it have been the Coronado Hotel?"

"I believe it was," said Mrs. Zabriski.

While Marissa's mind was busy recalling the central role played by a certain hotel in Philadelphia during the Legionnaires Disease outbreak, she asked about Dr. Zabriski's trip to Boston. But his wife did not know why he'd gone. Instead, she gave Marissa her husband's secretary's phone number, saying again that Judith would know that kind of thing.

Marissa took the number and asked whether Dr. Zabriski had been bitten by, or had been around, any monkeys recently.

"No, no," said Mrs. Zabriski. At least none that she knew of.

Marissa thanked the woman and apologized for bothering her. Armed with the secretary's home phone number, she went to call Judith.

Marissa had to explain twice who she was and why she was calling so late before the secretary would cooperate. Judith then confirmed what Mrs. Zabriski had told her: namely, that the doctor had stayed at the Coronado

Hotel while in San Diego, that Dr. Zabriski had not been bitten recently by any animal, and, as far as she knew, that he'd not been around any monkeys. When Marissa asked if Dr. Zabriski knew Dr. Richter, the answer was that the name had never appeared on any correspondence or on his phone list. Judith said the reason that Dr. Zabriski had gone to Boston was to help plan the Massachusetts Eye and Ear Infirmary's upcoming alumni meeting. She gave Marissa the name and phone number of Dr. Zabriski's colleague there. As Marissa wrote it down, she wondered if Zabriski had unknowingly transferred the virus to the Boston area. She decided that she'd have to discuss that possibility with Dubchek.

As she hung up, Marissa suddenly remembered that she hadn't called Ralph from the airport. He answered sleepily, and Marissa apologized both for waking him and for not getting in touch with him before she left Atlanta. After she explained what had happened, Ralph said that he would forgive her only if she promised to call him every couple of days to let him know what was going on. Marissa agreed.

Returning to the isolation ward, Marissa went back to the charts. The two later admissions were a Carol Montgomery and a Dr. Brian Cester. Both had come down with high fevers, splitting headaches and violent abdominal cramps. Although the symptoms sounded nonspecific, their intensity gave sufficient cause for alarm. There was no reference to travel or animal contact in either chart.

After gathering the material necessary for taking viral samples, Marissa dressed in protective gear and visited Carol Montgomery. The patient was a woman one year older than Marissa. Marissa found it hard not to identify with her. She was a lawyer who worked for one of the city's large corporate firms. Although she was lucid and able to talk, it was apparent that she was gravely ill.

Marissa asked if she had done any recent traveling. The answer was no. Marissa asked if she knew Dr. Zabriski. Carol said that she did. Dr. Zabriski was her ophthalmologist. Had she seen him recently? The answer was yes: she'd gone to him four days ago.

Marissa obtained the viral samples and left the room with a heavy heart. She hated making a diagnosis of a disease with no available treatment. The fact that she'd been able to uncover information that mirrored the earlier outbreak was small compensation. Yet the information reminded her of a question that had troubled her in L.A.: Why did some of Dr. Richter's patients catch the disease and others not?

After changing into fresh protective clothing, Marissa visited Dr. Brian Cester. She asked the same questions and got the same replies, except when she asked if he was one of Dr. Zabriski's patients.

"No," said Dr. Cester after a spasm of abdominal pain subsided. "I've never been to an ophthalmologist."

"Do you work with him?" asked Marissa.

"I occasionally give anesthesia for him," said Dr. Cester. His face contorted again in pain. When he recovered, he said, "I play tennis with him more often than I work with him. In fact I played with him just four days ago."

After obtaining her samples, Marissa left the man, more confused than ever. She had begun to think that fairly close contact—particularly with a mucous membrane—was needed to communicate the disease. Playing tennis with someone did not seem to fit that mold.

After sending off the second set of viral samples, Marissa went back to Dr. Zabriski's chart. She read over the history in minute detail and began the same type of diary she'd drawn up for Dr. Richter. She added what material she'd learned from Mrs. Zabriski and the secretary, knowing that she would have to go back to both of them. Although such work had not resulted in determining the reservoir of the virus in the L.A. outbreak, Marissa had hopes that by following the same procedure with Dr. Zabriski she might find some common element in addition to both doctors having been to the same eye conference in San Diego.

It was after twelve when Dubchek, Vreeland and Layne arrived. Marissa was relieved to see them, particularly because Dr. Zabriski's clinical condition had continued to deteriorate. The doctor taking care of him had demanded some routine blood work be done to determine the state of the patient's hydration, and Marissa had been caught between the conflicting demands of treating the patient and protecting the hospital. She finally allowed those tests that could be done in the patient's room.

After a cursory greeting, the CDC doctors all but ignored Marissa as they struggled to get the mobile isolation laboratory functioning and improve the isolation of the patients. Dr. Layne had some large exhaust fans brought in, while Dr. Vreeland immediately went down to the administration area to discuss improving the quarantine.

Marissa went back to her charts but soon exhausted the information they could supply. Getting up, she wandered to the isolation lab. Dubchek had removed his jacket and had rolled up his sleeves while he labored with the two CDC technicians. Some kind of electrical bug had developed in the automatic chemistry portion of the apparatus.

"Anything I can do?" called Marissa.

"Not that I can think of," said Dubchek without looking up. He immediately began conversing with one of the technicians, suggesting they change the sensing electrodes.

"I would like a minute to go over my findings with you," called Marissa, eager to discuss the fact that Dr. Zabriski had attended the same San Diego medical meeting as Dr. Richter had.

"It will have to wait," said Dubchek coolly. "Getting this lab functioning takes precedence over epidemiologic theories."

Going back to the nurses' station, Marissa seethed. She did not expect or deserve Dubchek's sarcasm. If he'd wanted to minimize her contribution, he had succeeded. Sitting down at the desk, Marissa considered her options. She could stay, hoping he might allow her ten minutes, at his convenience, or she could go and get some sleep. Sleep won out. She put her papers in her briefcase and went down to the first floor to rescue her suitcase.

The operator woke Marissa at seven o'clock. As she showered and dressed, she realized that her anger toward Dubchek had dissipated. After all, he was under a lot of stress. If Ebola raged out of control, it was his neck on the line, not hers.

When she arrived back at the isolation ward, one of the CDC lab techs told her that Dubchek had gone back to the hotel at 5:00 A.M. He didn't know where either Vreeland or Layne was.

At the nurses' station things were a bit chaotic. Five more patients had been admitted during the night with a presumptive diagnosis of Ebola Hemorrhagic Fever. Marissa collected the charts, but as she stacked them in order, she realized that Zabriski's was missing. She asked the day nurse where it was.

"Dr. Zabriski died just after four this morning."

Although she'd expected it, Marissa was still upset. Unconsciously, she had been hoping for a miracle. She sat down and put her face in her hands. After a moment she forced herself to go over the new charts. It was easier to keep busy. Without meaning to, she caught herself touching her neck for swelling. There was an area of tenderness. Could it be a swollen lymph node?

She was pleased to be interrupted by Dr. Layne, the Director of the CDC's Hospital Infectious Disease Program. It was obvious from the dark circles under his eyes, his drawn face and the stubble on his chin that he had pulled an "all-nighter." She smiled, liking his slightly heavyset, rumpled looks. He reminded her of a retired football player. He sat down wearily, massaging his temples.

"Looks like this is going to be just as bad as L.A.," he said. "We have another patient on the way up and another in the ER."

"I've just started looking at the new charts," said

Marissa, suddenly feeling guilty for having left the night before.

"Well, I can tell you one thing," said Dr. Layne. "All the new patients seem to have gotten their disease from the hospital. That's what bothers me so much."

"Are they all patients of Dr. Zabriski's?" asked Marissa.

"Those are," said Dr. Layne, pointing at the charts in front of Marissa. "They all saw Zabriski recently. He apparently inoculated them during his examinations. The new cases are both Dr. Cester's patients. He'd been the anesthesiologist when they had surgery during the last ten days."

"What about Dr. Cester?" asked Marissa. "Do you think that he contracted the disease the same way that Dr. Zabriski did?"

Dr. Layne shook his head. "Nope. I talked at length with the man, and I found out that he and Zabriski were tennis partners."

Marissa nodded. "But would such contact count?"

"About three days before Dr. Zabriski became ill, Dr. Cester borrowed his towel between sets. I think that's what did it. Transmission seems to depend on actual contact with body fluids. I think Zabriski is another index case, just like Dr. Richter."

Marissa felt stupid. She had stopped questioning Dr. Cester just one question short of learning a crucial fact. She hoped that she wouldn't make the same mistake again.

"If we only knew how the Ebola got into the hospital in the first place," said Dr. Layne rhetorically.

Dubchek, looking tired but clean-shaven and as carefully dressed as always, arrived at the nurses' station. Marissa was surprised to see him. If he'd left at five, he'd hardly had time to shower and change, much less get any sleep.

Before Dubchek could get involved in a conversation with Layne, Marissa quickly told both doctors that Zabriski had attended the same San Diego medical conference as Richter had and that they had stayed in the same hotel.

"It's too long ago to be significant," Dubchek said dogmatically. "That conference was over six weeks ago."

"But it appears to be the only association between the two doctors," protested Marissa. "I think I should follow up on it."

"Suit yourself," said Dubchek. "Meanwhile, I'd like you to go down to pathology and make sure they take every precaution when they post Zabriski this morning. And tell them that we want quick-frozen samples of liver, heart, brain and spleen for viral isolation."

"What about kidney?" interjected Layne.

"Yeah, kidney, too," said Dubchek.

Marissa went off feeling like an errand girl. She wondered if she would ever regain Dubchek's respect, then remembering why she'd lost it, her depression was wiped out by a surge of anger.

In pathology, a busy place at that time of day, Marissa was directed to the autopsy rooms, where she knew she'd find Dr. Rand. Remembering his pompous, overbearing manner, she was not looking forward to talking with him.

The autopsy rooms were constructed of white tile and gleaming stainless steel. There was a pervading aroma of formalin that made Marissa's eyes water. One of the technicians told her that Zabriski's post was scheduled for room three. "If you intend to go, you have to suit up. It's a dirty case."

With her general fear of catching Ebola, Marissa was more than happy to comply. When she entered the room, she found Dr. Rand just about to begin. He looked up from the table of horrific tools. Dr. Zabriski's body was still enclosed in a large, clear plastic bag. His body was a pasty white on the top, a livid purple on the bottom.

"Hi!" said Marissa brightly. She decided that she might as well be cheerful. Receiving no answer, she conveyed the CDC's requests to the pathologist, who agreed to supply the samples. Marissa then suggested the use of goggles. "A number of cases both here and in L.A. were apparently infected through the conjunctival membrane," she explained.

Dr. Rand grunted, then disappeared. When he returned he was wearing a pair of plastic goggles. Without saying anything he handed a pair to Marissa.

"One other thing," Marissa added. "The CDC recommends avoiding power saws on this kind of case because they cause significant aerosol formation."

"I was not planning to use any power tools," said Dr. Rand. "Although you may find this surprising, I have handled infectious cases during my career."

"Then I suppose I don't have to warn you about not cutting your fingers," said Marissa. "A pathologist died of viral hemorrhagic fever after doing just that."

"I recall," said Dr. Rand. "Lassa Fever. Are you about to favor us with any further suggestions?"

"No," said Marissa. The pathologist cut into the plastic bag and exposed Zabriski's body to the air. Marissa debated whether she should go or stay. Indecision resulted in inaction; she stayed.

Speaking into an overhead microphone activated by a foot pedal, Dr. Rand began his description of the external markings of the body. His voice had assumed that peculiar monotone Marissa remembered from her medical school days. She was startled back to the present when she heard Rand describe a sutured scalp laceration. That was something new. It hadn't been in the chart, nor had the cut on the right elbow or the circular bruise on the right thigh, a bruise about the size of a quarter.

"Did these abrasions happen before or after death?"

"Before," he answered, making no attempt to conceal his irritation at the interruption.

"How old do you think they are?" said Marissa, ignoring his tone. She bent over to look at them more carefully.

"About a week old, I'd say," Dr. Rand replied. "Give or take a couple of days. We'd be able to tell if we did microscopic sections. However, in view of the patient's condition, I hardly think they are important. Now, if you don't mind, I'd like to get back to work."

Forced to step back, Marissa thought about this evidence of trauma. There was probably some simple explanation; perhaps Dr. Zabriski had fallen playing tennis. What bothered Marissa was that the abrasion and the laceration were not mentioned on the man's chart. Where Marissa had trained, every physical finding went into the record.

As soon as Rand had finished and Marissa had seen

that the tissue samples were correctly done, she decided to track down the cause of the injuries.

Using the phone in pathology, Marissa tried Zabriski's secretary, Judith. She let the phone ring twenty times. No answer. Reluctant to bother Mrs. Zabriski, Marissa thought about looking for Dr. Taboso, but instead decided to check Dr. Zabriski's office, realizing it had to be right there in the hospital. She walked over and found Judith back at her desk.

Judith was a frail young woman in her mid-twenties. Mascara smudged her cheeks; Marissa could tell that she'd been crying. But she was more than sad; she was also terrified.

"Mrs. Zabriski is sick," she blurted out as soon as Marissa introduced herself. "I talked with her a little while ago. She's downstairs in the emergency room but she is going to be admitted to the hospital. They think she has the same thing that her husband had. My God, am I going to get it too? What are the symptoms?"

With some difficulty, Marissa calmed the woman enough to explain that in the L.A. outbreak the doctor's secretary had not come down with the illness.

"I'm still getting out of here," said Judith, opening a side drawer of her desk and taking out a sweater. She tossed it into a cardboard box. She'd obviously been packing. "And I'm not the only one who wants to go," she added. "I've talked with a number of the staff and they are leaving, too."

"I understand how you feel," said Marissa. She wondered if the entire hospital would have to be quarantined. At the Richter Clinic, it had been a logistical nightmare.

"I came here to ask you a question," said Marissa.

"So ask," said Judith. She continued to empty her desk drawers.

"Dr. Zabriski had some abrasions and a cut on his head, as if he'd fallen. Do you know anything about that?"

"That was nothing," said Judith, making a gesture of dismissal with her hand. "He was mugged about a week ago, in a local mall while he was shopping for a birthday gift for his wife. He lost his wallet and his gold Rolex. I think they hit him on the head."

So much for the mysterious question of trauma, thought Marissa. For a few minutes she stood watching Judith throw her things into the box, trying to think if she had any further questions. She couldn't think of any just then, so she said good-bye, then left, heading for the isolation ward. In many ways she felt as scared as Judith did.

The isolation ward had lost its previous tranquility. With all the new patients, it was fully staffed with overworked nurses. She found Dr. Layne writing in several of the charts.

"Welcome to Bedlam," he said. "We've got five more admissions, including Mrs. Zabriski."

"So I've heard," said Marissa, sitting down next to Dr. Layne. If only Dubchek would treat her as he did: like a colleague.

"Tad Schockley called earlier. It is Ebola."

A shiver ran down Marissa's spine.

"We're expecting the State Commissioner of Health to arrive any minute to impose quarantine," continued Dr. Layne. "Seems that a number of hospital personnel are abandoning the place: nurses, technicians, even some doctors. Dr. Taboso had a hell of a time staffing this ward. Have you seen the local paper?"

Marissa shook her head, indicating that she had not. She was tempted to say that she didn't want to stay either, if it meant being exposed.

"The headline is 'Plague Returns!'" Dr. Layne made an expression of disgust. "The media can be so god-damned irresponsible. Dubchek doesn't want anyone to talk with the press. He wants all questions directed to him."

The sound of the patient-elevator doors opening caught Marissa's attention. She watched as a gurney emerged, covered by a clear plastic isolation tent. As it went by, Marissa recognized Mrs. Zabriski. She shivered again, wondering if the local paper really had been exaggerating in their headline.

6

April 10

MARISSA TOOK ANOTHER FORKFUL of the kind of dessert that she allowed herself only on rare occasions. It was her second night back in Atlanta, and Ralph had taken her to an intimate French restaurant. After five weeks with little sleep, gulping down meals in a hospital cafeteria, the gourmet meal had been a true delight. She noticed that, not having had a drink since she'd left Atlanta, the wine had gone right to her head. She knew she was being very talkative, but Ralph seemed content to sit back and listen.

Winding down, Marissa apologized for chattering on about her work, pointing to her empty glass as the excuse.

"No need to apologize," Ralph insisted. "I could listen all night. I'm fascinated by what you have accomplished, both in L.A. and in St. Louis."

"But I've filled you in while I was away," protested Marissa, referring to their frequent phone conversations. While she'd been in St. Louis, Marissa had gotten into the habit of calling every few days. Talking with Ralph had provided a sounding board for her theories as well as a way to relieve her frustration at Dubchek's continued insistence on ignoring her. In both cases, Ralph had been understanding and supportive.

"I wish you'd tell me more about the community reaction," he said. "How did the administrators and medical staff of the hospital try to control the panic, considering that this time there were thirty-seven deaths?"

Taking him at his word, Marissa tried to describe the turmoil at the St. Louis hospital. The staff and patients were furious at the enforced quarantine, and Dr. Taboso had sadly told her he expected the hospital to close when it was lifted.

"You know, I'm still worried abut getting sick myself," admitted Marissa with a self-conscious laugh. "Every time I get a headache I think 'this is it.' And though we still have no idea where the virus came from, Dubchek's position is that the virus reservoir is somehow associated with medical personnel, which doesn't make me any more comfortable."

"Do you believe it?" asked Ralph.

Marissa laughed. "I'm supposed to," she said. "And if it is true, then you should consider yourself particularly at risk. Both index cases were ophthalmologists."

"Don't say that," laughed Ralph. "I'm superstitious."

Marissa leaned back as the waiter served a second round of coffee. It tasted wonderful, but she suspected she'd be sorry later on when she tried to sleep.

After the waiter left with the dessert dishes, Marissa continued: "If Dubchek's position is correct, then somehow both eye doctors came into contact with the mysterious reservoir. I've puzzled over this for weeks without coming up with a single explanation. Dr. Richter came in contact with monkeys; in fact he'd been bitten a week before he became ill, and monkeys have been associated with a related virus called Marburg. But Dr. Zabriski had no contact with any animals at all."

"I thought you told me that Dr. Richter had been to Africa," said Ralph. "It seems to me that is the crucial fact. After all, Africa is where this virus is endemic."

"True," said Marissa. "But the time frame is all wrong. His incubation period would have been six weeks, when all the other cases averaged only two to five days. Then consider the problem of relating the two outbreaks. Dr. Zabriski hadn't been to Africa, but the only point of connection was that the two doctors attended the same medical conference in San Diego. And again, that was six weeks before Dr. Zabriski got sick. It's crazy." Marissa waved her hand as if she were giving up.

"At least be happy you controlled the outbreaks as well as you did. I understand that it was worse when this virus appeared in Africa."

"That's true," agreed Marissa. "In the Zaire outbreak in 1976, whose index case may have been an American college student, there were three hundred eighteen cases and two hundred eighty deaths."

"There you go," said Ralph, feeling that the statistics should cheer Marissa. He folded his napkin and put it on the table. "How about stopping at my house for an after-dinner drink?"

Marissa looked at Ralph, amazed at how comfortable she'd become with him. The surprising thing was that the relationship had developed on the telephone. "An after-dinner drink sounds fine," she said with a smile.

On the way out of the restaurant, Marissa took Ralph's arm. When they got to his car, he opened the door for her. She thought that she could get used to such treatment.

Ralph was proud of his car. It was obvious in the loving way he touched the instruments and the steering wheel. The car was a new 300 SDL Mercedes. Marissa appreciated its luxuriousness as she settled back in the leather seat, but cars had never meant much to her. She also couldn't understand why people bought diesels since they had an uncomfortable rattle when they started and idled. "They are economical," said Ralph. Marissa looked around at the appointments. She marveled that someone could delude himself that an expensive Mercedes was economical.

They didn't speak for a while, and Marissa wondered if going to Ralph's house at that time of night was a good idea. But she trusted Ralph and was willing to let their relationship develop a little further. She turned to look at him in the half-light. He had a strong profile, with a prominent nose like her father's.

After they had settled on the couch in the parlor, with brandy snifters in hand, Marissa mentioned something she had been afraid to point out to Dubchek in his current patronizing mood. "There is one thing about the two index cases that I find curious. Both men were mugged just a few days before they got sick." Marissa waited for a response.

"Very suspicious," said Ralph with a wink. "Are you suggesting that there is an 'Ebola Mary' who robs people and spreads the disease?"

Marissa laughed. "I know it sounds stupid. That's why I haven't said anything to anyone else."

"But you have to think of everything," added Ralph. "The old medical-school training that taught you to ask everything, including what the maternal great-grandfather did for a living in the old country."

Deliberately, Marissa switched the conversation to Ralph's work and his house, his two favorite subjects. As the time passed, she noted that he did not make any moves toward her. She wondered if it were something about herself, like the fact that she'd been exposed to Ebola. Then, to make matters worse, he invited her to spend the night in the guest room.

Marissa was insulted. Perhaps just as insulted as if he'd tried to drag her dress over her head the moment they walked in the front door. She told him thank you, but she did not want to spend the night in his guest room; she wanted to spend the night in her own house with her dog. The last part was meant to be an affront, but it sailed over Ralph's head. He just kept on talking about redecorating plans he had for the first floor of the house, now that he'd lived there long enough to know what he wanted.

In truth, Marissa did not know what she would have done if Ralph had made any physical advances. He was a good friend, but she still didn't find him romantically attractive. In that respect, she thought Dubchek's looks distinctly more exciting.

Thinking of Cyrill reminded her of something. "How do you and Dr. Dubchek know each other?"

"I met him when he addressed the ophthalmology residents at the University Hospital," said Ralph. "Some of the rare viruses like Ebola and even the AIDS virus have been localized in tears and the aqueous humor. Some of them even cause anterior uveitis."

"Oh," said Marissa, nodding as if she understood. Actually she had no idea what anterior uveitis was, but she decided it was as good a point as any to ask Ralph to drive her home.

Over the next few days, Marissa adapted to a more normal life, although every time the phone rang, she half expected to be called out for another Ebola disaster. Remembering her resolve, she did pack a suitcase and kept it open in her closet, ready for her to toss in her cosmetics case. She could be out of her house in a matter of minutes, if the need arose.

At work, things were looking up. Tad helped her perfect her viral laboratory skills and worked with her to write up a research proposal on Ebola. Unable to come up with a working hypothesis for a possible reservoir for Ebola, Marissa concentrated instead on the issue of transmission. From the enormous amount of data that she'd amassed in L.A. and St. Louis, she had constructed elaborate case maps to show the spread of the illness from one person to another. At the same time, she'd compiled detailed profiles on the people who had been primary contacts but who had not come down with the disease. As Dr. Layne had suggested, close personal contact was needed, presumably viral contact with a mucous membrane, though, unlike AIDS, sexual transmission had only been a factor between Dr. Richter and the medical secretary and Dr. Zabriski and his wife. Given the fact that hemorrhagic fever could spread between strangers who shared a towel, or by the most casual close touch, Ebola made the AIDS scare seem like a tempest in a teapot.

What Marissa wanted to do was to validate her hypothesis by using guinea pigs. Of course such work required the use of the maximum containment lab, and she still had not obtained permission.

"Amazing!" exclaimed Tad, one afternoon when Marissa demonstrated a technique she'd devised to salvage bacteria-contaminated viral cultures. "I can't imagine Dubchek turning down your proposal now."

"I can," answered Marissa. She debated telling Tad about what had happened in the L.A. hotel, but once again she decided not to do so. It wouldn't accomplish anything and might cause problems in Tad's relationship with Cyrill.

She followed her friend into his office. As they relaxed over coffee, Marissa said, "Tad, you told me when we went into the maximum containment lab that there were all sorts of viruses stored in there, including Ebola."

"We have samples from every outbreak. There are even samples frozen and stored from your two outbreaks."

Marissa wasn't at all sure how she felt about people referring to the recent epidemics as "hers." But she kept that thought to herself, saying instead, "Is there any place else that the Ebola virus is stored, other than here at the CDC?"

Tad thought for a moment. "I'm not sure. Do you mean here in the U.S.?"

Marissa nodded.

"The army probably has some in Ft. Detrick at the Center for Biological Warfare. The fellow that runs the place used to be here at the CDC and he had an interest in viral hemorrhagic fevers."

"Does the army have a maximum containment lab?"

Tad whistled. "Man, they've got everything."

"And you say the man in charge at Ft. Detrick has an interest in viral hemorrhagic fever?"

"He was one of the people along with Dubchek who had been sent out to cover the initial Ebola outbreak in Zaire."

Marissa sipped her coffee, thinking that was an interesting coincidence. She was also beginning to get a germ of an idea, one so unpleasant that she knew she could not consider it a reasonable hypothesis.

"One moment, ma'am," said the uniformed sentry with a heavy Southern accent.

Marissa was stopped at the main gate to Ft. Detrick. Despite several days of trying to argue herself out of the suspicion that the army might have somehow been responsible for Ebola being loosened on an unsuspecting public, she had finally decided to use her day off to investigate for herself. Those two muggings continued to nag at her.

It had only been an hour-and-a-half flight to Maryland and a short drive in a rent-a-car. Marissa had pleaded her field experience with Ebola as an excuse to talk to anyone else familiar with the rare virus, and Colonel Woolbert had responded to her request with enthusiasm.

The sentry returned to Marissa's car. "You are expected at building number eighteen." He handed her a pass that she had to wear on the lapel of her blazer, then startled her with a crisp salute. Ahead of her, the black-and-white gate tipped up, and she drove onto the base.

Building #18 was a windowless concrete structure with a flat roof. A middle-aged man in civilian clothes waved as Marissa got out of her car. It was Colonel Kenneth Woolbert.

To Marissa, he looked more like a university professor than an army officer. He was friendly, even humorous, and was unabashedly pleased about Marissa's visit. He told her right off that she was the prettiest and the smallest EIS officer he'd ever met. Marissa took the good with the bad.

The building felt like a bunker. Entry was obtained through a series of sliding steel doors activated by remote control. Small TV cameras were mounted above each door. The laboratory itself, however, appeared like any other modern hospital facility, complete with the omnipresent coffeepot over the Bunsen burner. The only difference was the lack of windows.

After a quick tour, during which the presence of a maximum containment lab was not mentioned, Colonel Woolbert took Marissa to their snack shop, which was nothing more than a series of vending machines. He got her a donut and Pepsi, and they sat down at a small table.

Without any prompting, Colonel Woolbert explained that he'd started at the CDC as an EIS officer in the late fifties and had become increasingly interested in microbiology and ultimately virology. In the seventies, he'd gone back to school, at government expense, to get a Ph.D.

"It's been a hell of a lot better than looking at sore throats and clogged ears," said the Colonel.

"Don't tell me you were in pediatrics!" exclaimed Marissa.

They laughed when they realized they had both trained

at Boston's Children's Hospital. Colonel Woolbert went on to explain how he'd ended up at Ft. Detrick. He told Marissa that there had been a history of movement between Detrick and the CDC and that the army had come to him with an offer he couldn't refuse. He said that the lab and the equipment were superb, and best of all, he didn't have to grovel for funds.

"Doesn't the ultimate goal bother you?" asked Marissa.

"No," said Colonel Woolbert. "You have to understand that three-quarters of the work here involves defending the U.S. against biological attack, so most of my efforts are directed at neutralizing viruses like Ebola."

Marissa nodded. She'd not thought of that.

"Besides," continued Colonel Woolbert, "I'm given complete latitude. I can work on whatever I want to."

"And what is that just now?" asked Marissa innocently. There was a pause. The colonel's light-blue eyes twinkled.

"I suppose I'm not violating the confidentiality of the military by telling you, since I've been publishing a string of articles on my results. For the last three years my interest has been influenza virus."

"Not Ebola?" asked Marissa.

Colonel Woolbert shook his head. "No, my last research on Ebola was years ago."

"Is anyone here at the center working on Ebola?" asked Marissa.

Colonel Woolbert hesitated. Then he said, "I guess I can tell you, since there was a Pentagon policy paper published on it in *Strategic Studies* last year. The answer is no. No one is working on Ebola, including the Soviets, mainly because there is no vaccine or treatment for it. Once started, it was generally felt that Ebola Hemorrhagic Fever would spread like wildfire to both friendly and hostile forces."

"But it hasn't," said Marissa.

"I know," said Colonel Woolbert with a sigh. "I've read with great interest about the last two outbreaks. Someday we'll have to review our assessment of the organism."

"Please, not on my account," said Marissa. The last thing she wanted to do was encourage the army to work with Ebola. At the same time she was relieved to learn that the army was not fooling around with the virus just then.

"I understand you were part of the international team that was sent to Yambuku in 1976," she said.

"Which makes me appreciate what you're doing. I can tell you, when I was in Africa I was scared shitless."

Marissa grinned. She liked and trusted the man. "You are the first person to admit being afraid," she said. "I've been struggling with my fear from the first day I was sent to L.A."

"And for good reason," said Colonel Woolbert. "Ebola's a strange bug. Even though it seems it can be inactivated quite easily, it is extraordinarily infective, meaning that only a couple of organisms have to make entry to produce the disease. That's in marked contrast to something like AIDS, where billions of the virus have to be introduced, and even then there is only a low statistical chance that the individual will be infected."

"What about the reservoir?" asked Marissa. "I know

the official position is that no reservoir was discovered in Africa. But did you have an opinion?"

"I think it is an animal disease," said Colonel Woolbert. "I think it will eventually be isolated to some equatorial African monkey and is therefore a zoonosis, or a disease of vertebrate animals that occasionally gets transmitted to man."

"So you agree with the current CDC official position about these recent U.S. outbreaks?" asked Marissa.

"Of course," said Colonel Woolbert. "What other position is there?"

Marissa shrugged. "Do you have any Ebola here?"

"No," said Colonel Woolbert. "But I know where we can get it."

"I know, too," said Marissa. Well, that wasn't quite true, she thought. Tad had said that it was in the maximum containment lab, but exactly where, she did not know. When they'd made their covert visit, she'd forgotten to ask.

7

April 17

THE PHONE MUST HAVE been ringing for some time before Marissa finally rolled over to pick up the receiver. The CDC operator instantly apologized for waking her from such a deep sleep. As Marissa struggled to sit up, she learned that a call had come through from Phoenix, Arizona, and that the operator wanted permission to patch it through. Marissa agreed immediately.

While she waited for the phone to ring again, she slipped on her robe and glanced at the time. It was 4:00 A.M.; that meant it was 2:00 A.M. in Phoenix. There was little doubt in her mind that someone had discovered another suspected case of Ebola.

The phone jangled again. "Dr. Blumenthal," said Marissa.

The voice on the other end of the wire was anything but calm. The caller introduced himself as Dr. Guy Weaver, the Arizona State Epidemiologist. "I'm terribly sorry to be phoning at such an hour," he said, "but I've been called in on a severe problem at the Medica Hospital in Phoenix. I trust you are familiar with the Medica Hospital."

"Can't say I am."

"It's part of a chain of for-profit hospitals which have contracted with the Medica Medical Group to provide prepaid, comprehensive care in this part of Arizona. We're terrified that the hospital's been hit with Ebola."

"I trust that you've isolated the patient," said Marissa. "We've found that—"

"Dr. Blumenthal," interrupted Dr. Weaver. "It's not one case. It's eighty-four cases."

"Eighty-four!" she exclaimed in disbelief.

"We have forty-two doctors, thirteen RN's, eleven LPN's, four lab techs, six of the administrative staff, six food service personnel and two maintenance men."

"All at once?" asked Marissa.

"All this evening," said the epidemiologist.

At that time of night, there was no convenient service to Phoenix, though Delta promised the most direct flight available. As soon as she dressed, Marissa called the duty officer at the CDC to say that she was leaving for Phoenix immediately and to please brief Dr. Dubchek as soon as he came into the Center.

After writing a note to the Judsons asking them to please collect Taffy and pick up her mail, Marissa drove to the airport. The fact that the new outbreak had started with eighty-four cases overwhelmed her. She hoped Dubchek and his team would arrive by the afternoon.

The flight was uneventful, despite two stops, and was certainly not crowded. When it landed, Marissa was met by a short, round man, who nervously introduced himself as Justin Gardiner, the assistant director of the Medica Hospital.

"Here, let me take your bag," he said. But his hand was shaking so, the bag fell to the floor. Bending down to retrieve it, he apologized, saying that he was a bit upset.

"I can understand," said Marissa. "Have there been any further admissions?"

"Several, and the hospital is in a panic," said Mr. Gardiner, as they started down the concourse. "Patients started checking out—staff were leaving, too—until the State Health Commissioner declared a quarantine. The only reason I could meet you was that I was off yesterday."

Marissa's mouth felt dry with fear as she wondered what she was getting herself into. Pediatrics began to look a lot more attractive than this.

The hospital was another elaborate modern structure. It occurred to Marissa that Ebola favored such contemporary edifices. The clean, almost sterile lines of the building hardly seemed the proper setting for such a deadly outbreak.

Despite the early hour, the street in front of the hospital was crowded with TV trucks and reporters. In front of them stood a line of uniformed police, some of whom were actually wearing surgical masks. In the early light, the whole scene had a surreal look.

Mr. Gardiner pulled up behind one of the TV trucks. "You'll have to go inside and find the director," he said. "My orders are to stay outside to try to control the panic. Good luck!"

As she walked toward the entrance, Marissa got out her identification card. She showed it to one of the policemen, but he had to call over to his sergeant to ask if it was okay to let her pass. A group of the reporters, hearing that she was from the CDC, crowded around and asked for a statement.

"I have no direct knowledge of the situation," protested Marissa, as she felt herself buffeted by the surging journalists. She was grateful for the policeman, who shoved the press aside, then pulled one of the barricades open and allowed her through.

Unfortunately things on the inside of the hospital were even more chaotic. The lobby was jammed with people, and as Marissa entered, she was again mobbed. Apparently she was the first person to pass either in or out of the building for several hours.

A number of the people pressing in on her were patients, dressed in pajamas and robes. They were all simultaneously asking questions and demanding answers.

"Please!" shouted someone to Marissa's right. "Please! Let me through." A heavyset man with bushy eyebrows pushed his way to Marissa's side. "Dr. Blumenthal?"

"Yes," said Marissa with relief.

The heavyset man took her by the arm, ignoring the fact that she was carrying both a suitcase and briefcase. Pushing his way back through the crowd, he led her across the lobby to a door that he locked behind them. They were in a long, narrow hallway.

"I'm terribly sorry about all this turmoil," said the man. "I'm Lloyd Davis, director of the hospital, and we seem to have a bit of a panic on our hands."

Marissa followed Davis to his office. They entered through a side door, and Marissa noticed the main door was barricaded from the inside with a ladder-back chair, making her believe that the "bit of panic" had been an understatement.

"The staff is waiting to talk with you," said Mr. Davis, taking Marissa's belongings and depositing them next to his desk. He breathed heavily, as if the effort of bending over had exhausted him.

"What about the patients with suspected Ebola?" asked Marissa.

"For the moment they'll have to wait," said the director, motioning Marissa to return to the hallway.

"But our first priority has to be the proper isolation of the patients."

"They are well isolated," Mr. Davis assured her. "Dr. Weaver has taken care of that." He pressed his hand against the small of Marissa's back, propelling her toward the door. "Of course we'll follow any additional suggestions you have, but right now I would like you to talk with the staff before I'm faced with mutiny."

"I hope it's not that bad," said Marissa. It was one thing if the inpatients were upset, quite another if the professional staff was hysterical as well.

Mr. Davis closed his office door and led the way along another corridor. "A lot of people are terrified at being forced to stay in the hospital."

"How many more presumed cases have been diagnosed since you called the CDC?"

"Sixteen. No more staff; all the new cases are Medica Plan subscribers."

That suggested that the virus was already into its second generation, having been spread by the initially infected physicians. At least that was what had happened in the two previous outbreaks. Marissa herself quaked at the idea of being locked up in the same building with such a contagion, making her question how much consolation she would be able to extend to the staff. With so many people infected, she wondered if they would be able to contain the problem as they had in L.A. and St. Louis. The horror of the thought of Ebola passing into the general community was almost beyond comprehension.

"Do you know if any of the initial cases had been mugged recently?" asked Marissa, as much to distract herself as in hope of a positive answer. Davis just glanced at her and raised his eyebrows as if she were crazy. That seemed as much of a response he felt the question merited. So much for that observation, thought Marissa, remembering Ralph's response.

They stopped in front of a locked door. Davis took out his keys, unlocked the door and led Marissa onto the hospital auditorium's stage. It was not a big room: There was seating for approximately one hundred and fifty people. Marissa noticed all the seats were occupied, with still more people standing in the back. There was the buzz of a dozen simultaneous conversations. They trailed off into silence as Marissa nervously walked toward the podium, all eyes upon her. A tall, exceptionally thin man stood up from a chair behind the podium and shook her hand. Mr. Davis introduced him as Dr. Guy Weaver, the man she'd spoken to on the phone.

"Dr. Blumenthal," said Dr. Weaver, his deep voice a sharp contrast to his scrawny frame, "you have no idea how happy I am to see you."

Marissa felt that uncomfortable sense of being an imposter. And it got worse. After tapping the microphone to make certain it was "live," Dr. Weaver proceeded to introduce Marissa.

He did so in such glowing terms that she felt progressively more and more uneasy. From his comments, it was as if she were synonymous with the CDC, and that all the triumphs of the CDC were her triumphs. Then, with a sweep of his long arm, he turned the microphone over to Marissa.

Never feeling comfortable talking to a large group under the best of circumstances, Marissa was totally nonplussed in the current situation. She had no idea of what was expected of her, much less of what to say. She took the few moments required to bend the microphone down to her level, to think.

Glancing out at the audience, Marissa noted that about half were wearing surgical masks. She also noticed that a large portion of the people, both men and women, were ethnic appearing, with distinctive features and coloring. There was also a wide range of ages, making Marissa realize that what Mr. Davis meant by staff was anybody working for the hospital, not just physicians. They were all watching her expectantly, and she wished she had more confidence in her ability to affect what was happening at the hospital.

"The first thing we will do is ascertain the diagnosis," began Marissa in a hesitant voice several octaves above her normal pitch. As she continued speaking, not sure of which direction she would go, her voice became more normal. She introduced herself in reasonable terms, explaining her real function at the CDC. She also tried to assure the audience, even though she wasn't sure herself, that the outbreak would be controlled by strict isolation of the patients, complete barrier nursing, and reasonable quarantine procedures.

"Will we all get sick?" shouted a woman from the back of the room. A murmur rippled through the audience. This was their major concern.

"I have been involved in two recent outbreaks," said Marissa, "and I have not been infected, though I've come into contact with patients who had." She didn't mention her own continuing fear. "We have determined that close personal contact is necessary to spread Ebola. Airborne spread is apparently not a factor." Marissa noticed that a few of the people in the audience removed their masks. She glanced around at Dr. Weaver, who gave her an encouraging thumbs-up sign.

"Is it really necessary for us to remain within the hospital?" demanded a man in the third row. He was wearing a physician's long white coat.

"For the time being," said Marissa diplomatically. "The quarantine procedure that we followed in the previous outbreaks involved separating the contacts into primary and secondary groups." Marissa went on to describe in detail what they had done in L.A. and St. Louis. She concluded by saying that no one who'd been quarantined had come down with the illness unless they had previously had direct, hands-on contact with someone already ill.

Marissa then fielded a series of questions about the initial symptoms and the clinical course of Ebola Hemorrhagic Fever. The latter either terrified the audience into silence or satisfied their curiosity—Marissa couldn't decide which—but there were no further questions.

While Mr. Davis got up to talk to his staff, Dr.

Weaver led Marissa out of the auditorium. As soon as they were in the narrow hallway, she told him that she wanted to see one of the initial cases before she called the CDC. Dr. Weaver said he'd assumed as much and offered to take her himself. En route he explained that they had placed all the cases on two floors of the hospital, moving out the other patients and isolating the ventilation system. He had every reason to believe they'd made it a self-contained area. He also explained that the staff employed to man the floors were all specifically trained by his people, that laboratory work had been restricted to what could be done in a hastily set up unit on one of the isolated floors and that everything used by the patients was being washed with sodium hypochlorite before being directly incinerated.

As for the quarantine situation, he told Marissa that mattresses had been brought in from the outside and the outpatient department had been turned into a huge dormitory, separating primary and secondary contacts. All food and water was also being brought in. It was at that point that Marissa learned that Dr. Weaver had been an EIS officer at the CDC six years previously.

"Why did you introduce me as the expert?" asked Marissa, remembering his embarrassing exaggerations. Obviously he knew as much as or more than she did about quarantine procedures.

"For effect," admitted Dr. Weaver. "The hospital personnel needed something to believe in."

Marissa grunted, upset at being misrepresented, but impressed with Dr. Weaver's efficiency. Before entering the floor, they gowned. Then, before entering one of the rooms, they double gowned, adding hoods, goggles, masks, gloves and booties.

The patient Dr. Weaver brought Marissa to see was one of the clinic's general surgeons. He was an Indian, originally from Bombay. All Marissa's fears of exposure came back in a rush as she looked down at the patient. The man appeared moribund, even though he'd been sick for only twenty-four hours. The clinical picture mirrored the terminal phase of the cases in L.A. and St. Louis. There was high fever along with low blood pressure, and the typical skin rash with signs of hemorrhage from mucous membranes. Marissa knew the man would not last another twenty-four hours.

To save time, she drew her viral samples immediately, and Dr. Weaver arranged to have them properly packed and shipped overnight to Tad Schockley.

A glance at the man's chart showed the history to be fairly sketchy, but with eighty-four admissions in less than six hours she could hardly have hoped for a textbook writeup. She saw no mention of foreign travel, monkeys, or contact with the L.A. or St. Louis outbreaks.

Leaving the floor, Marissa first requested access to a telephone, then said she wanted to have as many physician volunteers as she could get to help her interview the patients. If many patients were as sick as the Indian doctor, they would have to work quickly if they were going to get any information at all.

Marissa was given the phone in Mr. Davis's office. It was already after eleven in Atlanta, and Marissa reached Dubchek immediately. The trouble was, he was irritated.

"Why didn't you call me as soon as the aid request

came in? I didn't know you had gone until I got into my office."

Marissa held her tongue. The truth was that she'd told the CDC operators that she should be called directly if a call came in suggestive of an Ebola outbreak. She assumed Dubchek could have done the same if he'd wanted to be called immediately, but she certainly wasn't going to antagonize him further by pointing out the fact.

"Does it look like Ebola?"

"It does," said Marissa, anticipating Dubchek's reaction to her next bomb. "The chief difference is in number of those infected. This outbreak involves one hundred cases at this point."

"I hope that you have instituted the proper isolation," was Dubchek's only reply.

Marissa felt cheated. She'd expected Dubchek to be overwhelmed. "Aren't you surprised by the number of cases?" she asked.

"Ebola is a relatively unknown entity," said Dubchek. "At this point, nothing would surprise me. I'm more concerned about containment; what about the isolation?"

"The isolation is fine," said Marissa.

"Good," said Dubchek. "The Vickers Lab is ready and we will be leaving within the hour. Make sure you have viral samples for Tad as soon as possible."

Marissa found herself giving assurances to a dead phone. The bastard had hung up. She hadn't even had a chance to warn him that the entire hospital was under quarantine—that if he entered, he'd not be allowed to leave. "It'll serve him right," she said aloud as she got up from the desk.

When she left the office, she discovered that Dr. Weaver had assembled eleven doctors to help take histories: five women and six men. All of them voiced the same motivation: as long as they had to be cooped up in the hospital, they might as well work.

Marissa sat down and explained what she needed: good histories on as many of the initial eighty-four cases as possible. She explained that in both the L.A. and the St. Louis incidents there had been an index case to which all other patients could be traced. Obviously, there in Phoenix it was different. With so many simultaneous cases there was the suggestion of a food- or waterborne disease.

"If it were waterborne, wouldn't more people have been infected?" asked one of the women.

"If the entire hospital supply was involved," said Marissa. "But perhaps a certain water fountain . . ." Her voice trailed off. "Ebola had never been a water- or food-borne infection," she admitted. "It is all very mysterious, and it just underlines the need for complete histories to try to find some area of commonality. Were all the patients on the same shifts? Were they all in the same areas of the hospital? Did they all drink coffee from the same pot, eat the same food, come in contact with the same animal?"

Pushing back her chair, Marissa went to a blackboard and began outlining a sequence of questions that each patient should be asked. The other doctors rose to the challenge and began giving suggestions. When they were done, Marissa added as an afterthought that they might ask if any of the patients had attended the eyelid surgery conference in San Diego that had been held about three months before.

Before the group disbanded, Marissa reminded everyone to adhere carefully to all the isolation techniques. Then she thanked them again and went to review the material that was already available.

As she had done in L.A., Marissa commandeered the chart room behind the nurses' station on one of the isolation floors as her command post. As the other doctors finished their history taking, they brought their notes to Marissa, who had begun the burdensome task of collating them. Nothing jumped out of the data except the fact that all the patients worked at the Medica Hospital, something that was already well known.

By midday, fourteen more cases had been admitted, which made Marissa extremely fearful that they had a full-blown epidemic on their hands. All the new patients, save one, were Medica subscribers who had been treated by one of the original forty-two sick physicians before the physicians developed symptoms. The other new case was a lab tech who had done studies on the first few cases before Ebola was suspected.

Just as the evening shift was coming on duty, Marissa learned that the other CDC physicians had arrived. Relieved, she went to meet them. She found Dubchek helping to set up the Vickers Lab.

"You might have told me the damn hospital was quarantined," he snapped when he caught sight of her.

"You didn't give me a chance," she said, skirting the fact that he had hung up on her. She wished there was something she could do to improve their relationship, which seemed to be getting worse instead of better.

"Well, Paul and Mark are not very happy," said Dubchek. "When they learned all three of us would be trapped for the length of the outbreak, they turned around and went back to Atlanta."

"What about Dr. Layne?" asked Marissa guiltily.

"He's already meeting with Weaver and the hospital administration. Then he will see if the State Health Commissioner can modify the quarantine for the CDC."

"I suppose I can't talk to you until you get the lab going," said Marissa.

"At least you have a good memory," said Dubchek, bending over to lift a centrifuge from its wooden container. "After I finish here and I've seen Layne about the isolation procedures, I'll go over your findings."

As Marissa headed back to her room, she mulled over a number of nasty retorts, all of which only would have made things worse. That was why she had said nothing.

After a meal of catered airplane food eaten in an area of the outpatient clinic reserved for staff in direct contact with the presumed Ebola patients, Marissa returned to her chart work. She now had histories on most of the initial eighty-four cases.

She found Dubchek leafing through her notes. He straightened up on seeing her. "I'm not sure it was a good idea to use the regular hospital staff to take these histories."

Marissa was caught off guard. "There were so many cases," she said defensively. "I couldn't possibly interview all of them quickly enough. As it is, seven people were too sick to speak and three have subsequently died."

"That's still not reason enough to expose doctors who aren't trained epidemiologists. The Arizona State Health Department has trained staff that should have been utilized. If any of these physicians you've drafted become ill, the CDC might be held responsible."

"But they—" protested Marissa.

"Enough!" interrupted Dubchek. "I'm not here to argue. What have you learned?"

Marissa tried to organize her thoughts and control her emotions. It was true that she'd not considered the legal implications, but she was not convinced there was a problem. The quarantined physicians were already considered contacts. She sat down at the desk and searched for the summary page of her findings. When she found it, she began reading in a flat monotone, without glancing up at Dubchek: "One of the initial patients is an ophthalmologist who attended the same San Diego conference as Drs. Richter and Zabriski. Another of the initial cases, an orthopedic surgeon, went on safari to East Africa two months ago. Two of the initial cases have used monkeys in their research but have not suffered recent bites.

"As a group, all eighty-four cases developed symptoms within a six-hour period, suggesting that they all were exposed at the same time. The severity of the initial symptoms suggests that they all received an overwhelming dose of the infective agent. Everyone worked at the Medica Hospital but not in the same area, which suggests the air-conditioning system was probably not the source. It seems to me we are dealing with a food- or waterborne infection, and in that regard, the only commonality that has appeared in the data is that all eighty-four people used the hospital cafeteria. In fact, as nearly as can be determined, all eighty-four people had lunch there three days ago."

Marissa finally looked up at Dubchek, who was staring at the ceiling. When he realized that she had finished speaking, he said, "What about contact with any of the patients in the L.A. or St. Louis episodes?"

"None," said Marissa. "At least none that we can discover."

"Have you sent blood samples to Tad?"

"Yes," said Marissa.

Cyrill headed for the door. "I think you should redouble your efforts to associate this outbreak with one of the other two. There has to be a connection."

"What about the cafeteria?" asked Marissa.

"You're on your own there," said Dubchek. "Ebola has never been spread by food, so I can't see how the cafeteria could be associated . . ." He pulled open the door. "Still, the coincidence is curious, and I suppose you'll follow your own instincts no matter what I recommend. Just be sure you exhaust the possibilities of a connection with L.A. or St. Louis."

For a moment Marissa stared at the closed door. Then she looked back at her summary sheet and the huge pile of histories. It was depressing.

Almost as if Cyrill's last words had been a challenge, Marissa decided to visit the cafeteria, which had been built as a separate wing over a garden courtyard. The double doors leading to the large room were closed, and on the right one a notice had been tacked up stating:

CLOSED BY ORDER OF STATE HEALTH COMMISSIONER. Marissa tried the door. It was unlocked.

Inside, the room was spotlessly clean and furnished in stainless steel and molded plastic. Directly ahead of Marissa was the steam table, with stacks of trays at one end and a cash register at the other.

A second set of double doors, with little round windows, was located behind the steam table and led to the kitchen. Just as Marissa was deciding whether to go through or not, they opened, and a stout but attractive middle-aged woman appeared and called out to Marissa that the cafeteria was closed. Marissa introduced herself and asked if she could ask the woman a few questions.

"Certainly," replied the woman, who explained with a faint Scandinavian accent that her name was Jana Beronson and that she was the cafeteria manager. Marissa followed her into her office, a windowless cubicle whose walls were filled with schedules and menus.

After some polite conversation, Marissa asked to see the lunch menu for three days ago. Miss Beronson got it out of the file, and Marissa scanned the page. It was a usual cafeteria menu, with three entrées, two soups and a selection of desserts.

"Is this all the food offered?"

"Those are all the specials," answered Miss Beronson. "Of course we always offer a selection of sandwiches and salads and beverages."

Marissa asked if she could have a copy of the menu, and Miss Beronson took the paper and left the office to Xerox it. Marissa decided that she would go back to each of the initial cases and ask what they had eaten for lunch three days ago. She would also question a control group made up of people who ate from the same menu but who did not become ill.

Miss Beronson returned with the copy. As she folded the paper, Marissa said, "One of your employees was stricken, wasn't she?"

"Maria Gonzales," said Miss Beronson.

"What was her job here?"

"She worked either the steam table or the salad bar," answered Miss Beronson.

"Could you tell me what she did on the day in question?" asked Marissa.

Getting up, Miss Beronson went over to one of the large scheduling boards on her wall. "Desserts and salads," she told Marissa.

Marissa wondered if they should test the whole cafeteria staff for Ebola antibodies. Although Ralph had been joking when he'd suggested an "Ebola Mary," perhaps it was possible, although it had not been the case in Africa.

"Would you like to see our facility?" asked Miss Beronson, trying to be helpful.

For the next thirty minutes Marissa was given a grand tour of the cafeteria, including both the kitchen and the dining area. In the kitchen, she saw the walk-in cooler, the food preparation area and the huge gas ranges. In the dining area, she walked along the steam table, peering into silverware bins and lifting the covers of the salad-dressing cannisters.

"Would you like to see the stock rooms?" Miss Beronson asked, when they were done.

Marissa declined, deciding it was time to start checking to see what the initial Ebola patients had chosen from the menu in her purse.

Marissa rocked back in the swivel chair and rubbed her eyes. It was 11:00 A.M. of her second day in Phoenix, and she'd only managed four hours of sleep the previous night. She'd been assigned one of the examination alcoves in the OB-GYN clinic, and every time someone went by, she'd been awakened.

Behind her, Marissa heard the door open. She turned and saw Dubchek holding up the front page of a local newspaper. The headline read: CDC BELIEVES HIDDEN SOURCE OF EBOLA IN U.S.A. Looking at his expression, Marissa guessed that he was, as usual, angry.

"I told you not to talk to the press."

"I haven't."

Dubchek smacked the paper. "It says right here that Dr. Blumenthal of the CDC said that there is a reservoir of Ebola in the U.S.A., and that the outbreak in Phoenix was spread by either contaminated food or water. Marissa, I don't mind telling you that you are in a lot of trouble!"

Marissa took the paper and read the article quickly. It was true that her name was mentioned, but only at second hand. The source of the information was a Bill Freeman, one of the doctors who'd helped take patient histories. She pointed this fact out to Dubchek.

"Whether you talk directly to the press, or to an intermediary who talks to the press, is immaterial. The effect is the same. It suggests that the CDC supports your opinions, which is not the case. We have no evidence of a food-related problem, and the last thing we want to do is cause mass hysteria."

Marissa bit her lower lip. It seemed that every time the man spoke to her, it was to find fault. If only she'd been able to handle the episode in the hotel room in L.A. in a more diplomatic way, perhaps he wouldn't be so angry. After all, what did he expect—that she wouldn't talk to anyone? Any team effort meant communication.

Controlling her temper, Marissa handed Dubchek a paper. "I think you should take a look at this."

"What is it?" he asked irritably.

"It's the result of a second survey of the initially infected patients. At least those who were able to respond. You'll notice that one fact jumps out. Except for two people who couldn't remember, all the patients had eaten custard in the hospital cafeteria four days ago. You'll remember that in my first survey, lunch in the cafeteria on that day was the only point of commonality. You'll also see that a group of twenty-one people who ate in the cafeteria on the same day but did not eat the custard remained healthy."

Dubchek put the paper down on the counter top. "This is a wonderful exercise for you, but you are forgetting one important fact: Ebola is not a food-borne disease."

"I know that," said Marissa. "But you cannot ignore the fact that this outbreak started with an avalanche of cases, then slowed to a trickle with isolation."

Dubchek took a deep breath. "Listen," he said condescendingly, "Dr. Layne has confirmed your finding that one of the initial patients had been to the San Diego conference with Richter and Zabriski. That fact forms the basis of the official position: Richter brought the virus back from its endemic habitat in Africa and spread it to other doctors in San Diego, including the unfortunate ophthalmologist here at the Medica Hospital."

"But that position ignores the known incubation period for hemorrhagic fever."

"I know there are problems," admitted Dubchek tiredly, "but at the moment that's our official position. I don't mind you following up the food-borne possibility, but for God's sake stop talking about it. Remember that you are here in an official capacity. I don't want you conveying your personal opinions to anyone, particularly the press. Understood?"

Marissa nodded.

"And there are a few things I'd like you to do," continued Dubchek. "I'd like you to contact the Health Commissioner's Office and ask that they impound the remains of some of the victims. We'll want some gross specimens to be frozen and sent back to Atlanta."

Marissa nodded again. Dubchek started through the door, then hesitated. Looking back he said more kindly, "You might be interested to know that Tad has started to compare the Ebola from the L.A., St. Louis and Phoenix outbreaks. His preliminary work suggests that they are all the same strain. That does support the opinion that it is really one related outbreak." He gave Marissa a brief, self-satisfied expression, then left.

Marissa closed her eyes and thought about what she could do. Unfortunately, no custard had been left over from the fatal lunch. That would have made things too easy. Instead, she decided to draw blood on all the food staff to check for Ebola antibodies. She also decided to send samples of the custard ingredients to Tad to check for viral contamination. Yet something told her that even if the custard were involved she wasn't going to learn anything from the ingredients. The virus was known to be extremely sensitive to heat, so it could only have been introduced into the custard after it had cooled. But how could that be? Marissa stared at her stacks of papers. The missing clue had to be there. If she'd only had a bit more experience, perhaps she'd be able to see it.

8

May 16

IT WAS NEARLY A month later, and Marissa was finally back in Atlanta in her little office at the CDC. The epidemic in Phoenix had finally been contained, and she, Dubchek and the other CDC doctors in the hospital had been allowed to leave, still without any final answers as to what caused the outbreak or whether it could be prevented from reoccurring.

As the outbreak had wound down, Marissa had become eager to get home and back to work at the Center. Yet now that she was there, she was not happy. With tear-filled eyes, due to a mixture of discouragement and anger, she was staring down at the memo which began, "I regret to inform you . . ." Once again Dubchek had turned down her proposal to work with Ebola in the maximum containment lab, despite her continued efforts to develop laboratory skills in relation to handling viruses and tissue cultures. This time she felt truly discouraged. She still felt that the outbreak in Phoenix had been connected to the custard dessert, and she desperately wanted to vindicate her position by utilizing animal systems. She thought that if she could understand the transmission of the virus she might develop an insight into where it came from in the first place.

Marissa glanced at the large sheets of paper that traced the transmission of the Ebola virus from one generation to another in all three U.S. outbreaks. She had also constructed less complete but similar diagrams concerning the transmission of Ebola in the first two outbreaks in 1976. Both had occurred almost simultaneously, one in Yambuku, Zaire, and the other in Nzara, Sudan. She'd gotten the material from raw data stored in the CDC archives.

One thing that interested her particularly about the African experience was that a reservoir had never been found. Even the discovery that the virus causing Lassa Hemorrhagic Fever resided in a particular species of domestic mouse had not helped in locating Ebola's reservoir. Mosquitoes, bedbugs, monkeys, mice, rats—all sorts of creatures were suspected and ultimately ruled out. It was a mystery in Africa just as it was in the United States.

Marissa tossed her pencil onto her desk with a sense of frustration. She had not been surprised by Dubchek's letter, especially since he had progressively distanced her from his work in Phoenix and had sent her back to Atlanta the day the quarantine had been lifted. He seemed determined to maintain the position that the Ebola virus had been brought back from Africa by Dr. Richter, who had then passed it on to his fellow ophthalmologists at the eyelid surgery conference in San Diego. Dubchek was convinced that the long incubation period was an aberration.

Impulsively, Marissa got to her feet and went to find

Tad. He'd helped her write up the proposal, and she was confident he'd allow her to cry on his shoulder now that it had been shot down.

After some protest, Marissa managed to drag him away from the virology lab to get an early lunch.

"You'll just have to try again," Tad said when she told him the bad news straight off.

Marissa smiled. She felt better already. Tad's naiveté was so endearing.

They crossed the catwalk to the main building. One benefit of eating early was that the cafeteria line was nonexistent.

As if to further torment Marissa, one of the desserts that day was caramel custard. When they got to a table and began unloading their trays, Marissa asked if Tad had had a chance to check the custard ingredients that she'd sent back from Arizona.

"No Ebola," he said laconically.

Marissa sat down, thinking how simple it would have been to find some hospital food supply company was the culprit. It would have explained why the virus repeatedly appeared in medical settings.

"What about the blood from the food service personnel?"

"No antibodies to Ebola," Tad said. "But I should warn you: Dubchek came across the work and he was pissed. Marissa, what's going on between you two? Did something happen in Phoenix?"

Marissa was tempted to tell Tad the whole story, but again she decided it would only make a bad situation worse. To answer his question, she explained that she'd been the inadvertent source of a news story that differed from the official CDC position.

Tad took a bite of his sandwich. "Was that the story that said there was a hidden reservoir of Ebola in the U.S.?"

Marissa nodded. "I'm certain the Ebola was in the custard. And I'm convinced that we're going to face further outbreaks."

Tad shrugged. "My work seems to back up Dubchek's position. I've been isolating the RNA and the capsid proteins of the virus from all three outbreaks, and astonishingly enough, they are all identical. It means that the exact same strain of virus is involved, which in turn means that what we are experiencing is one outbreak. Normally, Ebola mutates to some degree. Even the two original African outbreaks, in Yambuku and Nzara, which were eight hundred fifty kilometers apart, involved slightly different strains."

"But what about the incubation period?" protested Marissa. "During each outbreak, the incubation period of new cases was always two to four days. There were three months between the conference in San Diego and the problem in Phoenix."

"Okay," said Tad, "But that is no bigger a stumbling block than figuring out how the virus could have been introduced into the custard, and in such numbers."

"That's why I sent you the ingredients."

"But Marissa," said Tad, "Ebola is inactivated even at sixty degrees centigrade. Even if it had been in the ingredients the cooking process would have made it noninfective."

"The lady serving the dessert got sick herself. Perhaps she contaminated the custard."

"Fine," said Tad, rolling his pale blue eyes. "But how did she get a virus that lives only in darkest Africa."

"I don't know," admitted Marissa. "But I'm sure she didn't attend the San Diego eye meeting."

They ate in exasperated silence for a few minutes.

"There is only one place I know the dessert server could have gotten the virus," said Marissa at last.

"And where's that?"

"Here at the CDC."

Tad put down the remains of his sandwich and looked at Marissa with wide eyes. "Good God, do you know what you're suggesting?"

"I'm not suggesting anything," said Marissa. "I'm merely stating a fact. The only known reservoir for Ebola is in our own maximum containment lab."

Tad shook his head in disbelief.

"Tad," said Marissa in a determined tone, "I'd like to ask you for a favor. Would you get a printout from the Office of Biosafety of all the people going in and out of the maximum containment lab for the last year?"

"I don't like this," said Tad, leaning back in his seat.

"Oh, come on," said Marissa. "Asking for a printout won't hurt anyone. I'm sure you can think up a reason to justify such a request."

"The printout is no problem," said Tad. "I've done that in the past. What I don't like is encouraging your paranoid theory, much less getting between you and the administration, particularly Dubchek."

"Fiddlesticks," said Marissa. "Getting a printout hardly puts you between me and Dubchek. Anyway, how will he know? How will anybody know?"

"True," said Tad reluctantly. "Provided you don't show it to anybody."

"Good," said Marissa, as if the matter had been decided. "I'll stop over at your apartment this evening to pick it up. How's that?"

"Okay, I guess."

Marissa smiled at Tad. He was a wonderful friend, and she had the comfortable feeling that he'd do almost anything for her, which was reassuring, because she had yet another favor to ask him. She wanted to get back into the maximum containment lab.

After giving the emergency brake a good yank, Marissa alighted from her red Honda. The incline of the street was steep, and she'd taken the precaution of turning the wheels against the curb. Although she and Tad had gone out any number of times, Marissa had never been to his apartment. She climbed the front steps and struggled to make out the appropriate buzzer. It was almost 9:00 P.M. and was already dark.

The moment she saw Tad, Marissa knew that he had gotten what she wanted. It was the way he smiled when he opened the door.

Marissa plopped herself into an overstuffed sofa and waited expectantly as Tad's big tabby rubbed sensuously against her leg.

With a self-satisfied grin, Tad produced the computer printout. "I told them that we were doing an internal audit of frequency of entry," said Tad. "They didn't raise an eyebrow."

Turning back the first page, Marissa noted that there was an entry for each visit to the maximum containment lab, with name, time in and time out all duly noted. She traced down the list with her index finger, recognizing only a few of the names. The one that appeared most often was Tad's.

"Everybody knows I'm the only one who works at the CDC," he said with a laugh.

"I never expected the list to be so long," complained Marissa, flipping through the pages. "Does everyone on here still have access?"

Tad leaned against Marissa's shoulder and scanned the pages. "Go back to the beginning."

"That guy," said Tad, pointing to the name, "Gaston Dubois no longer has access. He was from the World Health Organization and was in town only for a short visit. And this fellow"—Tad pointed to an entry for one Harry Longford—"was a graduate student from Harvard, and he had access only for a specific project."

Marissa noticed Colonel Woolbert's name listed a number of times, as well as that of a man called Heberling, who seemed to have visited fairly regularly until September. Then his name disappeared. Marissa asked about him.

"Heberling used to work here," explained Tad. "He took another job six months ago. There's been a bit of mobility in academic virology of late because of the huge grants generated by the AIDS scare."

"Where'd he go?" asked Marissa, going on to the next page.

Tad shrugged. "Darned if I know. I think he wanted to go to Ft. Detrick, but he and Woolbert never hit it off. Heberling's smart but not the easiest guy in the world to get along with. There was a rumor he wanted the job

Dubchek got. I'm glad he didn't get it. He could have made my life miserable."

Marissa flipped through the list to January and pointed at a name that appeared several times over a two-week period: Gloria French. "Who's she?" asked Marissa.

"Gloria's from parasitic diseases. She uses the lab on occasion for work on vector-borne viral problems."

Marissa rolled up the list.

"Satisfied?" asked Tad.

"It's a little more than I expected," admitted Marissa. "But I appreciate your effort. There is another thing, though."

"Oh, no," said Tad.

"Relax," said Marissa. "You told me that the Ebola in L.A., St. Louis and Phoenix were all the identical strains. I'd sure like to see exactly how you determined that."

"But all that data is in the maximum containment lab," said Tad weakly.

"So?" said Marissa.

"But you haven't gotten clearance," Tad reminded her. He knew what was coming.

"I don't have clearance to do a study," said Marissa. "That means I can't go in by myself. But it's different if I'm with you, especially if there is no one else there. There wasn't any problem after my last visit, was there?"

Tad had to agree. There hadn't been any trouble, so why *not* do it again? He'd never been specifically told that he could not take other staff members into the lab, so he could always plead ignorance. Although he knew he was being manipulated, it was hard to withstand Marissa's charm. Besides, he was proud of his work and wanted to show it off. He was confident she'd be impressed.

"All right," he said. "When do you want to go?"

"How about right now?" said Marissa.

Tad looked at his watch. "I suppose it's as good a time as any."

"Afterwards we can go for a drink," said Marissa. "It'll be my treat."

Marissa retrieved her purse, noting that Tad's keys and his access card were on the same shelf by the door.

En route to the lab in Marissa's car, Tad began a complicated description of his latest work. Marissa listened, but just barely. She had other interests in the lab.

As before, they signed in at the front entrance of the CDC and took the main elevators as if they were going up to Marissa's office. They got off on her floor, descended a flight of stairs, then crossed the catwalk to the virology building. Before Tad had a chance to open the huge steel door, Marissa repeated his code number: 43-23-39.

Tad looked at her with respect. "God, what a memory!"

"You forget," said Marissa. "Those are my measurements."

Tad snorted.

When he switched on the lights and the compressors in the outer staging area, Marissa felt the same disquiet she'd felt on her first visit. There was something frightening about the lab. It was like something out of a science-fiction movie. Entering the dressing rooms, they changed in silence, first donning the cotton scrub suits, then the bulky plastic ones. Following Tad's lead, Marissa attached her air hose to the manifold.

"You're acting like an old pro," said Tad as he turned on the interior lights in the lab, then motioned for Marissa to detach her air hose and step into the next chamber.

As Marissa waited for Tad in the small room where they would get their phenolic-disinfectant shower on the way out, she experienced an uncomfortable rush of claustrophobia. She fought against it, and it lessened as they entered the more spacious main lab. Her practical work with viruses helped since a lot of the equipment was more familiar. She now recognized the tissue culture incubators and even the chromatography units.

"Over here," called Tad, after they'd both hooked up to an appropriate manifold. He took her to one of the lab benches, where there was a complicated setup of exotic glassware, and began explaining how he was separating out the RNA and the capsid proteins from the Ebola virus.

Marissa's mind wandered. What she really wanted to see was where they stored the Ebola. She eyed the bolted insulated door. If she had to guess, she'd guess someplace in there. As soon as Tad paused, she asked if he would show her where they kept it.

He hesitated for a moment. "Over there," he said, pointing toward the insulated door.

"Can I see?" asked Marissa.

Tad shrugged. Then he motioned for her to follow him. He waddled over to the side of the room and pointed out an appliance next to one of the tissue-culture incubators. He wasn't pointing at the insulated door.

"In there?" questioned Marissa with surprise and disappointment. She'd expected a more appropriate container, one that would be safely locked away behind a bolted door.

"It looks just like my parents' freezer."

"It is," said Tad. "We just modified it to take liquid-nitrogen coolant." He pointed to the intake and exhaust hoses. "We keep the temperature at minus seventy degrees centigrade."

Around the freezer and through the handle was a link chain secured by a combination lock. Tad lifted the lock and twirled the dial. "Whoever set this had a sense of humor. The magic sequence is 6-6-6."

"It doesn't seem very secure," said Marissa.

Tad shrugged. "Who's going to go in here, the cleaning lady?"

"I'm serious," said Marissa.

"No one can get in the lab without an access card," said Tad, opening the lock and pulling off the chain.

Big deal, thought Marissa.

Tad lifted the top of the freezer, and Marissa peered within, half expecting something to jump out at her. What she saw through a frozen mist were thousands upon thousands of tiny plastic-capped vials in metal trays.

With his plastic-covered hand, Tad wiped the frost off the inside of the freezer's lid, revealing a chart locating the various viruses. He found the tray number for Ebola, then rummaged in the freezer like a shopper looking for frozen fish.

"Here's your Ebola," he said, selecting a vial and pretending to toss it at Marissa.

In a panic, she threw her hands out to catch the vial. She heard Tad's laughter, which sounded hollow and distant coming from within his suit. Marissa felt a stab of irritation. This was hardly the place for such antics.

Holding the vial at arm's length, Tad told Marissa to take it, but she shook her head no. An irrational fear gripped her.

"Doesn't look like much," he said, pointing at the bit of frozen material, "but there's about a billion viruses in there."

"Well, now that I've seen it, I guess you may as well put it away." She didn't talk as he replaced the vial in the metal tray, closed the freezer and redid the bicycle lock. Marissa then glanced around the lab. It was an alien environment, but the individual pieces of equipment seemed relatively commonplace.

"Is there anything here that's not in any regular lab?"

"Regular labs don't have air locks and a negative pressure system," he said.

"No, I meant actual scientific equipment."

Tad looked around the room. His eyes rested on the protective hoods over the workbenches in the center island. "Those are unique," he said, pointing. "They're called type 3 HEPA filter systems. Is that what you mean?"

"Are they only used for maximum containment labs?" asked Marissa.

"Absolutely. They have to be custom constructed."

Marissa walked over to the hood in place over Tad's setup. It was like a giant exhaust fan over a stove. "Who makes them?" she asked.

"You can look," said Tad, touching a metal label

affixed to the side. It said: Lab Engineering, South Bend, Indiana. Marissa wondered if anyone had ordered similar hoods lately. She knew the idea in the back of her mind was crazy, but ever since she'd decided that the Phoenix episode had been related to the custard, she hadn't been able to stop wondering if any of the outbreaks had been deliberately caused. Or, if not, whether any physician had been doing some research which had gotten out of control.

"Hey, I thought you were interested in my work," said Tad suddenly.

"I am," insisted Marissa. "I'm just a little overwhelmed by this place."

After a hesitation for Tad to remember where he was in his lecture, he recommenced. Marissa's mind wandered. She made a mental note to write to Lab Engineering.

"So what do you think?" asked Tad when he finally finished.

"I'm impressed," said Marissa, ". . . and very thirsty. Now let's go get those drinks."

On the way out, Tad took her into his tiny office and showed her how closely all his final results matched each other, suggesting that all the outbreaks were really one and the same.

"Have you compared the American strain with the African ones?" she asked him.

"Not yet," admitted Tad.

"Do you have the same kind of charts or maps for them?"

"Sure do," said Tad. He stepped over to his file cabinet and pulled out the lower drawer. It was so full that he had trouble extracting several manila folders. "Here's the one for Sudan and here's Zaire." He stacked them on the desk and sat back down.

Marissa opened the first folder. The maps looked similar to her, but Tad pointed out significant differences in almost all of the six Ebola proteins. Then Marissa opened the second folder. Tad leaned forward and picked up one of the Zaire maps and placed it next to the ones he'd just completed.

"I don't believe this." He grabbed several other maps and placed them in a row on his desk.

"What?" asked Marissa.

"I'm going to have to run all these through a spectrophotometer tomorrow just to be sure."

"Sure of what?"

"There's almost complete structural homology here," said Tad.

"Please," said Marissa. "Speak English! What are you saying?"

"The Zaire '76 strain is exactly the same as the strain from your three outbreaks."

Marissa and Tad stared at one another for a few moments. Finally Marissa spoke. "That means there's been just one outbreak from Zaire 1976 through Phoenix 1987."

"That's impossible," said Tad, looking back at the maps.

"But that's what you're saying," said Marissa.

"I know," said Tad. "I guess it's just a statistical freak." He shook his head, his pale blue eyes returning to Marissa. "It's amazing, that's all I can say."

After they crossed the catwalk to the main building,

Marissa made Tad wait in her office while she sat and typed a short letter.

"Who's so important that you have to write him tonight?" asked Tad.

"I just wanted to do it while it was on my mind," said Marissa. She pulled the letter out of the machine and put it in an envelope. "There. It didn't take too long, did it?" She searched her purse for a stamp. The addressee was Lab Engineering in South Bend, Indiana.

"Why on earth are you writing to them?" Tad asked.

"I want some information about a type 3 HEPA filtration system."

Tad stopped. "Why?" he asked with a glimmer of concern. He knew Marissa was impulsive. He wondered if taking her back into the maximum containment lab had been a mistake.

"Come on!" laughed Marissa. "If Dubchek continues to refuse me authorization to use the maximum containment lab, I'll just have to build my own."

Tad started to say something, but Marissa grabbed his arm and pulled him toward the elevators.

9

May 17

MARISSA GOT UP EARLY with a sense of purpose. It was a glorious spring morning, and she took full advantage of it by going jogging with Taffy. Even the dog seemed to revel in the fine weather, running circles about Marissa as they crisscrossed the neighborhood.

Back home again, Marissa showered, watched a portion of the *Today Show* while she dressed, and was on her way to the Center by eight-thirty. Entering her office, she deposited her purse in her file cabinet and sat down at her desk. She wanted to see if there was enough information available on Ebola viruses for her to calculate the statistical probability of the U.S. strain being the same as the 1976 Zairean strain. If the chances were as infinitesimally small as she guessed, then she'd have a scientific basis for her growing suspicions.

But Marissa did not get far. Centered on her green blotter was an interoffice memo. Opening it, she found a terse message telling her to come to Dr. Dubchek's office immediately.

She crossed to the virology building. At night the enclosed catwalk made Marissa feel safe, but in the bright sun the wire mesh made her feel imprisoned. Dubchek's secretary had not come in yet, so Marissa knocked on the open door.

The doctor was at his desk, hunched over correspondence. When he looked up he told her to close the door and sit down. Marissa did as she was told, conscious the whole time of Dubchek's onyx eyes following her every move.

The office was as disorganized as ever, with stacks of reprinted scientific articles on every surface. Clutter was obviously Dubchek's style even though he personally was always impeccably dressed.

"Dr. Blumenthal," he began, his voice low and controlled. "I understand that you were in the maximum containment lab last night."

Marissa said nothing. Dubchek wasn't asking her a question; he was stating fact.

"I thought I made it clear that you were not allowed in there until you'd been given clearance. I find your disregard for my orders upsetting, to say the least, especially after getting Tad to do unauthorized studies on food samples from Medica Hospital."

"I'm trying to do my job as best I can," said Marissa. Her anxiety was fast changing to anger. It seemed Dubchek never intended to forget that she'd snubbed him in L.A.

"Then your best is clearly not good enough," snapped Dubchek. "And I don't think you recognize the extent of the responsibility that the CDC has to the public, especially given the current hysteria over AIDS."

"Well, I think you are wrong," said Marissa, returning Dubchek's glare. "I take our responsibility to the public very seriously, and I believe that minimizing the threat of Ebola is a disservice. There is no scientific reason to believe that we've seen the end of the Ebola outbreaks, and I'm doing my best to trace the source before we face another."

"Dr. Blumenthal, you are not in charge here!"

"I'm well aware of that fact, Dr. Dubchek. If I were, I surely wouldn't subscribe to the official position that Dr. Richter brought Ebola back from Africa and then experienced an unheard of six-week incubation period. And if Dr. Richter didn't bring back the virus, the only known source of it is here at the CDC!"

"It is just this sort of irresponsible conjecture that I will not tolerate."

"You can call it conjecture," said Marissa, rising to her feet. "I call it fact. Even Ft. Detrick doesn't have any Ebola. Only the CDC has the virus, and it is stored in a freezer closed with an ordinary bicycle lock. Some security for the deadliest virus known to man! And if you think the maximum containment lab is secure, just remember that even I was able to get into it."

Marissa was still trembling when she entered the University Hospital a few hours later and asked directions to the cafeteria. As she walked down the hallway she marveled at herself, wondering where she'd gotten the strength. She'd never been able to stand up to any authority as she'd just done. Yet she felt terrible, remembering Dubchek's face as he'd ordered her out of his office. Uncertain what to do and sure that her EIS career had come to an end, Marissa had left the Center and driven aimlessly around until she remembered Ralph and decided to ask his advice. She'd caught him between surgical cases, and he'd agreed to meet her for lunch.

The cafeteria at the University Hospital was a pleasant affair with yellow-topped tables and white tiled floor. Marissa saw Ralph waving from a corner table.

In typical style, Ralph stood as Marissa approached, and pulled out her chair. Although close to tears, Marissa smiled. His gallant manners seemed at odds with his scrub clothes.

"Thanks for finding time to see me," she said. "I know how busy you are."

"Nonsense," said Ralph. "I always have time for you. Tell me what's wrong. You sounded really upset on the phone."

"Let's get our food first," said Marissa.

The interruption helped; Marissa was in better control of her emotions when they returned with the trays. "I'm having some trouble at the CDC," she confessed. She told Ralph about Dubchek's behavior in Los Angeles and the incident in the hotel room. "From then on things have been difficult. Maybe I didn't handle things as well as I could have, but I don't think it was all my responsibility. After all, it was a type of sexual harassment."

"That doesn't sound like Dubchek," said Ralph with a frown.

"You do believe me, don't you?" asked Marissa.

"Absolutely," Ralph assured her. "But I'm still not sure you can blame all your problems on that unfortunate episode. You have to remember that the CDC is a government agency even if people try to ignore the fact." Ralph paused to take a bite of his sandwich. Then he said, "Let me ask you a question."

"Certainly," said Marissa.

"Do you believe that I am your friend and have your best interests at heart?"

Marissa nodded, wondering what was coming.

"Then I can speak frankly," said Ralph. "I have heard through the grapevine that certain people at the CDC are not happy with you because you've not been 'toeing the official line.' I know you're not asking my advice, but I'm giving it anyway. In a bureaucratic system, you have to keep your own opinions to yourself until the right time. To put it baldly, you have to learn to shut up. I know, because I spent some time in the military."

"Obviously you are referring to my stand on Ebola," said Marissa defensively. Even though she knew Ralph was right, what he'd just said hurt. She'd thought that in general she'd been doing a good job.

"Your stand on Ebola is only part of the problem. You simply haven't been acting as a team player."

"Who told you this?" asked Marissa challengingly.

"Telling you isn't going to solve anything," Ralph said.

"Nor is my staying silent. I cannot accept the CDC's position on Ebola. There are too many inconsistencies and unanswered questions, one of which I learned only last night during my unauthorized visit to the maximum containment lab."

"And what was that?"

"It's known that Ebola mutates constantly. Yet we are faced with the fact that the three U.S. strains are identical, and more astounding, they are the same as the strain in an outbreak in Zaire, in 1976. To me, it doesn't sound as if the disease is spreading naturally."

"You may be right," said Ralph. "But you are in a political situation and you have to act accordingly. And even if there is another outbreak, which I hope there won't be, I have full confidence that the CDC will be capable of controlling it."

"That is a big question mark," said Marissa. "The statistics from Phoenix were not encouraging. Do you realize there were three hundred forty-seven deaths and only thirteen survivors?"

"I know the stats," said Ralph. "But with eighty-four initial cases, I think you people did a superb job."

"I'm not sure you'd think it was so superb if the outbreak had been in your hospital," said Marissa.

"I suppose you're right," said Ralph. "The idea of further Ebola outbreaks terrifies me. Maybe that's why I want to believe in the official position myself. If it's correct, the threat may be over."

"Damn," said Marissa with sudden vehemence. "I've been so concerned about myself, I completely forgot about Tad. Dubchek must know it was Tad who took me into the maximum containment lab. I'd better get back and check on him."

"I'll let you go on one condition," said Ralph. "Tomorrow's Saturday. Let me take you to dinner."

"You are a dear. Dinner tomorrow night would be a treat."

Marissa leaned forward and kissed Ralph's forehead. He was so kind. She wished she found him more attractive.

As Marissa drove back to the CDC she realized her

anger at Dubchek had been replaced by fear for her job and guilt about her behavior. Ralph was undoubtedly correct: She'd not been acting as a team player.

She found Tad in the virology lab, back at work on a new AIDS project. AIDS was still the Center's highest priority. When he caught sight of Marissa he shielded his face with his arms in mock defensiveness.

"Was it that bad?" asked Marissa.

"Worse," said Tad.

"I'm sorry," said Marissa. "How did he find out?"

"He asked me," said Tad.

"And you told him?"

"Sure. I wasn't about to lie. He also asked if I was dating you."

"And you told him that, too?" asked Marissa, mortified.

"Why not?" said Tad. "At least it reassured him that I don't take just anybody off the street into the maximum containment lab."

Marissa took a deep breath. Maybe it was best to have everything out in the open. She put her hand on Tad's shoulder. "I'm really sorry I've caused you trouble. Can I try to make it up to you by fixing supper tonight?"

Tad's face brightened. "Sounds good to me."

At six o'clock Tad came by Marissa's office and then followed her in his car to the supermarket. Tad voted for double loin lamb chops for their meal and waited while the butcher cut them, leaving Marissa to pick up potatoes and salad greens.

When the groceries were stashed in Marissa's trunk, Tad insisted that he stop and pick up some wine. He said he'd meet her back at her house, giving her a chance to get the preparations going.

It had begun to rain, but as Marissa listened to the rhythm of the windshield wipers, she felt more hopeful than she had all day. It was definitely better to have everything out in the open, and she'd talk to Dubchek first thing Monday and apologize. As two adults, they surely could straighten things out.

She stopped at a local bakery and picked up two napoleons. Then, pulling in behind her house, she backed up toward the kitchen door to have the least distance to carry the groceries. She was pleased that she'd beat Tad. The sun had not set yet, but it was as dark as if it had. Marissa had to fumble with her keys to put the proper one in the lock. She turned on the kitchen light with her elbow before dumping the two large brown bags on the kitchen table. As she deactivated the alarm, she wondered why Taffy hadn't rushed to greet her. She called out for the dog, wondering if the Judsons had taken her for some reason. She called again, but the house remained unnaturally still.

Walking down the short hall to the living room, she snapped on the light next to the couch. "Ta-a-a-affy," she called, drawing out the dog's name. She started for the stairs in case the dog had inadvertently shut herself into one of the upstairs bedrooms as she sometimes did. Then she saw Taffy lying on the floor near the window, her head bent at a strange and alarming angle.

"Taffy!" cried Marissa desperately, as she ran to the dog and sank to her knees. But before she could touch the animal she was grabbed from behind, her head jerked upright with such force that the room spun. Instinctively, she reached up and gripped the arm, noticing that it felt like wood under the cloth of the suit. Even with all her strength she could not so much as budge the man's grip on her neck. There was a ripping sound as her dress tore. She tried to twist around to see her attacker, but she couldn't.

The panic button for the alarm system was in her jacket pocket. She reached in and juggled it in her fingers, desperately trying to depress the plunger. Just as she succeeded, a blow to her head sent her sprawling to the floor. Listening to the ear-splitting noise, Marissa tried to struggle to her feet. Then she heard Tad's voice shouting at the intruder. She turned groggily, to see him struggling with a tall, heavyset man.

Covering her ears against the incessant screech of the alarm, she rushed to the front door and threw it open, screaming for help from the Judsons. She ran across the lawn and through the shrubs that divided the properties. As she neared the Judsons' house, she saw Mr. Judson opening his front door. She yelled for him to call the police but didn't wait to explain. She turned on her heel and ran back to her house. The sound of the alarm echoed off the trees that lined the street. Bounding up the front steps two at a time, she returned to her living room, only to find it empty. Panicked, she rushed down the hall to the kitchen. The back door was ajar. Reaching over to the panel, she turned the alarm off.

"Tad," she shouted, going back to the living room and looking into the first-floor guest room. There was no sign of him.

Mr. Judson came running through the open front door,

brandishing a poker. Together they went through the kitchen and out the back door.

"My wife is calling the police," said Mr. Judson.

"There was a friend with me," gasped Marissa, her anxiety increasing. "I don't know where he is."

"Here comes someone," said Mr. Judson, pointing.

Marissa saw a figure approaching through the evergreen trees. It was Tad. Relieved, she ran to him and threw her arms around his neck, asking him what had happened.

"Unfortunately, I got knocked down," he told her, touching the side of his head. "When I got up, the guy was outside. He had a car waiting."

Marissa took Tad into the kitchen and cleaned the side of his head with a wet towel. It was only a superficial abrasion.

"His arm felt like a club," said Tad.

"You're lucky you're not hurt worse. You never should have gone after him. What if he'd had a gun?"

"I wasn't planning on being a hero," said Tad. "And all he had with him was a briefcase."

"A briefcase? What kind of burglar carries a briefcase?"

"He was well dressed," said Tad. "I'd have to say that about him."

"Did you get a good enough look at him to identify him?" asked Mr. Judson.

Tad shrugged. "I doubt it. It all happened so quickly."

In the distance, they heard the sound of a police siren approaching. Mr. Judson looked at his watch. "Pretty good response time."

"Taffy!" cried Marissa, suddenly remembering the dog. She ran back into the living room, with Tad and Mr. Judson close behind.

The dog had not moved, and Marissa bent down and gingerly lifted the animal. Taffy's head dangled limply. Her neck had been broken.

Up until that moment Marissa had maintained cool control of her emotions. But now she began to weep hysterically. Mr. Judson finally coaxed her into releasing the dog. Tad put his arms around her, trying to comfort her as best he could.

The police car pulled up with lights flashing. Two uniformed policemen came inside. To their credit, Marissa found them sensitive and efficient. They found the point of entry, the broken living room window, and explained to Marissa the reason why the alarm hadn't sounded initially: The intruder had knocked out the glass and had climbed through without lifting the sash.

Then, in a methodical fashion, the police took all the relevant information about the incident. Unfortunately, neither Marissa nor Tad could give much of a description of the man, save for his stiff arm. When asked if anything was missing, Marissa had to say that she had not yet checked. When she told them about Taffy, she began to cry again.

The police asked her if she'd like to go to the hospital, but she declined. Then, after saying they'd be in touch, the police left. Mr. Judson also departed, telling Marissa to call if she needed anything and not to concern herself about Taffy's remains. He also said he'd see about getting her window repaired tomorrow.

Suddenly Marissa and Tad found themselves alone,

sitting at the kitchen table with the groceries still in their bags.

"I'm sorry about all this," said Marissa, rubbing her sore head.

"Don't be silly," protested Tad. "Why don't we just go out for dinner?"

"I really am not up to a restaurant. But I don't want to stay here either. Would you mind if I fixed the meal at your place?"

"Absolutely not. Let's go!"

"Just give me a moment to change," said Marissa.

10

May 20

IT WAS MONDAY MORNING, and Marissa was filled with a sense of dread. It had not been a good weekend. Friday had been the worst day of her life, starting with the episode with Dubchek, then being attacked and losing Taffy. Right after the assault, she'd minimized the emotional impact, only to pay for it later. She'd made dinner for Tad and had stayed at his house, but it had been a turbulent evening filled with tears and rage at the intruder who'd killed her dog.

Saturday had found her equally upset, despite first Tad's and then the Judsons' attempts to cheer her up. Saturday night she'd seen Ralph as planned, and he'd suggested she ask for some time off. He even offered to take her to the Caribbean for a few days. He felt that a short vacation might let things at the CDC cool down. When Marissa insisted that she go back to work, he suggested she concentrate on something other than Ebola, but Marissa shook her head to that, too. "Well at least don't make more waves," Ralph counseled. In his opinion, Dubchek was basically a good man who was still recovering from the loss of the wife he'd adored.

Marissa should give him another chance. On this point at least, Marissa agreed.

Dreading another confrontation with Dubchek, but resolved to try her best to make amends, Marissa went to her office only to find another memorandum already waiting for her on her desk. She assumed it was from Dubchek, but when she picked up the envelope, she noticed it was from Dr. Carbonara, the administrator of the EIS program and hence Marissa's real boss. With her heart pounding, she opened the envelope and read the note which said that she should come to see him immediately. That didn't sound good.

Dr. Carbonara's office was on the second floor, and Marissa used the stairs to get there, wondering if she were about to be fired. The office was large and comfortable, with one wall dominated by a huge map of the world with little red pins indicating where EIS officers were currently assigned. Dr. Carbonara was a fatherly, soft-spoken man with a shock of unruly gray hair. He motioned for Marissa to sit while he finished a phone call. When he hung up, he smiled warmly. The smile made Marissa relax a little. He didn't act as though he were about to terminate her employment. Then he surprised her by commiserating with her about the assault and the death of her dog. Except for Tad, Ralph and the Judsons, she didn't think anyone knew.

"I'm prepared to offer you some vacation time," continued Dr. Carbonara. "After such a harrowing experience a change of scene might do you some good."

"I appreciate your consideration," said Marissa. "But to tell you the truth, I'd rather keep working. It will keep my mind occupied, and I'm convinced the outbreaks are not over."

Dr. Carbonara took up a pipe and went through the ritual of lighting it. When it was burning to his satisfaction he said, "Unfortunately, there are some difficulties relating to the Ebola situation. As of today we are transferring you from the Department of Virology to the Department of Bacteriology. You can keep your same office. Actually it's closer to your new assignment than it was to your old one. I'm certain you will find this new position equally as challenging as your last." He puffed vigorously on his pipe, sending up clouds of swirling gray smoke.

Marissa was devastated. In her mind the transfer was tantamount to being fired.

"I suppose I could tell you all sorts of fibs," said Dr. Carbonara, "but the truth of the matter is that the head of the CDC, Dr. Morrison, personally asked that you be moved out of virology and away from the Ebola problem."

"I don't buy that," snapped Marissa. "It was Dr. Dubchek!"

"No, it wasn't Dr. Dubchek," said Dr. Carbonara with emphasis. Then he added: ". . . although he was not against the decision."

Marissa laughed sarcastically.

"Marissa, I am aware that there has been an unfortunate clash of personalities between you and Dr. Dubchek, but—"

"Sexual harassment is more accurate," interjected Marissa. "The man has made it difficult for me ever since I stepped on his ego by resisting his advances."

"I'm sorry to hear you say that," said Dr. Carbonara calmly. "Perhaps it would be in everyone's best interests if I told you the whole story. You see, Dr. Morrison received a call from Congressman Calvin Markham, who is a senior member of the House Appropriations Subcommittee for the Department of Health and Human Services. As you know, that subcommittee handles the CDC's annual appropriations. It was the congressman who insisted that you be put off the Ebola team, not Dr. Dubchek."

Marissa was again speechless. The idea of a United States Congressman calling the head of the CDC to have her removed from the Ebola investigation seemed unbelievable. "Congressman Markham used my name specifically?" asked Marissa, when she found her voice.

"Yes," said Dr. Carbonara. "Believe me, I questioned it, too."

"But why?" asked Marissa.

"There was no explanation," said Dr. Carbonara. "And it was more of an order than a request. For political reasons, we have no choice. I think you can understand."

Marissa shook her head. "That's just it, I don't understand. But it does make me change my mind about that vacation offer. I think I need the time after all."

"Splendid," said Dr. Carbonara. "I'll arrange it—effective immediately. After a rest you can make a fresh start. I want to reassure you that we have no quarrel with your work. In fact we have been impressed by your performance. Those Ebola outbreaks had us all terrified. You'll be a significant addition to the staff working on enteric bacteria, and I'm sure you will enjoy the woman who heads the division, Dr. Harriet Samford."

Marissa headed home, her mind in turmoil. She'd counted on work to distract her from Taffy's brutal death; and while she'd thought there'd been a chance she'd be fired, she'd never considered she'd be given a vacation. Vaguely she wondered if she should ask Ralph if he was serious about that Caribbean trip. Yet such an idea was not without disadvantages. While she liked him as a friend, she wasn't sure if she were ready for anything more.

Her empty house was quiet without Taffy's exuberant greeting. Marissa had an overwhelming urge to go back to bed and pull the covers over her head, but she knew that would mean yielding to the depression she was determined to fight off. She hadn't really accepted Dr. Carbonara's story as an excuse for shuffling her off the Ebola case. A casual recommendation from a congressman usually didn't produce such fast results. She was sure if she checked she would discover Markham was a friend of Dubchek's. Eyeing her bed with its tempting ruffled pillows, she resolved not to give in to her usual pattern of withdrawal. The last reactive depression, after Roger left, was too fresh in her mind. Instead of just giving in and accepting the situation, which was what she'd done then, she told herself that she had to do something. The question was what.

Sorting her dirty clothes, intending to do a therapeutic load of wash, she spotted her packed suitcase. It was like an omen.

Impulsively, she picked up the phone and called Delta to make a reservation for the next flight to Washington, D.C.

"There's an information booth just inside the door," said the knowledgeable cab driver as he pointed up the stairs of the Cannon Congressional Office Building.

Once inside, Marissa went through a metal detector while a uniformed guard checked the contents of her purse. When she asked for Congressman Markham's office she was told that it was on the fifth floor. Following the rather complicated directions—it seemed that the main elevators only went to the fourth floor—Marissa was struck by the general dinginess of the interior of the building. The walls of the elevator were actually covered with grafitti.

Despite the circuitous route, she had no trouble finding the office. The outer door was ajar, so she walked in unannounced, hoping an element of surprise might work in her favor. Unfortunately, the congressman was not in.

"He's not due back from Houston for three days. Would you like to make an appointment?"

"I'm not sure," said Marissa, feeling a little silly after having flown all the way from Atlanta without checking to see if the man would be in town, let alone available.

"Would you care to talk with Mr. Abrams, the congressman's administrative assistant?"

"I suppose," said Marissa. In truth she hadn't been certain how to confront Markham. If she merely asked if he had tried to do Dubchek a favor by figuring out a way to remove her from the Ebola case, obviously he would deny it. While she was still deliberating, an earnest young man came up to her and introduced himself as Michael Abrams. "What can I do for you?" he asked, extending a hand. He looked about twenty-five, with dark, almost black, hair and a wide grin that Marissa suspected could not be as sincere as it first seemed.

"Is there somewhere we can talk privately?" she asked him. They were standing directly in front of the secretary's desk.

"By all means," said Michael. He guided her into the congressman's office, a large, high-ceilinged room with a huge mahogany desk flanked by an American flag on one side and a Texas state flag on the other. The walls were covered with framed photos of the congressman shaking hands with a variety of celebrities including all the recent presidents.

"My name is Dr. Blumenthal," began Marissa as soon as she was seated. "Does that name mean anything to you?"

Michael shook his head. "Should it?" he asked in a friendly fashion.

"Perhaps," said Marissa, unsure of how to proceed.

"Are you from Houston?" asked Michael.

"I'm from Atlanta," said Marissa. "From the CDC." She watched to see if there was any unusual response. There wasn't.

"The CDC," repeated Michael. "Are you here in an official capacity?"

"No," admitted Marissa. "I'm interested in the congressman's association with the Center. Is it one of his particular concerns?"

"I'm not sure 'particular' is the right word," said Michael warily. "He's concerned about all areas of health care. In fact Congressman Markham has introduced more health-care legislation than any other congressman. He's recently sponsored bills limiting the immigration of foreign medical school graduates, a bill for compulsory arbitration of malpractice cases, a bill establishing a federal ceiling on malpractice awards and a bill limiting federal subsidy of HMO—Health Maintenance Organization—development . . ." Michael paused to catch his breath.

"Impressive," said Marissa. "Obviously he takes a real interest in American medicine."

"Indeed," agreed Michael. "His daddy was a general practitioner, and a fine one at that."

"But as far as you know," continued Marissa, "he does not concern himself with any specific projects at the CDC."

"Not that I know of," said Michael.

"And I assume that not much happens around here without your knowing about it."

Michael grinned.

"Well, thank you for your time," said Marissa, getting to her feet. Intuitively, she knew she wasn't going to learn anything more from Michael Abrams.

Returning to the street, Marissa felt newly despondent. Her sense of doing something positive about her situation had faded. She had no idea if she should hang around Washington for three days waiting for Markham's return, or if she should just go back to Atlanta.

She wandered aimlessly toward the Capitol. She'd already checked into a hotel in Georgetown, so why not stay? She could visit some museums and art galleries. But as she gazed at the Capitol's impressive white dome, she couldn't help wondering why a man in Markham's position should bother with her, even if he were a friend of Dubchek's. Suddenly, she got the glimmer of an idea. Flagging a cab, she hopped in quickly and said, "Federal Elections Commission; do you know where that is?"

The driver was a handsome black who turned to her and said, "Lady, if there's some place in this city that I don't know, I'll take you there for nothin'."

Satisfied, Marissa settled back and let the man do the

driving. Fifteen minutes later they pulled up in front of a drab semimodern office building in a seedy part of downtown Washington. A uniformed guard paid little heed to Marissa other than to indicate she had to sign the register before she went in. Uncertain which department she wanted, Marissa ended up going into a first-floor office. Four women were typing busily behind gray metal desks.

As Marissa approached, one looked up and asked if she could be of assistance.

"Maybe," said Marissa with a smile. "I'm interested in a congressman's campaign finances. I understand that's part of the public record."

"Certainly is," agreed the woman, getting to her feet. "Are you interested in contributions or disbursements?"

"Contributions, I guess," said Marissa with a shrug.

The woman gave her a quizzical look. "What's the congressman's name?"

"Markham," said Marissa. "Calvin Markham."

The woman padded over to a round table covered with black loose-leaf books. She found the appropriate one and opened it to the *M*'s, explaining that the numbers following the congressman's name referred to the appropriate microfilm cassettes. She then led Marissa to an enormous cassette rack, picked out the relevant one and loaded it into the microfilm reader. "Which election are you interested in?" she asked, ready to punch in the document numbers.

"The last one, I suppose," said Marissa. She still wasn't sure what she was after—just some way to link Markham either to Dubchek or the CDC.

The machine whirred to life, documents flashing past

on the screen so quickly that they appeared as a continuous blur. Then the woman pressed a button and showed Marissa how to regulate the speed. "It's five cents a copy, if you want any. You put the money in here." She pointed to a coin slot. "If you run into trouble, just yell."

Marissa was intrigued by the apparatus as well as the information available. As she reviewed the names and addresses of all the contributors to Markham's considerable reelection coffers, Marissa noted that he appeared to get fiscal support on a national scale, not just from his district in Texas. She did not think that was typical, except perhaps for the Speaker of the House or the Chairman of the House Ways and Means Committee. She also noted that a large percentage of the donors were physicians, which made sense in light of Markham's record on health legislation.

The names were alphabetized, and though she carefully scanned the *D*'s, she failed to find Dubchek's name. It had been a crazy idea anyway, she told herself. Where would Cyrill get the money to influence a powerful congressman? He might have some hold on Markham, but not a financial one. Marissa laughed. To think she considered Tad naive!

Still, she made a copy of all the contributors, deciding to go over the list at her leisure. She noticed that one doctor with six children had donated the maximum amount allowable for himself and for each member of his family. That was real support. At the end of the individual contributors was a list of corporate supporters. One called the "Physicians' Action Congress Political Action Committee" had donated more money than any number of Texas oil companies. Going back to the previous election, Marissa found the same group. Clearly it was an established organization, and it had to be high on Markham.

After thanking the woman for her help, Marissa went outside and hailed a cab. As it inched through rush-hour traffic, Marissa looked again at the list of individual names. Suddenly, she almost dropped the sheets. Dr. Ralph Hempston's name leapt out from the middle of a page. It was a coincidence, to be sure, and made her feel what a small world it was, but thinking it over she was not surprised. One of the things that had always troubled her about Ralph was his conservatism. It would be just like him to support a congressman like Markham.

It was five-thirty when Marissa crossed the pleasant lobby of her hotel. As she passed the tiny newsstand, she saw the *Washington Post*'s headline: EBOLA STRIKES AGAIN!

Like iron responding to a magnet, Marissa was pulled across the room. She snatched up a paper and read the subhead: NEWEST SCOURGE TERRIFIES THE CITY OF BROTHERLY LOVE.

Digging up change from the bottom of her purse to buy the paper, she continued reading as she walked toward the elevators. There were three presumed cases of Ebola at the Berson Clinic Hospital in Abington, Pennsylvania, just outside of Philadelphia. The article described widespread panic in the suburban town.

As she pressed the button for her floor, Marissa saw that Dubchek was quoted as saying that he believed the outbreak would be contained quickly and that there was no need for concern: The CDC had learned a lot about controlling the virus from the three previous outbreaks.

Peter Carbo, one of Philadelphia's Gay Rights leaders, was quoted as saying that he hoped Jerry Falwell had noticed that not a single known homosexual had contracted this new and far more dangerous disease that had come from the same area of Africa as AIDS had.

Back in her room, Marissa turned to an inside photo section. The picture of the police barricade at the entrance to the Berson Hospital reminded her of Phoenix. She finished the article and put the paper down on the bureau, looking at herself in the mirror. Although she was on vacation and was officially off the Ebola team, she knew she had to get the details firsthand. Her commitment to the Ebola problem left her with little choice. She rationalized her decision to go by telling herself that Philadelphia was practically next door to Washington; she could even go by train. Turning into the room, Marissa began collecting her belongings.

Leaving the station in Philadelphia, Marissa took a cab to Abington, which turned out to be a far more expensive ride than she'd anticipated. Luckily she had some traveler's checks tucked in her wallet, and the driver was willing to accept them. Outside the Berson Hospital, she was confronted by the police barricade pictured in the newspaper. Before she attempted to cross, she asked a reporter if the place was quarantined. "No," said the man, who had been trying to interview a doctor who had just sauntered past. The police were there in case a quarantine was ordered. Marissa flashed her CDC identity card at one of the guards. He admitted her without question.

The hospital was a handsome, new facility much like the sites of the Ebola outbreaks in L.A. and Phoenix. As Marissa headed toward the information booth, she wondered why the virus seemed to strike these elegant new structures rather than the grubby inner-city hospitals in New York or Boston.

There were a lot of people milling about the lobby, but nothing like the chaos that she'd seen in Phoenix. People seemed anxious but not terrified. The man at the information booth told Marissa that the cases were in the hospital's isolation unit on the sixth floor. Marissa had started toward the elevators when the man called out, "I'm sorry, but there are no visitors allowed." Marissa flashed her CDC card again. "I'm sorry, Doctor. Take the last elevator. It's the only one that goes to six."

When Marissa got off the elevator, a nurse asked her to don protective clothing immediately. She didn't question Marissa as to why she was there. Marissa was particularly glad to put on the mask; it gave her anonymity as well as protection.

"Excuse me, are any of the CDC doctors available?" she asked, startling the two women gossiping behind the nurses' station.

"I'm sorry. We didn't hear you coming," said the older of the two.

"The CDC people left about an hour ago," said the other. "I think they said they were going down to the administrator's office. You could try there."

"No matter," said Marissa. "How are the three patients?"

"There are seven now," said the first woman. Then she asked Marissa to identify herself.

"I'm from the CDC," she said, purposely not giving her name. "And you?"

"Unfortunately, we're the RN's who normally run this unit. We're used to isolating patients with lowered resistance to disease, not cases of fatal contagious disease. We're glad you people are here."

"It *is* a little frightening at first," commiserated Marissa, as she boldly entered the nurses' station. "But if it's any comfort, I've been involved with all three previous outbreaks and haven't had any problems." Marissa did not admit to her own fear. "Are the charts here or in the rooms?"

"Here," said the older nurse, pointing to a corner shelf.

"How are the patients doing?"

"Terribly. I know that doesn't sound very professional, but I've never seen sicker people. We've used round-the-clock special-duty nursing, but no matter what we try, they keep getting worse."

Marissa well understood the nurse's frustration. Terminal patients generally depressed the staff.

"Do either of you know which patient was admitted first?"

The older nurse came over to where Marissa was sitting and pushed the charts around noisily before pulling out one and handing it to Marissa. "Dr. Alexi was the first. I'm surprised he's lasted the day."

Marissa opened the chart. There were all the familiar symptoms but no mention of foreign travel, animal experiments or contact with any of the three previous outbreaks. But she did learn that Alexi was the head of ophthalmology! Marissa was amazed; was Dubchek right after all?

Unsure of how long she dared stay in the unit, Marissa opted to see the patient right away. Donning an extra layer of protective clothing, including disposable goggles, she entered the room.

"Is Dr. Alexi conscious?" she asked the special-duty nurse, whose name was Marie. The man was lying silently on his back, mouth open, staring at the ceiling. His skin was already the pasty yellow shade that Marissa had learned to associate with near-death.

"He goes in and out," said the nurse. "One minute he's talking, the next he's unresponsive. His blood pressure has been falling again. I've been told that he's a 'no code.'"

Marissa swallowed nervously. She'd always been uncomfortable with the order not to resuscitate.

"Dr. Alexi," called Marissa, gingerly touching the man's arm. Slowly he turned his head to face her. She noticed a large bruise beneath his right eye.

"Can you hear me, Dr. Alexi?"

The man nodded.

"Have you been to Africa recently?"

Dr. Alexi shook his head "no."

"Did you attend an eyelid surgery conference in San Diego a few months back?"

The man mouthed the word "yes."

Perhaps Dubchek really was right. It was too much of a coincidence: each outbreak's primary victim was an ophthalmologist who'd attended that San Diego meeting.

"Dr. Alexi," began Marissa, choosing her words carefully. "Do you have friends in L.A., St. Louis or Phoenix? Have you seen them recently?"

But before Marissa had finished, he'd slipped back into unconsciousness.

"That's what he's been doing," said the nurse, moving to the opposite side of the bed to take another blood-pressure reading.

Marissa hesitated. Perhaps she'd wait a few minutes and try to question him again. Her attention returned to the bruise beneath the man's eye, and she asked the nurse if she knew how he'd gotten it.

"His wife told me he'd been robbed," said the nurse. Then she added, "His blood pressure is even lower." She shook her head in dismay as she put down the stethoscope.

"He was robbed just before he got sick?" asked Marissa. She wanted to be sure she'd heard correctly.

"Yes. I think the mugger hit him in the face even though he didn't resist."

An intercom sputtered to life. "Marie, is there a doctor from the CDC in your room?"

The nurse looked from the speaker to Marissa, then back to the speaker again. "Yes, there is."

Over the continued crackle of static, indicating that the line was still open, Marissa could hear a woman saying, "She's in Dr. Alexi's room." Another voice said, "Don't say anything! I'll go down and talk with her."

Marissa's pulse raced. It was Dubchek! Frantically, she looked around the room as if to hide. She thought of asking the nurse if there were another way out, but she knew it would sound ridiculous, and it was too late. She could already hear footsteps in the hall.

Cyrill walked in, adjusting his protective goggles.

"Marie?" he asked.

"Yes," said the nurse.

Marissa started for the door. Dubchek grabbed her by the arm. Marissa froze. It was ridiculous to have a confrontation of this sort in the presence of a dying man. She was scared of Dubchek's reaction, knowing how many rules she had probably broken. At the same time, she was angry at having been forced to break them.

"What the hell do you think you're doing?" he growled. He would not let go of her arm.

"Have some respect for the patient, if not for anyone else," said Marissa, finally freeing herself and leaving the room. Dubchek was right behind her. She pulled off the goggles, the outer hood and gown, then the gloves, and deposited them all in the proper receptacle. Dubchek did the same.

"Are you making a career out of flouting authority?" he demanded, barely controlling his fury. "Is this all some kind of game to you?"

"I'd rather not talk about it," said Marissa. She could tell that Dubchek, for the moment, was beyond any reasonable discussion. She started toward the elevators.

"What do you mean, you'd 'rather not talk about it'?" yelled Dubchek. "Who do you think you are?"

He grabbed Marissa's arm again and yanked her around to face him.

"I think we should wait until you are a little less upset," Marissa managed to say as calmly as she could.

"Upset?" exploded Dubchek. "Listen, young lady, I'm calling Dr. Morrison first thing in the morning to demand that he make you take a forced leave of absence rather than a vacation. If he refuses, I'll demand a formal hearing."

"That's fine by me," said Marissa maintaining a fragile control. "There is something extraordinary about these Ebola outbreaks, and I think you don't want to face it. Maybe a formal hearing is what we need."

"Get out of here before I have you thrown out," snapped Dubchek.

"Gladly," said Marissa.

As she left the hospital, Marissa realized she was shaking. She hated confrontations, and once again she was torn between righteous anger and guilty humiliation. She was certain she was close to the real cause of the outbreaks, but she still could not clearly formulate her suspicions—not even to her own satisfaction, much less someone else's.

Marissa tried to think it through on her way to the airport, but all she could think of was her ugly scene with Dubchek. She couldn't get it out of her head. She knew she had taken a risk by going into the Berson Hospital when she was specifically unauthorized to do so. Cyrill had every right to be enraged. She only wished she had been able to talk to him about the strange fact that each of the index cases had been mugged just before becoming ill.

Waiting for her plane back to Atlanta, Marissa went to a pay phone to call Ralph. He answered promptly, saying he'd been so worried about her that he'd gone to her house when she had failed to answer the phone. He asked her where she'd been, pretending to be indignant that she'd left town without telling him.

"Washington and now Philadelphia," explained Marissa, "but I'm on my way home."

"Did you go to Philly because of the new Ebola outbreak?"

"Yes," said Marissa. "A lot has happened since we talked last. It's a long story, but the bottom line is that I wasn't supposed to go, and when Dubchek caught me, he went crazy. I may be out of a job. Do you know anybody who could use a pediatrician who's hardly been used?"

"No problem," said Ralph with a chuckle. "I could get you a job right here at the University Hospital. What's your flight number? I'll drive out to the airport and pick you up. I'd like to hear about what was so important that you had to fly off without telling me you were going."

"Thanks, but it's not necessary," said Marissa. "My Honda is waiting for me."

"Then stop over on your way home."

"It might be late," said Marissa, thinking that it might be more pleasant at Ralph's than in her own empty house. "I'm planning on stopping by the CDC. There is something I'd like to do while Dubchek is out of town."

"That doesn't sound like a good idea," said Ralph. "What are you up to?"

"Believe me, not much," said Marissa. "I just want one more quick visit to the maximum containment lab."

"I thought you didn't have authorization."

"I can manage it, I think," she told him.

"My advice is to stay away from the CDC," said Ralph. "Going into that lab is what caused most of your problems in the first place."

"I know," admitted Marissa, "but I'm going to do it anyway. This Ebola affair is driving me crazy."

"Suit yourself, but stop over afterwards. I'll be up late."

"Ralph?" Marissa said, screwing up her courage to

ask the question. "Do you know Congressman Markham?"

There was a pause. "I know of him."

"Have you ever contributed to his campaign fund?"

"What an odd question, particularly for a long-distance call."

"Have you?" persisted Marissa.

"Yes," said Ralph. "Several times. I like the man's position on a lot of medical issues."

After promising again to see him that night, Marissa hung up feeling relieved. She was pleased she'd broached the subject of Markham and was even happier that Ralph had been so forthright about his contributions.

Once the plane took off, though, her sense of unease returned. The theory still undeveloped in the back of her mind was so terrifying, she was afraid to try to flesh it out.

More horrifying yet, she was beginning to wonder if her house being broken into and her dog killed was something more than the random attack she'd taken it for.

11

May 20—Evening

MARISSA LEFT THE AIRPORT and headed directly for Tad's house. She'd not called, thinking it would be better just to drop in, even though it was almost nine.

She pulled up in front of his house, pleased to see lights blazing in the living room on the second floor.

"Marissa!" said Tad, opening the front door of the building, a medical journal in his hand. "What are you doing here?"

"I'd like to see the man of the house," said Marissa. "I'm doing a home survey on peanut butter preference."

"You're joking."

"Of course I'm joking," said Marissa with exasperation. "Are you going to invite me in or are we going to spend the night standing here?" Marissa's new assertiveness surprised even herself.

"Sorry," said Tad, stepping aside. "Come on in."

He'd left his apartment door open, so after climbing the stairs Marissa entered ahead of him. Glancing at the shelf in the foyer, she saw that his lab access card was there.

"I've been calling you all day," said Tad. "Where have you been?"

"Out," said Marissa vaguely. "It's been another interesting day."

"I was told you'd been transferred from Special Pathogens," said Tad. "Then I heard a rumor that you were on vacation. What's happening?"

"I wish I knew," said Marissa, dropping onto Tad's low-slung sofa. His cat materialized out of nowhere and leaped into her lap. "What about Philadelphia? Is it Ebola?"

"I'm afraid so," said Tad, sitting down next to her. "The call came in on Sunday. I got samples this morning and they're loaded with the virus."

"Is it the same strain?"

"I won't know that for some time," said Tad.

"You still think it's all coming from that San Diego eye meeting?" she asked him.

"I don't know," said Tad with a slight edge to his voice. "I'm a virologist, not an epidemiologist."

"Don't be cross," said Marissa. "But you don't have to be an epidemiologist to recognize that something strange is happening. Do you have any idea why I've been transferred?"

"I'd guess that Dubchek requested it."

"Nope," said Marissa. "It was a U.S. Congressman from Texas named Markham. He called Dr. Morrison directly. He sits on the appropriations committee that decides on the CDC budget, so Morrison had to comply. But that's pretty weird, isn't it? I mean I'm only an EIS officer."

"I suppose it is," agreed Tad. He was becoming more and more nervous.

Marissa reached out and put her hand on his shoulder. "What's the matter?"

"All this worries me," said Tad. "I like you; you know that. But trouble seems to follow you around, and I don't want to be drawn into it. I happen to like my job."

"I don't want to involve you, but I need your help just one last time. That's why I came here so late."

Tad shook off her hand. "Please don't ask me to break any more rules."

"I have to get back into the maximum containment lab," said Marissa. "Only for a few minutes."

"No!" said Tad decisively. "I simply can't take the risk. I'm sorry."

"Dubchek is out of town," said Marissa. "No one will be there at this hour."

"No," said Tad. "I won't do it."

Marissa could tell he was adamant. "Okay," she said. "I understand."

"You do?" said Tad, surprised that she'd given in so easily.

"I really do, but if you can't take me into the lab, at least you could get me something to drink."

"Of course," said Tad, eager to please. "Beer, white wine. What's your pleasure?"

"A beer would be nice," said Marissa.

Tad disappeared into the kitchen. When she heard the sound of the refrigerator opening, Marissa stood and quickly tiptoed to the front door. Glancing at the shelf, she was pleased to see Tad had two access cards. Maybe he wouldn't even notice that she'd borrowed one, she thought to herself, as she slipped one of the two into her jacket pocket. She was back on the couch before Tad returned with the beers.

Tad handed Marissa a bottle of Rolling Rock, keeping one for himself. He also produced a package of potato chips that he popped open and set on the coffee table. To humor him, Marissa asked about his latest research, but it was obvious she wasn't paying close attention to his answers.

"You don't like Rolling Rock?" asked Tad, noticing that she'd hardly touched hers.

"It's fine," said Marissa, yawning. "I guess I'm more tired than thirsty. I suppose I ought to be going."

"You're welcome to spend the night," said Tad.

Marissa pushed herself to her feet. "Thanks, but I really should go home."

"I'm sorry about the lab," said Tad, bending to kiss her.

"I understand," said Marissa. She headed out the door before he could get his arms around her.

Tad waited until he heard the outer door close before going back inside his apartment. On the one hand, he was glad that he'd had the sense to resist her manipulations. On the other, he felt badly that he'd disappointed her.

From where Tad was standing he was looking directly at the shelf where he'd left his access card and keys. Still thinking about Marissa, he realized that one of his cards was gone. He carefully looked through all the junk he'd removed from his pockets and then searched the shelves above and below. His spare card was gone.

"Damn!" said Tad. He should have expected a trick when she'd given up so easily. Opening the door, he ran down the stairs and out into the street, hoping to catch her, but the street was empty. There wasn't even a breath of air in the humid night. The leaves on the trees hung limp and still.

Tad went back to his apartment, trying to decide what

to do. He checked the time, then went to the phone. He liked Marissa, but she'd gone too far. He picked up the phone and began dialing.

Driving to the Center, Marissa hoped Dubchek hadn't warned the guards she was no longer working in virology. But when she flashed her identity card the guard on duty just smiled and said, "Working late again?"

So far so good; but as a precaution, Marissa first went to her own office in case the man decided to follow her. She turned her light on and sat behind her desk, waiting, but there were no footsteps in the hall.

There were a few letters on her blotter: two advertisements from pharmaceutical houses and a third from Lab Engineering in South Bend. Marissa ripped this third one open. A salesman thanked her for her inquiry concerning their type 3 HEPA Containment Hoods and went on to say that such equipment was only built to custom specifications. If she was interested, she should retain an architectural firm specializing in health-care construction. He ended by answering the question that had prompted her letter: Lab Engineering had built only one system in the last year and that had been for Professional Labs in Grayson, Georgia.

Marissa looked at a map of the United States that her office's previous occupant had left hanging and which she'd never bothered to take down. Poring over Georgia, she tried to find Grayson. It wasn't there. She searched through her drawers, thinking she had a Georgia road map somewhere. Finally she found it in the file cabinet. Grayson was a small town a few hours east of Atlanta. What on earth were they doing with a type 3 HEPA Containment Hood?

After putting the road map back in the file cabinet and the letter in her blazer pocket, Marissa checked the hallway. It was quiet, and the elevator was still at her floor; it had not been used. She decided that the time was right to make her move.

Taking the stairs to descend one floor, Marissa left the main building and crossed to the virology building by the catwalk. She was pleased that there were no lights on in any of the offices. When she passed Dubchek's door, she stuck out her tongue. It was childish but satisfying. Turning the corner, she confronted the airtight security door. Involuntarily, she held her breath as she inserted Tad's card and tapped out his access number: 43-23-39. There was a resounding mechanical click and the heavy door swung open, Marissa caught a whiff of the familiar phenolic disinfectant.

Marissa felt her pulse begin to race. As she crossed the threshold, she had the uncomfortable feeling she was entering a house of horrors. The dimly lit cavernous two-story space, filled with its confusion of pipes and their shadows, gave the impression of a gigantic spider web.

As she'd seen Tad do on her two previous visits, Marissa opened the small cabinet by the entrance and threw the circuit breakers, turning on the lights, and activating the compressors and ventilation equipment. The sound of the machinery was much louder than she'd recalled, sending vibrations through the floor.

Alone, the futuristic lab was even more intimidating than Marissa remembered. It took all her courage to proceed, knowing in addition that she was breaking rules when she was already on probation. Every second, she feared that someone would discover her.

With sweaty palms, she grasped the releasing wheel

on the airtight door to the dressing rooms and tried to turn it. The wheel would not budge. Finally, using all her strength, she got it to turn. The seal broke with a hiss and the door swung outward. She climbed through, hearing the door close behind her with an ominous thud.

She felt her ears pop as she scrambled into a set of scrub clothes. The second door opened more easily, but the fewer problems she encountered, the more she worried about the real risks she was taking.

Locating a small plastic isolation suit among the twenty or so hanging in the chamber, Marissa found it much harder to get into without Tad's help. She was sweaty by the time she zipped it closed.

At the switch panel, she only turned on the lights for the main lab; the rest were unnecessary. She had no intention of visiting the animal area. Then, carrying her air hose, she crossed the disinfecting chamber and climbed through the final airtight door into the main part of the lab.

Her first order of business was to hook up to an appropriately positioned manifold and let the fresh air balloon out her suit and clear her mask. She welcomed the hissing sound. Without it the silence had been oppressive. Orienting herself in relation to all the high-tech hardware, she spotted the freezer. She was already sorry that she'd not turned on all the lights. The shadows at the far end of the lab created a sinister backdrop for the deadly viruses, heightening Marissa's fear.

Swinging her legs wide to accommodate the inflated and bulky isolation suit, Marissa started for the freezer, again marveling that with all the other "high-tech," up-to-the-minute equipment, they had settled for an ordinary household appliance. Its existence in the maximum containment lab was as unlikely as an old adding machine at a computer convention.

Just short of the freezer, Marissa paused, eyeing the insulated bolted door to the left. After learning the viruses were not stored behind it, she had wondered just what it did protect. Nervously, she reached out and drew the bolt. A cloud of vapor rushed out as she opened the door and stepped inside. For a moment she felt as if she had stepped into a freezing cloud. Then the heavy door swung back against her air hose, plunging her into darkness.

When her eyes adjusted, she spotted what she hoped was a light switch and turned it on. Overhead lights flicked on, barely revealing a thermometer next to the switch. Bending over she was able to make out that it registered minus fifty-one degrees centigrade.

"My God!" exclaimed Marissa, understanding the source of the vapor: as soon as the air at room temperature met such cold, the humidity it contained sublimated to ice.

Turning around and facing the dense fog, Marissa moved deeper into the room, fanning the air with her arms. Almost immediately a ghastly image caught her eye. She screamed, the sound echoing horribly within her suit. At first she thought she was seeing ghosts. Then she realized that, still more horrible, she was facing a row of frozen, nude corpses, only partially visible through the swirling mist. At first she thought they were standing on their own in a row, but it turned out they were hung like cadavers for an anatomy course—caliperlike devices thrust into the ear canals. As she came closer, Marissa recognized the first body. For a moment she thought she was going to pass out: it was the Indian doctor whom Marissa had seen in Phoenix, his face frozen into an agonized death mask.

There were at least a half-dozen bodies. Marissa didn't count. To the right, she saw the carcasses of monkeys and rats, frozen in equally grotesque positions. Although Marissa could understand that such freezing was probably necessary for the viral study of gross specimens, she had been totally unprepared for the sight. No wonder Tad had discouraged her from entering.

Marissa backed out of the room, turning off the light, and closing and bolting the door. She shivered both from distaste and actual chill.

Chastised for her curiosity, Marissa turned her attention to the freezer. In spite of the clumsiness afforded by the plastic suit and her own tremulousness, she worked the combination on the bicycle lock and got it off with relative ease. The link chain was another story. It was knotted, and she had to struggle to get it through the handle. It took longer than she would have liked, but at last it was free and she lifted the lid.

Rubbing the frost off the inner side of the lid, Marissa tried to decipher the index code. The viruses were in alphabetical order. "Ebola, Zaire '76 was followed by "97, E11-E48, F1-F12." Marissa guessed that the first number referred to the appropriate tray and that the letters and numbers that followed located the virus within the tray. Each tray held at least one thousand samples, which meant that there were fifty individual vials of the Zaire '76 strain.

As carefully as possible, Marissa lifted tray 97 free and set it on a nearby counter top while she scanned the slots. Each was filled with a small black-topped vial. Marissa was both relieved and disappointed. She located the Zaire '76 strain and lifted out sample E11. The tiny frozen ball inside looked innocuous, but Marissa knew that it contained millions of tiny viruses, any one or two of which, when thawed, were capable of killing a human being.

Slipping the vial back in its slot, Marissa lifted the next, checking to see if the ice ball appeared intact. She continued this process without seeing anything suspicious until finally she reached vial E39. The vial was empty!

Quickly, Marissa went through the rest of the samples: All were as they should be. She held vial E39 up to the light, squinting through her face mask to make sure she wasn't making a mistake. But there was no doubt: there was definitely nothing in the vial. Although one of the scientists might have misplaced a sample, she could think of no reason a vial might be empty. All her inarticulated fears that the outbreaks had stemmed from accidental or even deliberate misuse of a CDC vial filled with an African virus seemed to be confirmed.

A sudden movement caught Marissa's attention. The wheel to the door leading into the disinfecting chamber was turning! Someone was coming in!

Marissa was gripped with a paralyzing panic. For a moment she just stared helplessly. When she'd recovered enough to move, she put the empty vial back in the tray, returned it to the freezer and closed the lid. She thought about running, but there was no place to go. Maybe she could hide. She looked toward the darkened area by the animal cages. But there was no time. She heard the seal break on the door and two people entered the lab, dressed anonymously in plastic isolation suits. The smaller of the two seemed familiar with the lab, showing his larger companion where he should plug in his air hose.

Terrified, Marissa stayed where she was. There was always the faint chance that they were CDC scientists checking on some ongoing experiment. That hope faded quickly when she realized they were coming directly toward her. It was at that point she noticed that the smaller individual was holding a syringe. Her eyes flicked to his companion, who lumbered forward, his elbow fixed at an odd angle, stirring an unpleasant memory.

Marissa tried to see their faces, but the glare off the face plates made it impossible.

"Blumenthal?" asked the smaller of the two in a harsh, masculine voice. He reached out and rudely angled Marissa's mask against the light. Apparently he recognized her, because he nodded to his companion, who reached for the zipper on her suit.

"No!" screamed Marissa, realizing these men were not security. They were about to attack her just as she'd been attacked in her house. Desperately, she snatched the bicycle lock from the freezer and threw it. The confusion gave Marissa just enough time to detach her air hose and run toward the animal area.

The larger man was after her in less than a second, but as he was about to grab her, he was pulled up short by his air hose, like a dog on a leash.

Marissa moved as quickly as she could into the dark corridors between the stacked animal cages, hearing the frightened chatter of monkeys, rats, chickens and God knew what else. Trapped within the confines of the lab, she was desperate. Hoping to create a diversion, she began opening the monkey cages. The animals who weren't too sick to move, immediately fled. Soon, her breathing became labored.

Finding an air manifold, which was not easy in the darkness, Marissa plugged in, welcoming the rush of cool, dry air. It was obvious the larger man was unaccustomed to being in the lab, but she didn't really see that it would give her much of an advantage. She moved down the line of cages to where she could see into the main area of the room. Silhouetted against the light, he was moving toward her. She had no idea if he could see her or not, but she stayed still, mentally urging the man down a different aisle. But he was unswerving. He was walking right at her. The hairs on the back of her neck stood on end.

Reaching up, she detached her air hose and tried to move around the far end of the row of cages. Before she could, the man caught her left arm.

Marissa looked up at her assailant. All she could see was the slight gleam of his face plate. The strength of his grip made resistance seem useless, but over his shoulder she glimpsed a red handle marked Emergency Use Only.

In desperation, Marissa reached up with her free hand and pulled the lever down. Instantly an alarm sounded, and a sudden shower of phenolic disinfectant drenched the whole lab, sending up clouds of mist and reducing the visibility to zero. Shocked, the man released Marissa's arm. She dropped to the floor. Discovering that she could slither beneath the row of cages, she crawled away from the man, hoping she was headed back toward the main lab. She got to her feet, moving forward by feel. The disinfectant shower was apparently going to continue until someone replaced the lever. Her breathing was becoming painfully labored. She needed fresh air.

Something jumped in front of her, and she nearly screamed. But it was only one of the monkeys, tortured by the lethal atmosphere. The animal held onto her for a minute, then slid off her plastic-covered shoulder and disappeared.

Gasping, Marissa reached up and ran her hand along the pipes. Touching an air manifold, she connected her line.

Over the sound of the alarm, Marissa heard a commotion in the next aisle, then muffled shouts. She guessed that her pursuer could not find a manifold.

Gambling that the second man would go to the aid of his accomplice, Marissa detached her own air hose and moved toward the light, her arms stretched out in front of her like a blind man. Soon the illumination was uniform and she guessed she had reached the main part of the lab. Moving toward the wall, she banged into the freezer and remembered seeing a manifold just above it. She hooked up for several quick breaths. Then she felt her way to the door. The second she found it, she released the seai and pulled it open. A minute later she was standing in the disinfecting room.

Having already been drenched with phenolic disinfectant, she didn't wait through the usual shower. In the next room, she struggled out of her plastic suit, then ran into the room beyond, where she tipped the lockers holding the scrub clothes over against the pressure door. She didn't think it would stop the door from being opened, but it might slow her pursuers down.

Racing into her street clothes, she flicked all the circuit breakers, throwing even the dressing rooms into darkness and turning off the ventilation system.

Once outside the maximum containment lab, Marissa

ran the length of the virology building, across the catwalk, and to the stairs to the main floor, which she bounded down two at a time. Taking a deep breath, she tried to look relaxed as she went through the front lobby. The security guard was sitting at his desk to the left. He was on the phone, explaining to someone that a biological alarm had gone off, not a security door alarm.

Even though she doubted her pursuers would have enlisted security's help after having tried to kill her, she'd trembled violently while signing out. She heard the guard hang up after he explained to the person he was talking to that the operators were busy searching for the head of the virology department.

"Hey!" yelled the guard, as Marissa started for the door. Her heart leapt into her mouth. For a moment, she thought about fleeing; she was only six feet from the front door. Then she heard the guard say, "You forgot to put the time."

Marissa marched back and dutifully filled in the blank. A second later she was outside, running to her car.

She was halfway to Ralph's before she was able to stop shaking and think about her terrible discovery. The missing ball of frozen Ebola couldn't have been a coincidence. It was the same strain as each of the recent outbreaks across the country. Someone was using the virus, and whether intentionally or by accident, the deadly disease was infecting doctors and hospitals in disparate areas at disparate times.

That the missing sample from vial E39 was the mysterious reservoir for the Ebola outbreaks in the United States was the only explanation that answered the questions posed by the apparently long incubation periods and the fact that, though the virus tended to mutate, all of the outbreaks involved the same strain. Worse yet, someone did not want that information released. That was why she'd been taken off the Ebola team and why she had just been nearly killed. The realization that frightened her most was that only someone with maximum containment lab access—presumably someone on the CDC staff—could have found her there. She cursed herself for not having had the presence of mind to look in the log book as she signed out to see who'd signed in.

She had already turned down Ralph's street, anxious to tell him her fears, when she realized that it wasn't fair to involve him. She'd already taken advantage of Tad's friendship, and by the next day, when he saw her name on the log, she would be a total pariah. Her one hope was that her two assailants would not report her presence in the lab, since they would then be implicated in the attempt on her life. Even so, she couldn't count on their not devising a plausible lie about what had gone on. It would be their word against hers, and by tomorrow, her word wouldn't mean much at the CDC. Of that she was sure. For all she knew the Atlanta police might be looking for her by morning.

Remembering her suitcase was still in the trunk of her car, Marissa headed for the nearest motel. As soon as she reached the room assigned her, she put in a call to Ralph. He answered sleepily on the fifth ring.

"I stayed up as long as I could," he explained. "Why didn't you come by?"

"It's a long story," said Marissa. "I can't explain now, but I'm in serious trouble. I may even need a good criminal lawyer. Do you know of one?"

"Good God," said Ralph, suddenly not sleepy. "I think you'd better tell me what's going on."

"I don't want to drag you into it," said Marissa. "All I can say is that the whole situation has become decidedly serious and, for the moment, I'm not ready to go to the authorities. I guess I'm a fugitive!" Marissa laughed hollowly.

"Why don't you come over here?" said Ralph. "You'd be safe here."

"Ralph, I'm serious about not wanting to involve you. But I do need a lawyer. Could you find me one?"

"Of course," said Ralph. "I'll help you any way I can. Where are you?"

"I'll be in touch," said Marissa evasively. "And thanks for being my friend."

Marissa disconnected by pushing the button on top of the phone, trying to build up her courage to call Tad and apologize before he found out from someone else that she'd taken his access card. Taking a deep breath, she dialed. When there was no answer after several rings, she lost her nerve and decided not to wake him up.

Marissa took the letter from Lab Engineering from her pocket and smoothed it out. Grayson was going to be her next stop.

12

May 21

ALTHOUGH SHE WAS EXHAUSTED, Marissa slept poorly, tortured by nightmares of being chased through alien landscapes. When the early light coming through the window awakened her, it was a relief. She looked out and saw a man filling the coin-operated newspaper dispenser. As soon as he left, she ran out and bought the *Atlanta Journal and Constitution.*

There was nothing in it about the CDC, but halfway through the morning television news, the commentator said that there had been a problem at the Center. There was no mention of the maximum containment lab, but it was repeated that a technician had been treated at Emory University Hospital after inhaling phenolic disinfectant and then released. The segment continued with a phone interview with Dr. Cyrill Dubchek. Marissa leaned forward and turned up the volume.

"The injured technician was the only casualty," Cyrill said, his voice sounding metallic. Marissa wondered if he was in Philadelphia or Atlanta. "An emergency safety system was triggered by accident. Everything is under control, and we are searching for a Dr. Marissa Blumenthal in relation to the incident."

The anchorperson capped the segment with the comment that if anyone knew the whereabouts of Dr. Blumenthal, they should notify the Atlanta police. For about ten seconds they showed the photograph that had accompanied her CDC application.

Marissa turned off the TV. She'd not considered the possibility of seriously hurting her pursuers and she was upset, despite the fact that the man had been trying to harm her. Tad was right when he'd said that trouble seemed to follow her.

Although Marissa had joked about being a fugitive, she'd meant it figuratively. Now, having heard the TV announcer request information about her whereabouts, she realized the joke had become serious. She was a wanted person; at least by the Atlanta police.

Quickly getting her things together, Marissa went to check out of the motel. The whole time she was in the office, she felt nervous since her name was there in black and white for the clerk to see. But all he said was: "Have a nice day."

She grabbed a quick coffee and donut at a Howard Johnson's, and drove to her bank, which luckily had early hours that day. Although she tried to conceal her face at the drive-in window in case the teller had seen the morning news, the man seemed as uninterested as usual. Marissa extracted most of her savings, amounting to $4,650.

With the cash in her purse, she relaxed a little. Driving up the ramp to Interstate 78, she turned on the radio. She was on her way to Grayson, Georgia.

The drive was easy, although longer than she'd expected, and not terribly interesting. The only sight of note was that geological curiosity called Stone Mountain. It was a bubble of bare granite sticking out of the wooded Georgia hills, like a mole on a baby's bottom. Beyond the town of Snellville, Marissa turned northeast on 84, and the landscape became more and more rural. Finally she passed a sign: WELCOME TO GRAYSON. Unfortunately it was spotted with holes, as if someone had been using it for target practice, reducing the sincerity of the message.

The town itself was exactly as Marissa had imagined. The main street was lined with a handful of brick and wood-frame buildings. There was a bankrupt movie theater, and the largest commercial establishment was the hardware and feed store. On one corner, a granite-faced bank sported a large clock with Roman numerals. Obviously it was just the kind of town that needed a type 3 HEPA Containment Hood!

The streets were almost empty as Marissa slowly cruised along. She saw no new commercial structures and realized that Professional Labs was probably a little ways from town. She would have to inquire, but whom could she approach? She was not about to go to the local police.

At the end of the street, she made a U-turn and drove back. There was a general store that also boasted a sign that read U.S. Post Office.

"Professional Labs? Yeah, they're out on Bridge Road," said the proprietor. He was in the dry-goods section, showing bolts of cotton to a customer. "Turn yourself around and take a right at the firehouse. Then after Parsons Creek, take a left. You'll find it. It's the only thing out there 'cept for cows."

"What do they do?" asked Marissa.

"Darned if I know," said the storekeeper. "Darned if I care. They're good customers and they pay their bills."

Following the man's directions, Marissa drove out of the town. He was right about there being nothing around but cows. After Parsons Creek the road wasn't even paved, and Marissa began to wonder if she were on a wild-goose chase. But then the road entered a pine forest, and up ahead she could see a building.

With a thump, Marissa's Honda hit asphalt as the road widened into a parking area. There were two other vehicles: a white van with Professional Labs, Inc., lettered on the side, and a cream-colored Mercedes.

Marissa pulled up next to the van. The building had peaked roofs and lots of mirror glass, which reflected the attractive tree-lined setting. The fragrant smell of pine surrounded her as she walked to the entrance. She gave the door a pull, but it didn't budge. She tried to push, but it was as if it were bolted shut. Stepping back, she searched for a bell, but there was none. She knocked a couple of times, but realized she wasn't making enough noise for anyone inside to hear. Giving up on the front door, Marissa started to walk around the building. When she got to the first window, she cupped her hands and tried to look through the mirror glass. It was impossible.

"Do you know you are trespassing?" said an unfriendly voice.

Marissa's hands dropped guiltily to her sides.

"This is private property," said a stocky, middle-aged man dressed in blue coveralls.

"Ummm. . . ," voiced Marissa, desperately trying to think of an excuse for her presence. With his graying crew cut and florid complexion, the man looked exactly like a red-neck stereotype from the fifties.

"You did see the signs?" asked the man, gesturing to the notice by the parking lot.

"Well, yes," admitted Marissa. "But you see, I'm a doctor . . ." She hesitated. Being a physician didn't give her the right to violate someone's privacy. Quickly she went on: "Since you have a viral lab here, I was interested to know if you do viral diagnostic work."

"What makes you think this is a viral lab?" questioned the man.

"I'd just heard it was," said Marissa.

"Well, you heard wrong. We do molecular biology here. With the worry of industrial espionage, we have to be very careful. So I think that you'd better leave unless you'd like me to call the police."

"That won't be necessary," said Marissa. Involving the police was the last thing she wanted. "I certainly apologize. I don't mean to be a bother. I would like to see your lab, though. Isn't there some way that could be arranged?"

"Out of the question," the man said flatly. He led Marissa back to her car, their footsteps crunching on the crushed-stone path.

"Is there someone that I might contact to get a tour?" asked Marissa as she slid behind the wheel.

"I'm the boss," said the man simply. "I think you'd better go." He stepped back from the car, waiting for Marissa to leave.

Having run out of bright ideas, Marissa started the engine. She tried smiling good-bye, but the man's face remained grim as she drove off, heading back to Grayson.

He stood waiting until the little Honda was lost in the trees. With an irritated shake of his head, he turned and walked back to the building. The front door opened automatically.

The interior was as contemporary as the exterior. He went down a short tiled corridor and entered a small lab. At one end was a desk, at the other was an airtight steel door like the one leading into the CDC's maximum containment lab, behind which was a lab bench equipped with a type 3 HEPA filtration system.

Another man was sitting at the desk, torturing a paper clip into grotesque shapes. He looked up: "Why the hell didn't you let me handle her?" Speaking made him cough violently, bringing tears to his eyes. He raised a handkerchief to his mouth.

"Because we don't know who knows she was here," said the man in the blue coveralls. "Use a little sense, Paul. Sometimes you scare me." He picked up the phone and punched the number he wanted with unnecessary force.

"Dr. Jackson's office," answered a bright, cheerful voice.

"I want to talk to the doctor."

"I'm sorry, but he's with a patient."

"Honey, I don't care if he's with God. Just put him on the phone."

"Who may I say is calling?" asked the secretary coolly.

"Tell him the Chairman of the Medical Ethics Committee. I don't care; just put him on!"

"One moment, please."

Turning to the desk, he said: "Paul, would you get my coffee from the counter."

Paul tossed the paper clip into the wastebasket, then heaved himself out of his chair. It took a bit of effort because he was a big man and his left arm was frozen at the elbow joint. He'd been shot by a policeman when he was a boy.

"Who is this?" demanded Dr. Joshua Jackson at the other end of the phone.

"Heberling," said the man in the blue coveralls. "Dr. Arnold Heberling. Remember me?"

Paul gave Arnold his coffee, then returned to the desk, taking another paper clip out of the middle drawer. He pounded his chest, clearing his throat.

"Heberling!" said Dr. Jackson. "I told you never to call me at my office!"

"The Blumenthal girl was here," said Heberling, ignoring Jackson's comment. "She drove up pretty as you please in a red car. I caught her looking through the windows."

"How the hell did she find out about the lab?"

"I don't know and I don't care," said Heberling. "The fact of the matter is that she was here, and I'm coming into town to see you. This can't go on. Something has to be done about her."

"No! Don't come here," said Jackson frantically. "I'll come there."

"All right," said Heberling. "But it has to be today."

"I'll be there around five," said Jackson, slamming down the receiver.

* * *

Marissa decided to stop in Grayson for lunch. She was hungry, and maybe someone would tell her something about the lab. She stopped in front of the drugstore, went in and sat down at the old-fashioned soda fountain. She ordered a hamburger, which came on a freshly toasted roll with a generous slice of Bermuda onion. Her Coke was made from syrup.

While Marissa ate, she considered her options. They were pretty meager. She couldn't go back to the CDC or the Berson Clinic Hospital. Figuring out what Professional Labs was doing with a sophisticated 3 HEPA filtration system was a last resort, but the chances of getting in seemed slim: the place was built like a fortress. Perhaps it was time to call Ralph and ask if he'd found a lawyer, except . . .

Marissa took a bite of her dill pickle. In her mind's eye she pictured the two vehicles in the lab's parking lot. The white van had had Professional Labs, Inc., printed on its side. It was the Inc. that interested her.

Finishing her meal, Marissa walked down the street to an office building she remembered passing. The door was frosted glass: RONALD DAVIS, ATTORNEY AND REALTOR, was stenciled on it in gold leaf. A bell jangled as she entered. There was a cluttered desk, but no secretary.

A man dressed in a white shirt, bow tie and red suspenders, came out from an inside room. Although he appeared to be no more than thirty, he was wearing wire-rimmed glasses that seemed almost grandfatherly. "Can I help you?" he asked, with a heavy Southern accent.

"Are you Mr. Davis?" asked Marissa.

"Yup." The man hooked his thumbs through his suspenders.

"I have a couple of simple questions," said Marissa. "About corporate law. Do you think you could answer them?"

"Maybe," said Mr. Davis. He motioned for Marissa to come in.

The scene looked like a set for a 1930s movie, complete with the desk-top fan that slowly rotated back and forth, rustling the papers. Mr. Davis sat down and leaned back, putting his hands behind his head. Then he said: "What is it you want to know?"

"I want to find out about a certain corporation," began Marissa. "If a business is incorporated, can someone like myself find out the names of the owners?"

Mr. Davis tipped forward, resting his elbows on the desk. "Maybe and maybe not," he said, smiling.

Marissa groaned. It seemed that a conversation with Mr. Davis was going to be like pulling teeth. But before she could rephrase her question, he continued: "If the company in question is a public corporation, it would be hard to find out all the stockholders, especially if a lot of the stock is held in trust with power of attorney delegated to a third party. But if the company is a partnership, then it would be easy. In any case, it is always possible to find out the name of the service agent if you have in mind to institute some sort of litigation. Is that what you have in mind?"

"No," said Marissa. "Just information. How would I go about finding out if a company is a partnership or a public corporation?"

"Easy," said Mr. Davis, leaning back once more.

"All you have to do is go to the State House in Atlanta, visit the Secretary of State's office and ask for the corporate division. Just tell the clerk the name of the company, and he can look it up. It's a matter of public record, and if the company is incorporated in Georgia, it will be listed there."

"Thank you," said Marissa, seeing a glimmer of light at the end of the dark tunnel. "How much do I owe you?"

Mr. Davis raised his eyebrows, studying Marissa's face. "Twenty dollars might do it, unless . . ."

"My pleasure," said Marissa, pulling out a twenty-dollar bill and handing it over.

Marissa returned to her car and drove back toward Atlanta. She was pleased to have a goal, even if the chances of finding significant information were not terribly good.

She stayed just under the speed limit. The last thing she wanted was to be stopped by the police. She made good time and was back in the city by 4:00. Parking in a garage, she walked to the State House.

Distinctly uncomfortable in the presence of the capitol police, Marissa sweated nervously as she started up the front steps, certain she would be recognized.

"Dr. Blumenthal," called a voice.

For a split second, Marissa considered running. Instead, she turned to see one of the CDC secretaries, a bright young woman in her early twenties, walking toward her.

"Alice MacCabe, Doctor Carbonara's office. Remember me?"

Marissa did, and for the next few nerve-racking minutes was forced to engage in small talk. Luckily, Miss MacCabe was oblivious to the fact that Marissa was a "wanted" person.

As soon as she could, Marissa said good-bye and entered the building. More than ever, she just wanted to get whatever information she could and leave. Unfortunately, there was a long line at the corporate division. With dwindling patience, Marissa waited her turn, keeping a hand to her face with the mistaken notion that it might keep her from being recognized.

"What can I do for you?" asked the white-haired clerk when it was finally Marissa's turn.

"I'd like some information about a corporation called Professional Labs."

"Where is it located?" asked the clerk. He slipped on his bifocals and entered the name at a computer terminal.

"Grayson, Georgia," said Marissa.

"Okay," said the clerk. "Here it is. Incorporated just last year. What would you like to know?"

"Is it a partnership or a public corporation?" asked Marissa, trying to remember what Mr. Davis had said.

"Limited partnership, subchapter S."

"What does that mean?" asked Marissa.

"It has to do with taxes. The partners can deduct the corporate losses, if there are any, on their individual returns."

"Are the partners listed?" asked Marissa, excitement overcoming her anxiety for the moment.

"Yup," said the clerk. "There's Joshua Jackson, Rodd Becker . . ."

"Just a second," said Marissa. "Let me write this down." She got out a pen and began writing.

"Let's see," said the clerk, staring at the computer screen. "Jackson, Becker; you got those?"

"Yes."

"There's Sinclair Tieman, Jack Krause, Gustave Swenson, Duane Moody, Trent Goodridge and the Physicians' Action Congress."

"What was that last one?" asked Marissa, scribbling furiously.

The clerk repeated it.

"Can an organization be a limited partner?" She had seen the name Physicians' Action Congress on Markham's contributions list.

"I'm no lawyer, lady, but I think so. Well, it must be so or it wouldn't be in here. Here's something else: a law firm by the name of Cooper, Hodges, McQuinllin and Hanks."

"They're partners too?" asked Marissa, starting to write down the additional names.

"No," said the clerk. "They're the service agent."

"I don't need that," said Marissa. "I'm not interested in suing the company." She erased the names of Cooper and Hodges.

Thanking the clerk, Marissa beat a hasty retreat and hurried back to the parking garage. Once inside her car, she opened her briefcase and took out the photocopies of Markham's contributors list. Just as she'd remembered, the Physicians' Action Congress (PAC) was listed. On the one hand it was a limited partner in an economic venture, on the other, a contributor to a conservative politician's reelection campaign.

Curious, Marissa looked to see if any of the other partners of Professional Labs were on Markham's list.

To her surprise, they all were. More astonishing, the partners, like Markham's contributors, came from all over the country. From Markham's list, she had all their addresses.

Marissa put her key in the ignition, then hesitated. Looking back at Markham's list she noted that the Physicians' Action Congress was listed under corporate sponsors. Much as she hated to tempt fate by passing the capitol police again, she forced herself to get out of the car and walk back. She waited in line for the second time, for the same clerk, and asked him what he could tell her about the Physicians' Action Congress.

The clerk punched in the name on his terminal, waited for a moment, then turned to Marissa. "I can't tell you anything. It's not in here."

"Does that mean it's not incorporated?"

"Not necessarily. It means it's not incorporated in Georgia."

Marissa thanked the man again, and again ran out of the building. Her car felt like a sanctuary. She sat for a few minutes, trying to decide what to do next. She really didn't have all that much information, and she was getting rather far afield from the Ebola outbreaks. But her intuition told her that in some weird way everything she had learned was related. And if that were the case, then the Physicians' Action Congress was the key. But how could she investigate an organization she'd never heard of?

Her first thought was to visit the Emory Medical School library. Perhaps one of the librarians might know where to look. But then, remembering running into Alice MacCabe, she decided the chance of being recognized was too great. She would do much better to go out of town for a few days. But where?

Starting the car, Marissa had an inspiration: the AMA! If she couldn't get information about a physicians' organization at the AMA, then it wasn't available. And Chicago sounded safe. She headed south toward the airport, hoping the meager supply of clothing in her suitcase would hold up.

Joshua Jackson's heavy sedan thundered over the wood-planked bridge spanning Parsons Creek, then veered sharply to the left, the tires squealing. The pavement stopped, and the car showered the shoulder of the road with pebbles as it sped down the tree-lined lane. Inside, Jackson's fury mounted with each mile he traveled. He didn't want to visit the lab, but he had no intention of being seen in town with Heberling. The man was proving increasingly unreliable, and even worse, unpredictable. Asked to create minor confusion, he resorted to atomic warfare. Hiring him had been a terrible decision, but there wasn't much any of them could do about the fact now.

Pulling up to the lab, Jackson parked across from Heberling's Mercedes. He knew that Heberling had bought it with some of the funds he'd been given for technical equipment. What a waste!

Jackson walked up to the front of the building. It was an impressive affair, and Jackson, perhaps better than anyone, knew how much money it had all cost. The Physicians' Action Congress had built Dr. Arnold Heberling a personal monument, and for what: a hell of a lot of trouble, because Heberling was a nut.

There was a click, the door opened and Jackson stepped inside.

"I'm in the conference room," shouted Heberling.

Jackson knew the room Heberling meant, and it was hardly a conference room. Jackson paused at the door, taking in the high ceiling, glass wall and stark furnishings. Two Chippendale couches faced one another on a large Chinese rug. There was no other furniture. Heberling was on one of the couches.

"I hope this is important," said Jackson, taking the initiative. The two men sat facing each other. Physically, they couldn't have been more different. Heberling was stocky with a bloated face and coarse features. Jackson was tall and thin with an almost ascetic face. Their clothes helped heighten the contrast: Heberling in coveralls; Jackson in a banker's pinstripes.

"The Blumenthal girl was right here in the yard," said Heberling, pointing over his shoulder for effect. "Obviously she didn't see anything, but just the fact that she was here suggests that she knows something. She's got to be removed."

"You had your chance," snapped Jackson. "Twice! And each time, you and your thugs made a mess of things. First at her house and then last night at the CDC."

"So we try again. But you've called it off."

"You're darn right. I found out you were going to give her Ebola."

"Why not?" said Heberling. "She's been exposed. There'd be no questions."

"I don't want an Ebola outbreak in Atlanta," shouted

Jackson. "The stuff terrifies me. I've got a family of my own. Leave the woman to us. We'll take care of her."

"Oh, sure," scoffed Heberling. "That's what you said when you got her transferred off Special Pathogens. Well, she's still a threat to the whole project, and I intend to see that she's eliminated."

"You are not in charge here," said Jackson menacingly. "And when it comes to fixing blame, none of us would be in this mess if you'd stuck to the original plan of using influenza virus. We've all been in a state of panic since we learned you took it upon yourself to use Ebola!"

"Oh, we're back to that complaint," said Heberling disgustedly. "You were pretty pleased when you heard the Richter Clinic was closing. If PAC wanted to undermine the public's growing confidence in prepaid health clinics, they couldn't have done better. The only difference from the original plan was that I got to carry out some field research that will save me years of lab research time."

Jackson studied Heberling's face. He'd come to the conclusion the man was a psychopath, and loathed him. Unfortunately the realization was a bit late. Once the project had started, there was no easy way to stop it. And to think that the plan had sounded so simple back when the PAC executive committee had first suggested it.

Jackson took a deep breath, knowing he had to control himself despite his anger. "I've told you a dozen times the Physicians' Action Congress is not pleased and, on the contrary, is appalled at the loss of life. That had never been our intent and you know it, Dr. Heberling!"

"Bullshit!" shouted Heberling. "There would have

been loss of life with influenza, given the strains we would have had to use. How many would you have tolerated? A hundred? And what about the loss of life you rich practitioners cause when you turn your backs on unnecessary surgery, or allow incompetent doctors to keep their hospital privileges?''

''We do not sanction unnecessary surgery or incompetence,'' snapped Jackson. He'd had about as much of this psychopath as he could tolerate.

''You do nothing to stop them,'' said Heberling, with disgust. ''I haven't believed any of this crap you and PAC feed me about your concern for the negative drift of American medicine away from its traditional values. Give me a break! It's all an attempt to justify your own economic interests. All of a sudden there are too many doctors and not enough patients. The only reason I've cooperated with you is because you built me this lab.'' Heberling made a sweeping gesture with his hand. ''You wanted the image of prepaid health plans tarnished, and I delivered. The only difference is that I did it my way for my own reasons.''

''But we ordered you to stop,'' yelled Jackson. ''Right after the Richter Clinic outbreak.''

''Half-heartedly, I might add,'' said Heberling. ''You were pleased with the results. Not only did the Richter Clinic fold, but new subscribers to California health plans have leveled off for the first time in five years. The Physicians' Action Congress feels an occasional twinge of conscience, but basically you're all happy. And I've vindicated my beliefs that Ebola is a premier biological weapon despite the lack of vaccine or treatment. I've shown that it is easily introduced, relatively easy to contain and devastatingly contagious to small populations. Dr. Jackson, we are both getting what we want. We just have to deal with this woman before she causes real trouble."

"I'm telling you once and for all," said Jackson. "We want no further use of Ebola. That's an order!"

Heberling laughed. "Dr. Jackson," he said, leaning forward, "I have the distinct impression that you are ignoring the facts. PAC is no longer in a position to give me orders. Do you realize what would happen to your careers if the truth gets out? And I'm telling you that it will unless you let me handle Blumenthal in my own way."

For a moment, Jackson struggled with his conscience. He wanted to grab Heberling by the neck and choke him. But he knew the man was right: PAC's hands were tied. "All right," he said reluctantly. "Do whatever you think is best about Dr. Blumenthal. Just don't tell me about it and don't use Ebola in Atlanta."

"Fine." Heberling smiled. "If that will make you feel better, I'll give you my word on both accounts. After all, I'm a very reasonable man."

Jackson stood up. "One other thing. I don't want you phoning my office. Call me at home on my private line if you have to reach me."

"My pleasure," said Heberling.

Since the Atlanta–Chicago run was heavily traveled, Marissa only had to wait half an hour for the next available flight. She bought a Dick Francis novel, but she couldn't concentrate. Finally, she decided to call Tad and at least attempt an apology. She wasn't sure how much to tell him about her growing suspicions, but decided to play it by ear. She dialed the lab, and as she suspected, he was working late.

"This is Marissa," she said when he answered. "Are you mad at me?"

"I'm furious."

"Tad, I'm sorry . . ."

"You took one of my access cards."

"Tad, I'm truly sorry. When I see you, I'll explain everything."

"You actually went into the maximum containment lab, didn't you?" Tad said, his voice uncharacteristically hard.

"Well, yes."

"Marissa, do you know that the lab is a shambles, all the animals are dead, and someone had to be treated at Emory Emergency?"

"Two men came into the lab and attacked me."

"Attacked you?"

"Yes," said Marissa. "You have to believe me."

"I don't know what to believe. Why does everything happen to you?"

"Because of the Ebola outbreaks. Tad, do you know who got hurt?"

"I assume one of the techs from another department."

"Why don't you find out. And maybe you could also find out who else went into the lab last night."

"I don't think that's possible. No one will tell me anything right now because they know we're friends. Where are you?"

"I'm at the airport," said Marissa.

"If what you say about being attacked is true, then

you should come back here and explain. You shouldn't be running away."

"I'm not running away," insisted Marissa. "I'm going to the AMA in Chicago to research an organization called the Physicians' Action Congress. Ever hear of them? I believe they are involved somehow."

"Marissa, I think you should come directly back to the Center. You're in real trouble, in case you don't know."

"I do, but for the time being what I'm doing is more important. Can't you please ask the Office of Biosafety who else went into the maximum containment lab last night?"

"Marissa, I'm in no mood to be manipulated."

"Tad, I . . ." Marissa stopped speaking. Tad had hung up. Slowly she replaced the receiver. She couldn't really blame him.

She glanced at the clock. Five minutes until boarding. Making up her mind, she dialed Ralph's home number.

He picked up on the third ring. In contrast to Tad, he was concerned, not angry. "My God, Marissa, what is going on? Your name is in the evening paper. You're in serious trouble, the Atlanta police are looking for you!"

"I can imagine," said Marissa, thinking that she'd been wise to use a false name and pay cash when she'd bought her airline ticket. "Ralph, have you gotten the name of a good lawyer yet?"

"I'm sorry. When you asked, I didn't realize it was an emergency."

"It's becoming an emergency," said Marissa. "But I'll be out of town for a day or two. So if you could do it tomorrow I'd really appreciate it."

"What's going on?" asked Ralph. "The paper gave no details."

"Like I said last night, I don't want to involve you."

"I don't mind," Ralph insisted. "Why don't you come over here. We can talk and I can get you a lawyer in the morning."

"Have you ever heard of an organization called the Physicians' Action Congress?" asked Marissa, ignoring Ralph's offer.

"No," said Ralph. "Marissa, please come over. I think it would be better to face this problem, whatever it is. Running away makes you look bad."

Marissa heard her flight called.

"I'm going to the AMA to find out about the organization I just mentioned," said Marissa quickly. "I'll call tomorrow. I've got to run." She hung up, picked up her briefcase and book and boarded the plane.

13

May 22

ARRIVING IN CHICAGO, MARISSA decided to treat herself to a nice hotel and was happy to find the Palmer House had a room. She risked using her credit card and went straight upstairs to bed.

The next morning, she ordered fresh fruit and coffee from room service. While waiting, she turned on the *Today Show* and went into the bathroom to shower. She was drying her hair when she heard the anchorman mention Ebola. She rushed into the bedroom, expecting to see the news commentator giving an update on the situation in Philadelphia. Instead, he was describing a new outbreak. It was at the Rosenberg Clinic on upper Fifth Avenue in New York City. A doctor by the name of Girish Mehta had been diagnosed as having the disease. Word had leaked to the press, and a widespread panic had gripped the city.

Marissa shivered. The Philadelphia outbreak was still in progress and another one had already started. She put on her makeup, finished fixing her hair and ate her breakfast. Marissa got the AMA's address and set out for Rush Street.

A year ago if someone had told her she'd be visiting the association, she never would have believed it. But there she was, going through the front door.

The woman at the information booth directed her to the Public Relations office. The director, a James Frank, happened by as Marissa was trying to explain her needs to one of the secretaries. He invited her to his office.

Mr. Frank reminded Marissa of her high-school guidance counselor. He was of indeterminate age, slightly overweight and going bald, but his face had a lived-in look that exuded friendliness and sincerity. His eyes were bright, and he laughed a lot. Marissa liked him instantly.

"Physicians' Action Congress," he repeated when Marissa asked about the organization. "I've never heard of it. Where did you come across it?"

"On a congressman's contributions list," said Marissa.

"That's funny," said Mr. Frank. "I'd have sworn that I knew all the active political action committees. Let me see what my computer says."

Mr. Frank punched in the name. There was a slight delay, then the screen blinked to life. "What do you know! You're absolutely right. It's right here." He pointed to the screen. "Physicians' Action Congress Political Action Committee. It's a registered separate segregated fund."

"What does that mean?" asked Marissa.

"Less than it sounds. It just means that your Physicians' Action Congress is an incorporated membership organization because it has legally set up a committee to dispense funds as campaign contributions. Let's see who they have been supporting."

"I can tell you one candidate," said Marissa. "Calvin Markham."

Mr. Frank nodded. "Yup, here's Markham's name along with a number of other conservative candidates. At least we know the political bent."

"Right wing," said Marissa.

"Probably very right wing," said Mr. Frank. "I'd guess they are trying to knock off DRGs—Diagnosis-Related Groups—limit immigration of foreign medical school graduates, stop HMO start-up subsidies and the like. Let me call someone I know at the Federal Elections Commission."

After some chitchat, he asked his friend about the Physicians' Action Congress. He nodded a few times while he listened, then hung up and turned to Marissa. "He doesn't know much about PAC either, except he looked up their Statement of Organization and told me they are incorporated in Delaware."

"Why Delaware?" questioned Marissa.

"Incorporation is cheapest there."

"What are the chances of finding out more about the organization?" asked Marissa.

"Like what? Who the officers are? Where the home office is? That kind of stuff?"

"Yes," said Marissa.

Picking up the phone again, Frank said: "Let's see what we can learn from Delaware."

He was quite successful. Although initially a clerk in the Delaware State House said that he'd have to come in person for the information, Mr. Frank managed to get a supervisor to bend the rules.

Mr. Frank was on the line for almost fifteen minutes, writing as he listened. When he was done, he handed

Marissa a list of the board of directors. She looked down: President, Joshua Jackson, MD; vice-president, Rodd Becker, MD; treasurer, Sinclair Tieman, MD; secretary, Jack Krause, MD; directors, Gustave Swenson, MD; Duane Moody, MD; and Trent Goodridge, MD. Opening her briefcase, she took out the list of partners for Professional Labs. They were the same names!

Marissa left the AMA with her head spinning. The question that loomed in her mind was almost too bizarre to consider: what was an ultraconservative physicians' organization doing with a lab that owned sophisticated equipment used only for handling deadly viruses? Purposely, Marissa did not answer her own question.

Her mind churning, Marissa began walking in the direction of her hotel. Other pedestrians jostled her, but she paid no heed.

Trying to pick holes in her own theory, Marissa ticked off the significant facts: each of the outbreaks of Ebola had occurred in a private group prepaid health-care facility; most of the index patients had foreign-sounding names; and in each case where there was an index patient, the man had been mugged just prior to getting sick. The one exception was the Phoenix outbreak, which she still believed was food borne.

Out of the corner of her eye, she saw a display of Charles Jourdan shoes—her one weakness. Stopping abruptly to glance in the store window, she was startled when a man behind her almost knocked her over. He gave her an angry look, but she ignored him. A plan was forming in her mind. If her suspicions had any merit, and the previous outbreaks had not been the result of chance, then the index patient in New York was probably working for a prepaid health-care clinic and had been mugged a few days previous to becoming ill. Marissa decided she had to go to New York.

Looking around, she tried to figure out where she was in relation to her hotel. She could see the el in front of her and remembered that the train traveled the Loop near the Palmer House.

She began walking briskly when she was suddenly overwhelmed with fear. No wonder she'd been attacked in her home. No wonder the man who'd caught her in the maximum containment lab had tried to kill her. No wonder Markham had had her transferred. If her fears were true, then a conspiracy of immense proportions existed and she was in extreme jeopardy.

Up until that moment she'd felt safe in Chicago. Now, everywhere she looked she saw suspicious characters. There was a man pretending to window-shop she was sure was watching her in the reflection. She crossed the street, expecting the man to follow. But he didn't.

Marissa ducked into a coffee shop and ordered a cup of tea to calm down. She sat at a window table and stared out at the street. The man who had scared her came out of the store with a shopping bag and hailed a cab. So much for him. It was at that moment that she saw the businessman. It was the way he was carrying his briefcase that caught her attention, his arm at an awkward angle, as though he couldn't flex his elbow.

In a flash, Marissa was back in her own home, desperately fighting the unseen figure whose arm seemed frozen at the joint. And then there was the nightmare in the lab . . .

As Marissa watched, the man took out a cigarette and lit it, all with one hand, the other never leaving his briefcase. Marissa remembered that Tad had said the intruder had carried a briefcase.

Covering her face with her hands, Marissa prayed she was imagining things. She sat rubbing her eyes for a minute, and when she looked again, the man was gone.

Marissa finished her tea, then asked directions to the Palmer House. She walked quickly, nervously switching her own briefcase from hand to hand. At the first corner, she looked over her shoulder: the same businessman was coming toward her.

Immediately changing directions, Marissa crossed the street. Out of the corner of her eye, she watched the man continue to the middle of the block and then cross after her. With a rising sense of panic, she looked for a taxi, but the street was clear. Instead, she turned around and ran back to the elevated train. Hurriedly she climbed the stairs, catching up to a large group. She wanted to be in a crowd.

Once on the platform, she felt better. There were lots of people standing about, and Marissa walked a good distance away from the entrance. Her heart was still pounding, but at least she could think. Was it really the same man? Had he been following her?

As if in answer to her question, the man popped into her line of vision. He had large features and coarse skin and a heavy five-o'clock shadow. His teeth were square and widely spaced. He coughed into a closed fist.

Before she could move, the train thundered into the station, and the crowd surged forward, taking Marissa along with the rest. She lost sight of the man as she was carried into the car.

Fighting to stay near the door, Marissa hoped she could detrain at the last moment as she'd seen people do in spy movies, but the crush of people hampered her, and the doors closed before she could get to them. Turning, she scanned the faces around her, but she did not see the man with the stiff elbow.

The train lurched forward, forcing her to reach for a pole. Just as she grabbed it, she saw him again. He was right next to her, holding onto the same pole with the hand of his good arm. He was so close, Marissa could smell his cologne. He turned and their eyes met. A slight smile formed at the corners of his mouth as he let go of the pole. He coughed and reached into his jacket pocket.

Losing control, Marissa screamed. Frantically, she tried to push away from the man, but she was again hindered by the crush of people. Her scream died, and no one moved or spoke. They just stared at her. The wheels of the train shrieked as they hit a sharp bend, and Marissa and the man had to grab the pole to keep from falling. Their hands touched.

Marissa let go of the pole as if it were red hot. Then, to her utter relief, a transit policeman managed to shove his way over to her.

"Are you all right?" yelled the policeman over the sounds of the train.

"This man has been following me," said Marissa, pointing.

The policeman looked at the businessman. "Is this true?"

The man shook his head. "I've never seen her before. I don't know what she's talking about."

The policeman turned back to Marissa as the train began to slow. "Would you care to file a complaint?"

"No," yelled Marissa, "as long as he leaves me alone."

The screech of the wheels and the hiss of the air brakes made it impossible to hear until the train stopped. The doors opened instantly.

"I'll be happy to get off if it would make the lady feel better," said the businessman.

A few people got off. Everyone else just stared. The policeman kept the door from closing with his body and looked questioningly at Marissa.

"I would feel better," said Marissa, suddenly unsure of her reactions.

The businessman shrugged his shoulders and got off. Almost immediately, the doors closed and the train lurched forward once again.

"You all right now?" asked the policeman.

"Much better," said Marissa. She was relieved the businessman was gone, but afraid the cop might ask for her identification. She thanked him then looked away. He took the hint and moved on.

Realizing that every eye within sight was still on her, Marissa was acutely embarrassed. As soon as the train pulled into the next station, she got off. Descending to the street, and irrationally afraid the man had found a way to follow her, she caught the first cab she could to take her to the Palmer House.

Within the security of the taxi, Marissa was able to regain a degree of control. She knew she was in over her head, but she had no idea to whom in authority she could go. She was presupposing a conspiracy but had no idea of its extent. And worst of all, she had no proof; nothing—just a few highly suggestive facts.

She decided she might as well continue on to New York. If her suspicions about that outbreak proved to be correct, she'd decide there who to contact. Meanwhile, she hoped that Ralph had found her a good lawyer. Maybe he could handle the whole thing.

As soon as she got back to the hotel, Marissa went directly to her room. With her present paranoia, she wanted out as soon as possible, criticizing herself for having used a credit card and, hence, her own name. She'd used an assumed name and paid cash for the flight from Atlanta to Chicago, and she should have done the same at the hotel.

Going up in the elevator, Marissa had decided she would pack her few things and go right to the airport. She opened her door and headed straight for the bathroom, tossing her purse and briefcase onto the desk. Out of the corner of her eye, she saw movement and ducked automatically. Even so, she was struck so hard she was knocked forward over the nearest twin bed, ending up on the floor between them. Looking up, she saw the man from the train coming toward her.

Frantically, she tried to scramble beneath one of the beds, but the man got ahold of her skirt with his good arm and yanked her back.

Marissa rolled over, kicking furiously. Something fell out of the man's hand and hit the floor with a metallic thud. A gun, thought Marissa, compounding her terror.

The man bent to retrieve the gun, and Marissa slithered beneath the bed closest to the door. The man returned, checking first under one bed, then under the one where Marissa was cowering. His large hand reached for her. When he couldn't grab her, he got down on his knees and lunged under the bed, catching Marissa by an ankle and pulling her toward him.

For the second time that day, Marissa screamed. She kicked again and loosened the man's grip. In a flash she was back under the bed.

Tiring of the tug of war, he dropped his gun onto the bed and came after her. But Marissa rolled out the other side. She scrambled to her feet and ran for the door. She had just wrenched it open when the man leaped across the bed and caught her hair. Whipping her around, he threw her against the bureau with such force that the mirror fell with a crash.

The man checked the hall quickly, then closed and secured the door. Marissa ran to the bathroom, grabbing what she thought was the gun off the far bed. She had almost managed to get the bathroom door closed before the man reached it.

Marissa wedged her back against the sink and tried to keep her attacker from opening the door farther. But, little by little, his greater strength prevailed. The door cracked open, enabling him to get the arm with the frozen elbow hooked around the jamb.

Marissa eyed the wall phone but couldn't reach it without taking her feet off the door. She looked at the weapon in her hand, wondering if it would scare the man if she were to fire a bullet at the wall. That was when she realized she was holding an air-powered vaccination gun of the kind used for mass inoculations in her old pediatrics clinic.

The door had opened enough for the man to move his arm more freely. He blindly groped until he got a grip on one of Marissa's ankles. Feeling she had little choice,

Marissa pressed the vaccination gun against the man's forearm and discharged it. The man screamed. The arm was withdrawn, and the door slammed shut.

She heard him run across the room, open the door to the hall and rush out. Going back into the bedroom, Marissa breathed a sigh of relief, only to be startled by a strong odor of phenolic disinfectant. Turning the vaccinator toward herself with a shaky hand, she examined the circular business end. Intuitively, she sensed the gun contained Ebola virus, and she guessed that the disinfectant she smelled was part of a mechanism to prevent exposure to the operator. Now she was truly terrified. Not only had she possibly killed a man, she might also have triggered a new outbreak. Forcing herself to remain calm, she carefully placed the gun in a plastic bag that she took from the wastebasket and then got another plastic bag from the basket under the desk and placed it over the first, knotting it closed. For a moment she hesitated, wondering if she should call the police. Then she decided there was nothing they could do. The man was far away by now, and if the vaccination gun did contain Ebola, there was no way they could find him quietly if he didn't want to be found.

Marissa looked out into the hall. It was clear. She put a Do Not Disturb sign on the door, then carried her belongings, including the plastic bag with the vaccination gun, down to housekeeping. There were no cleaning people in sight. She found a bottle of Lysol and disinfected the outside of the plastic bag. Then she washed and disinfected her hands. She couldn't think of anything else to do prophylactically.

In the lobby, where there were enough people to make

Marissa feel reasonably safe, she called the Illinois State Epidemiologist. Without identifying herself, she explained that room 2410 at the Palmer House might have been contaminated with Ebola virus. Before the man could gasp out a single question, she hung up.

Next, she called Tad. All this activity was enabling her to avoid thinking about what had just happened. Tad's initial coolness thawed when he realized that she was on the verge of hysteria.

"What on earth is going on now?" he asked. "Marissa, are you all right?"

"I have to ask two favors. After the trouble I've caused you, I'd vowed that I wouldn't bother you again. But I have no choice. First, I need a vial of the convalescent serum from the L.A. outbreak. Could you send it by overnight carrier to Carol Bradford at the Plaza Hotel in New York?"

"Who the hell is Carol Bradford?"

"Please don't ask any questions," said Marissa, struggling to keep from bursting into tears. "The less you know at this point, the better." Carol Bradford had been one of Marissa's college roommates; it was the name she'd used on the flight from Atlanta to Chicago.

"The next favor involves a parcel I'm sending you by overnight carrier. Please, do not open it. Take it inside the maximum containment lab and hide it." Marissa paused.

"Is that it?" asked Tad.

"That's it," said Marissa. "Will you help me, Tad?"

"I guess," said Tad. "Sounds reasonably innocuous."

"Thank you," said Marissa. "I'll be able to explain everything in a few days."

She hung up and called the Westin Hotel toll-free number and reserved a room at the Plaza for that night under the name of Carol Bradford. That accomplished, she scanned the Palmer House lobby. No one seemed to be paying her any heed. Trusting that the hotel would bill her on her credit card, she did not bother to check out.

The first stop was a Federal Express office. The people were extremely nice when she told them it was a special vaccine needed in Atlanta by the next day. They helped her pack her plastic bags in an unbreakable metal box and even addressed it, when they saw how badly her hand was trembling.

Back on the street, she flagged a cab to O'Hare. As soon as she was seated, she began checking her lymph nodes and testing her throat for soreness. She'd been close to Ebola before, but never this close. She shuddered to think that the man had intended to infect her with the virus. It was a cruel irony that the only way she'd escaped was to have infected him. She hoped that he realized the convalescent serum had a protective effect if it was given prior to the appearance of symptoms. Maybe that was why the man had left so precipitously.

During the long ride to the airport, she began to calm down enough to think logically. The fact that she'd been attacked again gave more credence to her suspicions. And if the vaccination gun proved to contain Ebola, she'd have her first real piece of evidence.

The taxi driver dropped Marissa at the American Airlines terminal, explaining that they had hourly flights to New York. Once she got her ticket, passed through security and hiked the long distance to the gate, she found she had nearly half an hour to wait. She decided to call

Ralph. She badly needed to hear a friendly voice, and she wanted to ask about the lawyer.

Marissa spent several minutes struggling with Ralph's secretary, who guarded him as if he were the Pope, pleading with the woman to at least let him know she was on the line. Finally, Ralph picked up the phone.

"I hope you're back in Atlanta," he said before she could say hello.

"Soon," promised Marissa. She explained that she was at the American terminal in Chicago, on her way to New York, but that she'd probably be back in Atlanta the following day, particularly if he'd found her a good lawyer.

"I made some discreet inquiries," said Ralph, "and I think I have just the man. His name is McQuinllin. He's with a large firm here in Atlanta."

"I hope he's smart," said Marissa. "He's going to have his hands full."

"Supposedly he's one of the best."

"Do you think that he will require a lot of money up front?"

"Chances are he'll want a retainer of some sort," said Ralph. "Will that be a problem?"

"Could be," said Marissa. "Depends on how much."

"Well, don't worry," said Ralph. "I'll be happy to lend a hand."

"I couldn't ask you to do that," said Marissa.

"You're not asking, I'm offering," said Ralph. "But in return, I'd like you to stop this crazy trip. What's so important in New York? I hope it's not the new Ebola outbreak. You don't want a repeat of Philadelphia. Why don't you just fly back to Atlanta. I'm worried about you."

"Soon," said Marissa. "I promise."

After hanging up, Marissa kept her hand on the receiver. It always made her feel good to talk with Ralph. He cared.

Like most of the businesspeople who comprised ninety percent of the passengers, Marissa ordered herself a drink. She was still a bundle of nerves. The vodka tonic calmed her considerably, and she actually got into one of those "where you from?" and "what do you do?" conversations with a handsome young bond dealer from Chicago, named Danny. It turned out he had a sister who was a doctor in Hawaii. He chatted so enthusiastically, Marissa finally had to close her eyes and feign sleep in order to find time to put her thoughts in order.

The question that loomed in her mind was: how had the man with the frozen arm known she was in Chicago? And, assuming it was the same man, how had he known when she'd been in the maximum containment lab? To answer both questions, Marissa's mind reluctantly turned to Tad. When Tad had discovered the missing card, he must have known she would use it that night. Maybe he told Dubchek to avoid getting into trouble himself. Tad had also known she was flying to Chicago, but she simply couldn't believe he had intentionally set a murderer on her trail. And much as she resented Dubchek, she respected him as a dedicated scientist. It was hard to connect him with the financially oriented, right-wing Physicians' Action Congress.

Thoroughly confused as to what was intelligent deduction and what paranoid delusion, Marissa wished she hadn't let the vaccination gun out of her hands. If Tad was somehow involved, then she'd lost her only hard evidence, provided it tested positive for Ebola.

As her plane touched down at La Guardia airport, Marissa decided that if the New York outbreak confirmed her theories about the origin of the Ebola outbreaks, she would go directly to Ralph's lawyer and let him and the police sort things out. She just wasn't up to playing Nancy Drew any longer. Not against a group of men who thought nothing of risking entire populations.

When the plane stopped and the seat-belt sign went off, indicating that they had arrived at the gate, Marissa stood and wrestled her suitcase out of the overhead bin. Danny insisted on helping her down the jetway, but when they said good-bye, Marissa vowed she would be more careful in the future. No more conversations with strangers, and she would not tell anyone her real name. In fact, she decided not to check into the Plaza as Carol Bradford. Instead, she'd stay overnight at the nearby Essex House, using the name of her old high-school chum, Lisa Kendrick.

George Valhala stood by the Avis Rent-a-Car counter and casually scanned the crowds in the baggage area. His employers had nicknamed him The Toad, not because of any physical characteristic, but rather because of his unusual patience, enabling him to sit still for hours on a stakeout, like a toad waiting for an insect.

But this job was not going to utilize his special talent. He'd only been at the airport for a short time, and his information was that the girl would arrive on the five o'clock or the six o'clock flight from Chicago. The five o'clock had just landed, and a few passengers were beginning to appear around the appropriate carousel.

The only minor problem that George foresaw was that the description he'd been given was vague: a cute, short, thirty-year-old female with brown hair. Usually he worked with a photo, but in this case there hadn't been time to get one.

Then he saw her. It had to be her. She was almost a foot shorter than everyone else in the army of attaché-case-toting travelers swarming the baggage area. And he noticed that she was bypassing the carousel, having apparently carried her suitcase off the plane.

Pushing off the Avis counter, George wandered toward Marissa to get a good fix on her appearance. He followed her outside, where she joined the taxi queue. She definitely was cute, and she definitely was little. George wondered how on earth she'd managed to overpower Paul in Chicago. The idea that she was some kind of martial-arts expert flitted through his mind. One way or another, George felt some respect for this little trick. He knew Al did too, otherwise Al wouldn't be going through all this trouble.

Having gotten a look at her up close, George crossed the street in front of the terminal and climbed into a taxi waiting opposite the taxi stand.

The driver twisted around, looking at George. "You see her?" He was a skinny fellow with birdlike features, quite a contrast to George's pear-shaped obesity.

"Jake, do I look like an idiot? Start the car. She's in the taxi line."

Jake did as he was told. He and George had been

working for Al for four years, and they got along fine, except when George started giving orders. But that wasn't too often.

"There she is," said George, pointing. Marissa was climbing into a cab. "Pull up a little and let her cab pass us."

"Hey, I'm driving," said Jake. "You watch, I drive." Nonetheless, he put the car in gear and started slowly forward.

George watched out the rear window, noticing Marissa's cab had a dented roof, he said, "That will be easy to follow." The taxi passed them on the right, and Jake pulled out behind. He allowed one car to get between them before they entered the Long Island Expressway.

There was no problem keeping Marissa's cab in sight even though the driver took the Queensborough Bridge, which was crowded with rush-hour traffic. After forty minutes they watched her get out in front of the Essex House. Jake pulled over to the curb fifty feet beyond the hotel.

"Well, now we know where she's staying," said Jake.

"Just to be certain, I'm going in to see that she registers," said George. "I'll be right back."

14

May 23

MARISSA DID NOT SLEEP WELL. After the incident in the room at the Palmer House, she might never feel comfortable in a hotel again. Every noise in the hall made her fearful, thinking someone would try to break in. And there were plenty of noises, what with people returning late and ordering from room service.

She also kept imagining symptoms. She could not forget the feel of the vaccination gun in her hand, and each time she woke up, she was certain she had a fever or was otherwise ill.

By the next morning, she was totally exhausted. She ordered fresh fruit and coffee, which arrived with a complimentary *New York Times*. The front page carried an article about the Ebola outbreaks. In New York, the number of cases had risen to eleven with one death, while in Philadelphia the count stood at thirty-six with seventeen deaths. The single death in New York was the initial case, Dr. Girish Mehta.

Starting at ten, Marissa repeatedly called the Plaza Hotel to inquire after a parcel for Carol Bradford. She intended to keep calling until noon: the overnight carriers generally guaranteed delivery by that time. If the parcel arrived, she would be less wary of Tad's betraying her and would then go up to the Rosenberg Clinic. Just after eleven, she was told that the package was there and that it was being held for the guest's arrival.

As Marissa prepared to leave the hotel, she didn't know whether to be surprised that Tad had sent the serum or not. Of course the package could be empty, or its arrival only a ruse to get her to reveal her whereabouts. Unfortunately, there was no way for Marissa to be sure, and she wanted the serum enough to make her doubts academic. She would have to take a chance.

Taking only her purse, Marissa tried to think of a way of obtaining the package that would involve the least risk. Unfortunately, she didn't have any bright ideas other than to have a cab waiting and to be sure there were plenty of people around.

George Valhala had been in the lobby of the Essex House since early that morning. This was the kind of situation that he loved. He'd had coffee, read the papers and ogled some handsome broads. All in all, he'd had a great time, and none of the house detectives had bothered him, dressed as he was in an Armani suit and genuine alligator shoes.

He was considering ducking into the men's room when he saw Marissa get off the elevator. He dropped his *New York Post* and beat her out the revolving door. Dodging Fifty-ninth Street traffic, he jogged across to the taxi where Jake was waiting and climbed into the front seat.

Jake had spotted Marissa and had already started the

car. "She looks even cuter in daylight," he said, preparing to make a U-turn.

"You sure that's Blumenthal?" asked the man who had been waiting in the backseat. His name was Alphonse Hicktman, but few people teased him about his first name, just calling him Al, as he requested. He'd grown up in East Germany and had fled to the West over the Berlin Wall. His face was deceptively youthful. His hair was blond, and he wore it short in a Julius Caesar-style shag. His pale blue eyes were as cold as a winter sky.

"She registered under the name of Lisa Kendrick, but she fits the description," said George. "It's her all right."

"She's either awfully good or awfully lucky," said Al. "We've got to isolate her without any slipups. Heberling says she could blow the whole deal."

They watched as Marissa climbed into a taxi and headed east.

Despite the traffic, Jake made his U-turn, then worked his way up to a position only two cars behind Marissa's taxi.

"Look, lady, you got to tell me where you want to go," said Marissa's driver, eyeing her in his rearview mirror.

Marissa was twisted around, still watching the entrance to the Essex House. No one had come out who appeared to be following her. Facing forward, she told the driver to go around the block. She was still trying to think of a safe way to get the serum.

The driver muttered something under his breath as he

proceeded to turn right at the corner. Marissa looked at the Fifth Avenue entrance to the Plaza. There were loads of cars, and the little park in front of the hotel was crowded with people. Horse-drawn hansom cabs lined the curb, waiting for customers. There were even several mounted policemen with shiny blue and black helmets. Marissa felt encouraged. There was no way anybody could surprise her in such a setting.

As they came back down Fifty-ninth Street, Marissa told the driver that she wanted him to stop at the Plaza and wait while she ran inside.

"Lady, I think . . ."

"I'll only be a moment," said Marissa.

"There are plenty of cabs," pointed out the driver. "Why don't you get another?"

"I'll add five dollars to the metered fare," said Marissa, "and I promise I won't be long." Marissa treated the man to the largest smile she could muster under the circumstances.

The driver shrugged. His reservations seemed adequately covered by the five-dollar tip and the smile. He pulled up to the Plaza. The hotel doorman opened the door and Marissa got out.

She was extremely nervous, expecting the worst at any second. She watched as her cab pulled up about thirty feet from the entrance. Satisfied, she went inside.

As she'd hoped, the ornate lobby was busy. Without hesitating, Marissa crossed to a jewelry display window and pretended to be absorbed. Scanning the reflection in the glass, she checked the area for signs anyone was watching her. No one seemed to notice her at all.

Crossing the lobby again, she approached the concierge's desk and waited, her heart pounding.

"May I see some identification?" asked the man, when Marissa requested the parcel.

Momentarily confused, Marissa said she didn't have any with her.

"Then your room key will be adequate," said the man, trying to be helpful.

"But I haven't checked in yet," said Marissa.

The man smiled. "Why don't you check in and then get your parcel. I hope you understand. We do have a responsibility."

"Of course," said Marissa, her confidence shaken. She obviously had not thought this out as carefully as she should have. Recognizing she had little choice, she walked to the registration desk.

Even that process was complicated when she said she didn't want to use a credit card. The clerk made her go to the cashier to leave a sizable cash deposit before he would give her a room key. Finally, armed with the key, she got her Federal Express package.

Tearing open the parcel as she walked, Marissa lifted out the vial and glanced at it. It seemed authentic. She threw the wrapping in a trash can and pocketed the serum. So far so good.

Emerging from the revolving door, Marissa hesitated while her eyes adjusted to the midday glare. Her cab was still where she'd last seen it. The doorman asked if she wanted transportation, and Marissa smiled and shook her head.

She looked up and down Fifty-ninth Street. If anything, the traffic had increased. On the sidewalk hundreds of people rushed along as if they were all late for some important meeting. It was a scene of bright sun and purposeful bustle. Satisfied, Marissa descended the few steps to the street and ran the short distance to her cab.

Reaching the car and grasping the rear door handle, she cast one last look over her shoulder at the Plaza entrance. No one was following her. Her fears about Tad had been unfounded.

She was about to slide inside when she found herself staring into the muzzle of a gun held by a blond man who'd apparently been lying on the backseat. The man started to speak, but Marissa didn't give him time. She swung herself clear of the cab and slammed the door. The weapon discharged with a hiss. It was some kind of sophisticated air gun. The cab window shattered, but Marissa was no longer looking. She took off, running as she'd never run before. Out of the corner of her eye, she noticed that the cab driver had bolted out of his car and was running diagonally away from her. The next time she looked over her shoulder, she saw the blond man headed in her direction, pushing his way through the crowds.

The sidewalk was an obstacle course of people, luggage, pushcarts, baby carriages and dogs. The blond man had pocketed his weapon, but she no longer was convinced the crowds provided the protection she had hoped for. Who would even notice the air gun's soft hiss? She'd just fall to the ground, and her attacker would escape before anyone realized she'd been shot.

People shouted as she crashed by them, but she kept going. The confusion she caused hampered the blond man, but not dramatically. He was gaining on her.

Running across the drive east of the Plaza, Marissa dodged taxis and limos, reaching the edge of the small park with its central fountain. She was in a full panic with no destination. But she knew she had to do something. It was at that moment that she saw the mounted policeman's horse. It was loosely tethered to the link chain fence that bordered the tiny patch of grass in the park. As Marissa ran toward the horse, she searched desperately for the policeman. She knew he had to be near, but there was so little time. She could hear the blond man's heels strike the sidewalk, then hesitate. He'd arrived at the drive separating the park from the hotel.

Reaching the horse, Marissa grabbed the reins and ducked underneath as the animal nervously tossed its head. Looking back, Marissa saw the man was in the street, rounding a limo.

Frantically, Marissa's eyes swept the small park. There were plenty of people, many of them looking in her direction, but no policeman. Giving up, she turned and started running across the park. There was no chance to hide. Her pursuer was too close.

A good crowd was seated by the fountain, watching her with studied indifference. New Yorkers, they were accustomed to any form of excess, including panic-filled flight.

As Marissa rounded the side of the fountain, the blond man was so close she could hear him breathe. Turning again, Marissa collided with the people streaming into the park. Pushing and shoving, Marissa forced her way through the pedestrians, hearing people muttering, "Hey, you!" "The nerve," and worse.

Breaking into a clear space, she thought she was free, until she realized she was in the center of a circle of several hundred people. Three muscular blacks were break dancing to a rap song. Marissa's desperate eyes met those of the youths. She saw only anger: She'd crashed their act.

Before anyone could move, the blond man stumbled into the circle, coming to an off-balance halt. He started to raise his air gun, but he didn't get far. With a practiced kick, one of the infuriated dancers sent the weapon on a low arc into the crowd. People began to move away as Marissa's pursuer countered with a kick of his own. The dancer caught the blow on his forearm and fell to the ground.

Three of his friends who'd been watching from the sidelines leaped to their feet and rushed the blond man from behind.

Marissa didn't wait. She melted into the crowd that had backed away from the sudden brawl. Most of the people were crossing Fifth Avenue, and she did the same. Once north of Fifty-ninth Street, she hailed another taxi and told the driver she wanted the Rosenberg Clinic. As the cab turned on Fifty-ninth, Marissa could see a sizable crowd near the fountain. The mounted policeman was finally back on his horse, and she hoped he would keep the blond man occupied for several weeks.

Once again, Marissa looked over at the Plaza entrance. There was no unusual activity going on as far as she could see. Marissa sat back and closed her eyes. Instead of fear she was suddenly consumed with anger. She was furious with everyone, particularly with Tad. There could be little doubt now that he was telling her pursuers her whereabouts. Even the serum that she'd gone to so much trouble to obtain was useless. With her current suspicions, there was no way she'd inject herself with it. Instead, she'd have to take her chances that the vaccination gun had been designed to adequately protect the user.

For a short time, she considered skipping her visit to the Rosenberg Clinic, but the importance of proving, at least to herself, that the Ebola was being deliberately spread won out. She had to be sure. Besides, after the last elaborate attack, no one would be expecting her.

Marissa had the cab drop her off a little way from the clinic and went the remaining block on foot. The place certainly was not hard to find. It was a fancy, renovated structure that occupied most of a city block. A mobile TV truck and several police cruisers were parked out front. A number of officers lounged on the granite steps. Marissa had to flash her CDC identity card before they let her through.

The lobby was in the same state of confusion as the other hospitals that had suffered an Ebola outbreak. As she threaded her way through the crowd, she began to lose her resolve. The anger she'd felt in the taxi waned, replaced with the old fear of exposing herself to Ebola. Also, her exhilaration at escaping her pursuer faded. In its stead was the reality of being caught in a dangerous web of conspiracy and intrigue. She stopped, eyeing the exit. For a moment she debated leaving, but decided her only hope was to be absolutely sure. She had to remove any of her own doubts before she could possibly convince anyone else.

She thought she would check the easiest piece of information first. She walked down to the business office, where she found a desk with a sign, New Subscribers.

Although it was unoccupied, it was loaded with printed literature. It only took a moment for her to learn that the Rosenberg Clinic was an HMO, just as she'd suspected.

The next questions she wanted answered would be more difficult since the initial patient had already died. Retracing her steps back to the main lobby, Marissa stood watching the stream of people coming and going until she figured out where the doctor's coatroom was. Timing her approach, Marissa arrived at the door along with a staff doctor who paused to signal the man at the information booth. The coatroom door buzzed open and Marissa entered behind the doctor.

Inside, she was able to obtain a long white coat. She put it on and rolled up the sleeves. There was a name tag on the lapel that said Dr. Ann Elliott. Marissa took it off and placed it in the coat's side pocket.

Going back to the lobby, Marissa was startled to see Dr. Layne. Turning away, she expected any moment to hear a cry of recognition. Luckily, when she glanced back, Dr. Layne was leaving the hospital.

Seeing him had made Marissa more nervous than ever. She was terrified of running into Dubchek as she had in Philadelphia, but she knew she had to find out more about the dead index case.

Going over to the directory, she saw that the Department of Pathology was on the fourth floor. Marissa took the next elevator. The Rosenberg Clinic was an impressive place. Marissa had to walk through the chemistry lab to get to the pathologists' offices. En route, she noticed that they had the latest and most expensive automated equipment.

Going through a pair of double doors, Marissa found

herself surrounded by secretaries busily typing from dictaphones. This was the center of the pathology department, where all the reports were prepared.

One of the women removed her ear piece as Marissa approached. "May I help you?"

"I'm one of the doctors from the CDC," Marissa said warmly. "Do you know if any of my colleagues are here?"

"I don't think so," said the secretary, starting to rise. "I can ask Dr. Stewart. He's in his office."

"I'm right here," said a big, burly man with a full beard. "And to answer your question, the CDC people are down on the third floor in our isolation wing."

"Well, perhaps you can help me," said Marissa, purposely avoiding introducing herself. "I've been looking into the Ebola outbreaks from the beginning, but unfortunately I was delayed getting to New York. I understand that the first case, a Dr. Mehta, has already died. Did you do a post?"

"Just this morning."

"Would you mind if I asked a few questions?"

"I didn't do the autopsy," said Dr. Stewart. Then, turning to the secretary, he asked, "Helen, see if you can round up Curt."

He led Marissa to a small office furnished with a modern desk and white Formica lab bench, holding a spanking new double-headed Zeiss binocular microscope.

"Did you know Dr. Mehta?" asked Marissa.

"Quite well," said Stewart, shaking his head. "He was our medical director, and his death will be a great loss." Stewart went on to describe Dr. Mehta's contributions in establishing the Rosenberg Clinic and his enormous popularity among staff and patients alike.

"Do you know where he did his training?" asked Marissa.

"I'm not certain where he went to medical school," said Stewart. "I think it was in Bombay. But I know he did his residency in London. Why do you ask?"

"I was just curious if he was a foreign medical school graduate," said Marissa.

"Does that make a difference?" asked Stewart, frowning.

"It might," said Marissa vaguely. "Are there a large percentage of foreign medical school graduates on staff here?"

"Of course," said Stewart. "All HMOs started by hiring a large proportion of foreign medical graduates. American graduates wanted private practice. But that's changed. These days we can recruit directly from the top residencies."

The door opened and a young man came in.

"This is Curt Vandermay," said Stewart.

Reluctantly, Marissa gave her own name.

"Dr. Blumenthal has some questions about the autopsy," explained Dr. Stewart. He pulled a chair away from his microscope bench for Dr. Vandermay, who sat down and gracefully crossed his legs.

"We haven't processed the sections yet," explained Dr. Vandermay. "So I hope the gross results will do."

"Actually, I'm interested in your external exam," said Marissa. "Were there any abnormalities?"

"For sure," said Dr. Vandermay. "The man had extensive hemorrhagic lesions in his skin."

"What about trauma?" asked Marissa.

"How did you guess?" said Dr. Vandermay, surprised. "He had a broken nose. I'd forgotten about that."

"How old?" asked Marissa.

"A week, ten days. Somewhere in that range."

"Did the chart mention a cause?"

"To tell the truth, I didn't look," said Dr. Vandermay. "Knowing the man died of Ebola Hemorrhagic Fever took precedence. I didn't give the broken nose a lot of thought."

"I understand," said Marissa. "What about the chart? I assume it's here in pathology. Can I see it?"

"By all means," said Vandermay. He stood up. "Why don't you come down to the autopsy area. I have some Polaroids of the broken nose, if you'd like to see them."

"Please," said Marissa.

Stewart excused himself, saying he had a meeting to attend, and Marissa followed Vandermay as he explained that the body had been disinfected and then double-bagged in special receptacles to avoid contamination. The family had requested that the body be shipped home to India, but that permission had been refused. Marissa could understand why.

The chart wasn't as complete as Marissa would have liked, but there was reference to the broken nose. It had been set by one of Dr. Mehta's colleagues, an ENT surgeon. Marissa also learned that Dr. Mehta was an ENT surgeon himself, a terrifying fact given the way the epidemic had spread in the previous outbreaks. As far as the cause of the broken nose was concerned, there was nothing.

Vandermay suggested that they phone the man who set it. While he put through the call, Marissa went through the rest of the chart. Dr. Mehta had no history of recent travel, exposure to animals or connection to any of the other Ebola outbreaks.

"The poor man was robbed," said Dr. Vandermay, hanging up the phone. "Punched out and robbed in his own driveway. Can you believe it? What a world we live in!"

If you only knew, thought Marissa, now absolutely certain that the Ebola outbreaks were deliberately caused. A wave of fear swept over her, but she forced herself to continue questioning the pathologist. "Did you happen to notice a nummular lesion on Dr. Mehta's thigh?"

"I don't recall," said Dr. Vandermay. "But here are all the Polaroids." He spread a group of photos out as if he were laying out a poker hand.

Marissa looked at the first one. They brutally portrayed the naked corpse laid out on the stainless-steel autopsy table. Despite the profusion of hemorrhagic lesions, Marissa was able to pick out the same circular lesion she had seen on Dr. Richter's thigh. It corresponded in size to the head of a vaccination gun.

"Would it be possible for me to take one of these photos?" asked Marissa.

Dr. Vandermay glanced at them. "Go ahead. We've got plenty."

Marissa slipped the photo into her pocket. It wasn't as good as the vaccination gun, but it was something. She thanked Dr. Vandermay and got up to leave.

"Aren't you going to tell me your suspicions?" Vandermay asked. There was a slight smile on his face, as if he knew that something was up.

An intercom system crackled to life, informing Dr. Vandermay that he had a phone call on line six. He picked up, and Marissa overheard him say, "That's a coincidence, Dr. Dubchek, I'm talking with Dr. Blumenthal right this moment . . ."

That was all Marissa needed to hear. She got up and ran for the elevators. Vandermay called after her, but she didn't stop. She passed the secretaries at a half-jog and raced through the double doors, clutching the pens in the pocket of the white coat to keep them from falling out.

Facing the elevators and fire stairs, she decided to risk the elevator. If Dubchek had been on the third floor, he probably would think it faster to use the stairs. She pushed the Down button. A lab tech was waiting with his tray of vacu-containers. He watched Marissa frantically push the already illuminated elevator button several more times. "Emergency?" he asked as their eyes met.

An elevator stopped and Marissa squeezed on. The doors seemed to take forever to close, and she expected at any moment to see Dubchek running to stop them. But finally they started down, and Marissa began to relax only to find herself stopping on three. She moved deeper into the car, for once appreciating her small stature. It would have been difficult to see her from outside the elevator.

As the elevator began to move again, she asked a gray-haired technician where the cafeteria was. He told her to turn right when she got off the elevator and follow the main corridor.

Marissa got off and did as she had been told. A short

distance down the hall, she smelled the aroma of food. For the rest of the way she followed her nose.

She had decided it was too dangerous to risk the front entrance to the clinic. Dubchek could have told the police to stop her. Instead, she ran into the cafeteria, which was crowded with people having lunch. She headed directly for the kitchen. The staff threw her a few questioning looks, but no one challenged her. As she'd imagined, there was a loading dock, and she exited directly onto it, skirting a dairy truck that was making a delivery.

Dropping down to the level of the driveway, Marissa walked briskly out onto Madison Avenue. After going north for half a block, she turned east on a quiet tree-lined street. There were few pedestrians, which gave Marissa confidence that she was not being trailed. When she got to Park Avenue, she hailed a cab.

To be sure that no one was following her, Marissa got off at Bloomingdales, walked through the store to Third Avenue and hailed a second cab. By the time she pulled up at the Essex House, she was confident that she was safe, at least for the time being.

Outside her room, with its Do Not Disturb sign still in place, Marissa hesitated. Even though no one knew she was registered under an assumed name, the memory of Chicago haunted her. She opened the door carefully, scanning the premises before going in. Then she propped the door open with a chair and warily searched the room. She checked under the beds, in the closet and in the bathroom. Everything was as she'd left it. Satisfied, Marissa closed and locked her door, using all the bolts and chains available.

15

May 23—continued

MARISSA ATE SOME OF the generous portion of fruit she'd ordered from room service for her breakfast that morning, peeling an apple with the sharp paring knife that had come with it. Now that her suspicions appeared to be true, she wasn't sure what to do next. The only thing she could think of was to go to Ralph's lawyer and tell him what she believed: that a small group of right-wing physicians were introducing Ebola into privately owned clinics to erode public trust in HMOs. She could hand over the meager evidence she had and let him worry about the rest of the proof. Maybe he could even suggest a safe place for her to hide while things were being sorted out.

Putting down the apple, she reached for the phone. She felt much better having come to a decision. She dialed Ralph's office number and was pleasantly surprised to be immediately put through to him.

"I gave my secretary specific instructions," explained Ralph. "In case you don't know it, I'm concerned about you."

"You're sweet," said Marissa, suddenly touched by

Ralph's sympathy. It undermined the tight control she'd been holding over her emotions. For a second she felt like the child who didn't cry after a fall until she saw her mother.

"Are you coming home today?"

"That depends," said Marissa, biting her lip and taking a deep breath. "Do you think I can talk to that lawyer today?" Her voice wavered.

"No," said Ralph. "I called his office this morning. They said he had to go out of town but that he's expected back tomorrow."

"Too bad," said Marissa, her voice beginning to shake.

"Marissa, are you all right?" asked Ralph.

"I've been better," admitted Marissa. "I've had some awful experiences."

"What happened?"

"I can't talk now," said Marissa, knowing if she tried to explain, she'd burst into tears.

"Listen to me," said Ralph. "I want you to come here immediately. I didn't want you going to New York in the first place. Did you run into Dubchek again?"

"Worse than that," said Marissa.

"Well, that settles it," said Ralph. "Get the next flight home. I'll come and pick you up."

The idea had a lot of appeal, and she was about to say as much when there was a knock on her door. Marissa froze.

The knock was repeated.

"Marissa, are you there?"

"Just a minute," said Marissa into the phone. "There's someone at the door. Stay on the line."

She put the phone down on the night table and warily approached the door. "Who is it?"

"A delivery for Miss Kendrick." Marissa opened the door a crack but kept the safety catch on. One of the uniformed bellmen was standing there, holding a large package covered with white paper.

Flustered, she told the bellman to wait while she went back to the phone. She told Ralph that someone was at her door and that she'd call back as soon as she knew what flight she was taking home to Atlanta that evening.

"You promise?" asked Ralph.

"Yes!" said Marissa.

Returning to the door, Marissa looked out into the hall again. The bellman was leaning against the wall opposite, still holding the package. Who could have sent "Miss Kendrick" flowers when as far as Marissa knew her friend was living happily on the West Coast?

Returning to the phone, she called the desk and asked if she'd gotten any flowers. The concierge said, yes, they were on their way up.

Marissa felt a little better, but not enough to take off the chain. Instead, she called through the crack, "I'm terribly sorry, but would you mind leaving the flowers? I'll get them in a few minutes."

"My pleasure, madam," said the bellman, setting down the package. Then he touched his hat and disappeared down the hall.

Removing the chain, Marissa quickly picked up the basket and relocked the door. She ripped off the paper and found a spectacular arrangement of spring blossoms. On a green stake pushed into the Styrofoam base was an envelope addressed to Lisa Kendrick.

Removing it, Marissa pulled out a folded card addressed to Marissa Blumenthal! Her heart skipped a beat as she began to read:

> Dear Dr. Blumenthal,
> Congratulations on your performance this morning. We were all impressed. Of course, we will have to make a return visit unless you are willing to be reasonable. Obviously, we know where you are at all times, but we will leave you alone if you return the piece of medical equipment you borrowed.

Terror washed over Marissa. For a moment she stood transfixed in front of the flowers, looking at them in disbelief. Then in a sudden burst of activity, she began to pack her belongings, opening the drawers of the bureau, pulling out the few things that she'd placed there. But then she stopped. Nothing was exactly where she'd left it. They had been in her room, searching through her belongings! Oh, God! She had to get away from there.

Rushing into the bathroom, she snatched up her cosmetics, dumping them haphazardly into her bag. Then she stopped again. The implications of the note finally dawned on her. If they did not have the vaccination gun, that meant Tad was not involved. And neither he nor anyone else knew she was staying at the Essex House under a second assumed name. The only way they could have found her was by following her from the airport in Chicago.

The sooner she was out of the Essex House the better. After flinging the rest of her things into her suitcase, she found she had packed so badly it wouldn't close. As she sat on it, struggling with the latch, her eyes drifted back to the flowers. All at once she understood. Their purpose was to frighten her into leading her assailants to the vaccination gun, which was probably just what she would have done.

She sat on the bed and forced herself to think calmly. Since her adversaries knew she didn't have the vaccination gun with her, and were hoping she would lead them to it, she felt she had a little room to maneuver. Marissa decided not to bother taking the suitcase with her. She stuffed a few essentials in her purse and pulled the various papers she needed from her briefcase so she could leave that, too.

The only thing that Marissa felt absolutely certain of was that she would be followed. Undoubtedly her pursuers expected her to leave in a panic, making it that much easier for them. Well, thought Marissa, they were in for a surprise.

Looking again at the magnificent flowers, she decided she might well use the same strategy her enemies had. Thinking along those lines, she began to develop a plan that might give the answers that would provide the solution to the whole affair.

Unfolding the list of officers of the Physicians' Action Congress, Marissa reassured herself that the secretary was based in New York. His name was Jack Krause, and he lived at 426 East Eighty-fourth Street. Marissa decided that she'd pay the man an unannounced visit. Maybe all the doctors didn't know what was going on. It was hard to think of a group of physicians being willing to spread plague. In any case, her appearance on his doorstep should spread a lot more panic than any bouquet.

Meanwhile, she decided to take some steps to protect her departure. Going to the phone, she called the hotel manager, and in an irritated voice, complained that the desk had given her room number to her estranged boyfriend and that the man had been bothering her.

"That's impossible," said the manager. "We do not give out room numbers."

"I have no intention of arguing with you," snapped Marissa. "The fact of the matter is that it happened. Since the reason I stopped seeing him was because of his violent nature, I'm terrified."

"What would you like us to do?" asked the manager, sensing that Marissa had something specific in mind.

"I think you could at least move me to another room," said Marissa.

"I'll see to it myself," said the manager.

"One other thing," said Marissa. "My boyfriend is blond, athletic looking, sharp features. Perhaps you could alert your people."

"Certainly," said the manager.

Alphonse Hicktman took one last draw on his cigarette and tossed it over the granite wall that separated Central Park from the sidewalk. Looking back at the taxi with its off-duty light on, Al could just make out George's features. He was hunkered down, relaxed as usual. Waiting never seemed to bother the man. Looking across the street at the Essex House entrance, Al hoped to God that Jake was properly situated in the lobby so that Marissa could not leave unseen by a back entrance.

Al had been so sure that the flowers would send the woman flying out of the hotel. Now he was mystified. Either she was super smart or super stupid.

Walking over to the taxi, he whacked its roof with an open palm, making a noise like a kettledrum. George was instantly half out of the car on the other side.

Al smiled at him. "Little tense, George?" His patience made Al's frustration that much harder to bear.

"Jesus Christ!" exclaimed George.

The two men got into the cab.

"What time is it?" asked Al, taking out another cigarette. He'd already gone through most of a pack that afternoon.

"Seven-thirty."

Al flicked the used match out the open window. The job was not going well. Since the vaccination gun had not been in the woman's hotel room, his orders were to follow her until she retrieved it, but it was all too apparent that Dr. Blumenthal was not about to accommodate them, at least not immediately.

At that moment a group of revelers came stumbling out of the Essex House, arm in arm, swaying, laughing and generally making fools of themselves. They were obviously conventioneers, dressed in dark suits with name tags, and wearing plastic sun visors that said SANYO.

The doorman signaled a group of limousines waiting just up the street. One by one, they drove to the door to pick up their quota.

Al slapped George on the shoulder, frantically pointing toward the largest group to emerge through the revolving door. Among them two men were supporting a woman wearing a Sanyo visor who seemed too drunk to walk. "Is that the mark hanging onto those guys?" he asked.

George squinted, and before he could answer, the woman in question disappeared into one of the limousines. He turned back to Al. "I don't think so. Her hair was different. But I couldn't be sure."

"Damn!" said Al. "Neither could I." After a moment's hesitation, Al jumped out of the taxi. "If she comes out, follow her." Al then dodged the traffic and raced across to get in another cab.

From the back of the limousine, Marissa watched the entrance to the hotel. Out of the corner of her eye she saw someone alight from a parked taxi and run across the street. Just as her limousine pulled in front of a bus, blocking her view, she saw the man climbing into another taxi, a vintage Checker.

Marissa turned to face forward. She was certain she was being followed. She had several options, but with almost a full block's head start, she decided it would be best to get out.

As soon as the limousine turned on Fifth, Marissa shocked her companions by shouting at the driver to pull over.

The driver complied, figuring she was about to be sick, but before any of the men knew what was happening, she had the door open and jumped out, telling the driver to go on without her.

Spying a Doubleday bookstore, which, happily, was keeping late hours, she ducked inside. From the store window she saw the Checker cab speed by and caught a glimpse of a blond head in the backseat. The man was sitting forward, staring straight ahead.

The house looked more like a medieval fortress than a New York luxury townhouse. Its leaded windows were narrow and covered with twisted wrought-iron grilles. The front door was protected by a stout iron gate that was fashioned after a portcullis. The fifth floor was set back and the resulting terrace was crenellated like a castle tower.

Marissa eyed the building from across the street. It was hardly a hospitable sight, and for a moment she had second thoughts about visiting Dr. Krause. But safely ensconced in her new room at the Essex House that afternoon, she'd made some calls and learned that he was a prominent Park Avenue internist. She could not imagine that he would be capable of harming her directly. Perhaps through an organization like PAC, but not with his own two hands.

She crossed the street and climbed the front steps. Casting one last glance up and down the quiet street, she rang the bell. Behind the gate was the heavy wooden door, its center decorated with a family crest carved in relief.

She waited a minute and rang again. All at once a bright light went on, blinding her so that she could not see who was opening the door.

"Yes?" said a woman's voice.

"I would like to see Dr. Krause," said Marissa, trying to sound authoritative.

"Do you have an appointment?"

"No," admitted Marissa. "But tell the doctor that I'm

here on emergency Physicians' Action Congress business. I think he'll see me."

Marissa heard the door close. The hard light illuminated most of the street. After a couple of minutes, the door was reopened.

"The doctor will see you." Then there was the painful sound of the iron gate opening on hinges that needed oil.

Marissa went inside, relieved to get away from the glare. She watched the woman, who was dressed in a maid's black uniform, close the gate, then come toward her.

"If you'll follow me, please."

Marissa was led through a marbled and chandeliered entrance, down a short corridor to a paneled library.

"If you'll wait here," said the woman, "the doctor will be with you shortly."

Marissa glanced around the room, which was beautifully furnished with antiques. Bookcases lined three of the walls.

"Sorry to keep you waiting," said a mellow voice.

Marissa turned to look at Dr. Krause. He had a fleshy face with deep lines, and as he gestured for her to sit, she noticed his hands were unusually large and square, like those of an immigrant laborer. When they were sitting, she could see him better. The eyes were those of an intelligent, sympathetic man, reminding her of some of her internal medicine professors. Marissa was amazed that he could have gotten mixed up in something like the Physicians' Action Congress.

"I'm sorry to bother you at such an hour," she began.

"No problem," said Dr. Krause. "I was just reading. What can I do for you?"

Marissa leaned forward to watch the man's face. "My name is Dr. Marissa Blumenthal."

There was a pause as Dr. Krause waited for Marissa to continue. His expression did not change. Either he was a good actor or her name was not familiar.

"I'm an Epidemiology Intelligence Service officer at the CDC," added Marissa. His eyes narrowed just a tad.

"My maid said that you were here on PAC business," said Dr. Krause, a measure of the hospitality disappearing from his voice.

"I am," said Marissa. "Perhaps I should ask if you are aware of anything that PAC might be doing that could concern the CDC."

This time, Krause's jaw visibly tightened. He took a deep breath, started to speak, then changed his mind. Marissa waited as if she had all the time in the world.

Finally, Dr. Krause cleared his throat. "PAC is trying to rescue American medicine from the economic forces that are trying to destroy it. That's been its goal from the start."

"A noble goal," admitted Marissa. "But how is PAC attempting to accomplish this mission?"

"By backing responsible and sensible legislation," said Dr. Krause. He stood up, presumably to escape Marissa's stare. "PAC is providing an opportunity for more conservative elements to exert some influence. And it's about time; the profession of medicine is like a runaway train." He moved over to the fireplace, his face lost in shadow.

"Unfortunately, it seems PAC is doing more than sponsoring legislation," said Marissa. "That's what concerns the CDC."

"I think we have nothing more to discuss," said Dr. Krause. "If you'll excuse me—"

"I believe PAC is responsible for the Ebola outbreaks," blurted Marissa, standing up herself. "You people have some misguided idea that spreading disease in HMOs will further your cause."

"That's absurd!" said Dr. Krause.

"I couldn't agree more," said Marissa. "But I have papers linking you and the other officers of PAC to Professional Labs in Grayson, Georgia, which has recently purchased equipment to handle the virus. I even have the vaccination gun used to infect the index cases."

"Get out of here," ordered Dr. Krause.

"Gladly," said Marissa. "But first let me say that I intend to visit all the officers of PAC. I can't imagine they all agreed to this idiotic scheme. In fact, it's hard for me to imagine that a physician like yourself—any physician—could have allowed it."

Maintaining a calm she did not feel, Marissa walked to the door. Dr. Krause did not move from the fireplace. "Thank you for seeing me," said Marissa. "I'm sorry if I've upset you. But I'm confident that one of the PAC officers I see will want to help stop this horror. Perhaps by turning state's evidence. It could be you. I hope so. Good night, Dr. Krause."

Marissa forced herself to walk slowly down the short corridor to the foyer. What if she misjudged the man and he came after her? Luckily, the maid materialized and let her out. As soon as Marissa was beyond the cone of light, she broke into a run.

For a few moments Dr. Krause didn't move. It was as if his worst nightmare were coming true. He had a gun upstairs. Maybe he should just kill himself. Or he could call his lawyer and ask for immunity in return for turning state's evidence. But he had no idea what that really meant.

Panic followed paralysis. He rushed to his desk, opened his address book and, after looking up a number, placed a call to Atlanta.

The phone rang almost ten times before it was picked up. Joshua Jackson's smooth accent oiled its way along the wires as he said hello and asked who was calling.

"Jack Krause," said the distraught doctor. "What the hell is going on? You swore that aside from Los Angeles, PAC had nothing to do with the outbreaks of Ebola. That the further outbreaks sprang from accidental contact with the initial patients. Joshua, you gave me your word."

"Calm down," said Jackson. "Get ahold of yourself!"

"Who is Marissa Blumenthal?" asked Krause in a quieter voice.

"That's better," said Jackson. "Why do you ask?"

"Because the woman just showed up on my doorstep accusing me and PAC of starting all the Ebola epidemics."

"Is she still there?"

"No. She's gone," said Krause. "But who the hell is she?"

"An epidemiologist from the CDC who got lucky. But don't worry, Heberling is taking care of her."

"This affair is turning into a nightmare," said Krause. "I should remind you that I was against the project even when it only involved influenza."

"What did the Blumenthal girl want with you?" asked Jackson.

"She wanted to frighten me," said Krause. "And she did a damn good job. She said she has the names and addresses of all the PAC officers, and she implied that she was about to visit each one."

"Did she say who was next?"

"Of course she didn't. She's not stupid," said Krause. "In fact she's extremely clever. She played me like a finely tuned instrument. If she sees us all, somebody's going to fold. Remember Tieman in San Fran? He was even more adamantly against the project than I was."

"Try to relax," urged Jackson. "I understand why you're upset. But let me remind you that there is no real evidence to implicate anyone. And as a precautionary measure, Heberling has cleaned out his whole lab except for his bacterial studies. I'll tell him that the girl plans to visit the other officers. I'm sure that will help. In the meantime, we'll take extra precautions to keep her away from Tieman."

Krause hung up. He felt a little less anxious, but as he stood up and turned off the desk lamp, he decided he'd phone his attorney in the morning. It couldn't hurt to inquire about the procedure for turning state's evidence.

As her cab whizzed over the Triborough Bridge, Marissa was mesmerized by Manhattan's nighttime skyline. From that distance it was beautiful. But it soon dropped behind, then out of sight altogether as the car descended into the sunken portion of the Long Island Expressway. Marissa forced her eyes back to the list of names and addresses of the PAC officers, which she had taken from her purse. They were hard to make out as the taxi shot from one highway light to the next.

There was no logical way to choose who to visit after Krause. The closest would be easiest, but also probably the most obvious to her pursuers, and therefore the most dangerous. For safety's sake, she decided to visit the man farthest away, Doctor Sinclair Tieman in San Francisco.

Leaning forward, Marissa told the driver she wanted Kennedy rather than LaGuardia airport. When he asked what terminal, she chose at random: United. If they didn't have space on a night flight, she could always go to another terminal.

At that time in the evening there were few people at the terminal, and Marissa got rapid service. She was pleased to find a convenient flight to San Francisco with just one stop, in Chicago. She bought her ticket with cash, using yet another false name, bought some reading material from a newsstand and went to the gate. She decided to use the few moments before takeoff to call Ralph. As she anticipated, he was upset she hadn't called him back sooner, but was pleased at first to learn she was at the airport.

"I'll forgive you this one last time," he said, "but only because you are on your way home."

Marissa chose her words carefully: "I wish I could see you tonight, but . . ."

"Don't tell me you are not coming," said Ralph, feigning anger to conceal his disappointment. "I made arrangements for you to meet with Mr. McQuinllin tomorrow at noon. You said you wanted to see him as soon as possible."

"It will have to be postponed," said Marissa. "Something has come up. I must go to San Francisco for a day or two. I just can't explain right now."

"Marissa, what on earth are you up to?" said Ralph in a tone of desperation. "Just from the little you've told me, I'm absolutely certain you should come home, see the lawyer; then, if Mr. McQuinllin agrees, you can still go to California."

"Ralph, I know you're worried. The fact you care makes me feel so much better, but everything is under control. What I'm doing will just make my dealings with Mr. McQuinllin that much easier. Trust me."

"I can't," pleaded Ralph. "You're not being rational."

"They're boarding my plane," said Marissa. "I'll call as soon as I can."

Marissa replaced the receiver with a sigh. He might not be the world's most romantic man, but he certainly was sensitive and caring.

Al told Jake to shut up. He couldn't stand the man's incessant gab. If it wasn't about baseball, it was about the horses. It never stopped. It was worse than George's eternal silence.

Al was sitting with Jake in the taxi while George still waited in the Essex House lobby. Something told Al that things were screwed up. He'd followed the limo all the way to a restaurant in Soho, but then the girl he'd seen get in didn't get out. Coming back to the hotel, he'd had Jake check to see if Miss Kendrick was still registered. She was, but when Al went up and walked past the room, he'd seen it being cleaned. Worse, he'd been spotted by the house detectives, who claimed he was the broad's boyfriend and that he'd better leave her alone. You didn't have to be a brain surgeon to know something was wrong. His professional intuition told him that the girl had fled and that they were wasting their time staking out the Essex House.

"You sure you don't want to put a small bet on the fourth at Belmont today?" said Jake.

Al was about to bounce a couple of knuckles off the top of Jake's head when his beeper went off. Reaching under his jacket, he turned the thing off, cursing. He knew who it was.

"Wait here," he said gruffly. He got out of the car and ran across the street to the Plaza where he used one of the downstairs pay phones to call Heberling.

Heberling did not even try to hide his contempt. "For Chrissake, the woman's only a hundred pounds or so. It's not like I'm asking you to take out Rambo. Why the hell is PAC paying you fellows a thousand dollars a day?"

"The woman's been lucky," said Al. He'd be patient, but only to a point.

"I don't buy that," said Heberling. "Now tell me, do you have any idea where she is at this moment?"

"I'm not positive," admitted Al.

"Meaning you've lost her," snapped Heberling. "Well, I can tell you where she's been. She's seen Dr. Krause and scared him shitless. Now we're afraid she's planning to visit the other PAC officers. Dr. Tieman's the most vulnerable. I'll worry about the other physicians. I want you and your orangutans to get your asses to San Francisco. See if she's there, and whatever you do, don't let her get to Tieman."

16

May 24

IT WAS JUST BEGINNING to get light as Al followed Jake and George down the jetway to San Francisco's central terminal. They'd taken an American flight that first stopped for an hour and a half at Dallas, then was delayed in Las Vegas on what should have been a brief touchdown.

Jake was carrying the suitcase with the vaccination gun they'd used on Mehta. Al wondered if he looked as bad as his colleagues. They needed to shave and shower, and their previously sharply pressed suits were badly wrinkled.

The more Al thought about the current situation, the more frustrated he became. The girl could be in any one of at least four cities. And it wasn't even a simple hit. If they did find her, they first had to get her to tell them where she'd hidden the vaccination gun.

Leaving Jake and George to get the luggage, he rented a car, using one of the several fake IDs he always carried. He decided the only thing they could do was stake out Tieman's house. That way, even if they didn't find the girl, she wouldn't get to the doctor. After making sure he could get a car with a cellular phone, he spread out the map the girl at Budget had given him. Tieman lived in some out-of-the-way place called Sausalito. At least there wouldn't be much traffic; it wasn't even 7:00 A.M. yet.

The operator at the Fairmont placed Marissa's wake-up call at 7:30 as she'd requested. Marissa had been lucky the night before. A small convention group had canceled out at the last minute, and she'd had no trouble getting a room.

Lying in bed waiting for her breakfast she wondered what Dr. Tieman would be like. Probably not much different from Krause: a selfish, greedy man whose attempt to protect his own wallet had gotten out of control.

Getting up, she opened the drapes to a breathtaking scene that included the Bay Bridge, the hills of Marin County, with Alcatraz Island looking like a medieval fortress in the foreground. Marissa only wished that she was visiting under more pleasant circumstances.

By the time she'd showered and wrapped herself in the thick white terry cloth robe supplied by the hotel, her breakfast had arrived, an enormous selection of fresh fruit and coffee.

Peeling a peach, she noticed they had given her an old-fashioned paring knife—wood handled and very sharp. As she ate, she looked at Tieman's address and wondered if it wouldn't be better to visit him at his office rather than at home. She was sure someone had contacted him after her visit to Dr. Krause, so she couldn't count on really surprising the man. Under such conditions, it seemed safer to go to his office.

The Yellow Pages was in one of the desk drawers. Marissa opened it to Physicians and Surgeons, found Tieman's name and noted that his practice was limited to OB-GYN.

Just to be certain the man was in town, Marissa dialed his office. The service operator said that the office didn't open until eight-thirty. That was about ten minutes away.

Marissa finished dressing and dialed again. This time she got the receptionist, who told her the doctor wasn't expected until three. This was his day for surgery at San Francisco General.

Hanging up, Marissa stared out at the Bay Bridge while she considered this new information. In some ways confronting Tieman in the hospital might even be better than at his office. It would certainly be safer if the doctor had any idea of trying to stop her himself.

She looked at herself in the mirror. Except for her underwear, she had been wearing the same clothes for two days, and she realized she'd have to stop somewhere and get some fresh things.

She put up the Do Not Disturb sign as she left the room, less nervous here than in New York since she was certain she was several jumps ahead of her pursuers.

The site of San Francisco General was gorgeous, but once inside, the hospital was like any other large city hospital, with the same random mixture of old and modern. There was also that overwhelming sense of bustle and disorganization characteristic of such institutions. It was easy for Marissa to walk unnoticed into the doctor's locker room.

As she was selecting a scrub suit, an attendant came over and asked, "Can I help you?"

"I'm Dr. Blumenthal," said Marissa. "I'm here to observe Dr. Tieman operate."

"Let me give you a locker," said the attendant without hesitation, and gave her a key.

After Marissa changed, her locker key pinned to the front of her scrub dress, she walked to the surgical lounge. There were about twenty people there, drinking coffee, chatting and reading newspapers.

Passing through the lounge, Marissa went directly into the operating area. In the vestibule, she put on a hood and booties, then stopped in front of the big scheduling board. Tieman's name was listed for room eleven. The man was already on his second hysterectomy.

"Yes?" inquired the nurse behind the OR desk. Her voice had that no-nonsense tone of a woman in charge.

"I'm here to watch Dr. Tieman," said Marissa.

"Go on in. Room eleven," said the nurse, already devoting her attention to another matter.

"Thank you," said Marissa, starting down the wide central corridor. The operating rooms were on either side, sharing scrub and anesthesia space. Through the oval windows in the doors, Marissa caught glimpses of gowned figures bent over their patients.

Entering the scrub area between rooms eleven and twelve, Marissa put on a mask and pushed into Tieman's operating room.

There were five people besides the patient. The anesthesiologist was sitting at the patient's head, two surgeons were standing on either side of the table, a scrub nurse perched on a footstool and there was one circulating nurse. As Marissa entered, the circulating nurse was sitting in the corner, waiting for orders. She got up and asked Marissa what she needed.

"How much longer for the case?"

"Three-quarters of an hour," shrugged the nurse. "Dr. Tieman is fast."

"Which one is Dr. Tieman?" asked Marissa. The nurse gave her a strange look.

"The one on the right," she said. "Who are you?"

"A doctor friend from Atlanta," said Marissa. She didn't elaborate. Moving around to the head of the table and looking at Dr. Tieman, she understood why the nurse had been surprised by her question: the man was black.

How odd, thought Marissa. She would have suspected that all the PAC officers were old-guard, white and probably racially prejudiced.

For a while she stood above the ether screen and watched the course of the operation. The uterus was already out, and they were starting repair. Tieman was good. His hands moved with that special economy of motion that could not be taught. It was a talent, a gift from God, not something to be learned even with practice.

"Start the damn car," said Al hanging up the cellular phone. They were parked across from a sprawling redwood house that clung to the hillside above the town of Sausalito. Between the eucalyptus trees they could see blue patches of the Bay.

Jake turned the key in the ignition. "Where to?" He

knew Al was pissed, and when he was in that kind of mood, it was better to say as little as possible.

"Back to the city."

"What did Tieman's office say?" asked George from the backseat.

Jake wanted to tell George to shut up, but he was afraid to speak.

"That the doctor was in surgery at San Francisco General," said Al, almost white with anger. "His first operation was scheduled for seven-thirty, and he's not expected at the office until three."

"No wonder we missed him," said George disgustedly. "The guy must have left his house an hour before we got here. What a waste of time. We should have gone to a hotel like I said."

With blinding speed Al twisted around in the front seat and grabbed George's pink Dior tie. George's eyes bulged and his face turned red. "If I want your advice, I'll ask for it. Understand?"

Al released the tie and shoved George back down in his seat. Jake hunkered down like a turtle into his sports jacket. He hazarded a glance in Al's direction.

"And what are you gawking at?" demanded Al.

Jake didn't say a word, and after what had just happened, he hoped George had learned the wisdom of silence.

They were almost at the bridge before anyone spoke.

"I think we should get another car," Al said, his voice as calm as if the outburst had never happened. "Just in case we run into a problem and have to split up. Then we'll go to San Francisco General. The sooner we spot Tieman the better."

With plenty of time to spare and feeling confident that she'd have no problem recognizing Dr. Tieman now that she'd seen him, Marissa left the operating room as the assistant was closing. She changed back to her street clothes. She wanted to be able to leave right after she spoke to the man. Going into the surgical lounge, she found a seat by the window. A few people smiled at her but no one spoke.

A half hour went by before Dr. Tieman appeared, coming into the room with the same effortless grace that had characterized his surgical technique.

Marissa walked over to where he was pouring a cup of coffee. In his short-sleeved scrub top, Marissa could see his beautifully muscled arms. His color was a rich brown, like polished walnut.

"I'm Dr. Marissa Blumenthal," she said, watching the man for a reaction.

He had a broad, masculine face with a well-trimmed mustache and sad eyes, as if he'd seen more of life than he cared to know. He looked down at Marissa with a smile. It was obvious from his expression that he had no idea who she was.

"May I speak to you in private?" asked Marissa.

Tieman glanced at his assistant, who was just approaching. "I'll see you in the OR," Tieman said, leading Marissa away.

He took her to one of the dictation cubicles separated from the lounge by two swinging doors. There was one chair, and Dr. Tieman turned it around, gesturing for Marissa to sit. He leaned against a counter, holding his coffee in his right hand.

Acutely conscious of her short stature and its psychological handicap, Marissa pushed the chair back to him, insisting that he sit since he'd been standing in surgery since early that morning.

"Okay, okay," he said with a short laugh. "I'm sitting. Now what can I do for you?"

"I'm surprised you don't recognize my name," said Marissa, watching the man's eyes. They were still questioning, still friendly.

"I'm sorry," said Dr. Tieman. He laughed again, but with a tinge of embarrassment. He was studying Marissa's face. "I do meet a lot of people . . ."

"Hasn't Dr. Jack Krause called you about me?" asked Marissa.

"I'm not even sure I know a Dr. Krause," said Dr. Tieman, directing his attention to his coffee.

The first lie, thought Marissa. Taking a deep breath, she told the doctor exactly what she'd told Krause. From the moment she mentioned the L.A. Ebola outbreak, he never lifted his eyes. She could tell that he was nervous. The surface of the coffee shook slightly in the cup in his hand, and Marissa was suddenly glad she was not the man's next patient.

"I haven't the slightest idea why you are telling me this," said Dr. Tieman, starting to rise. "And unfortunately I have another case."

With uncharacteristic forwardness, Marissa gently touched his chest, forcing him back in his seat. "I'm not finished," she said, "and whether you realize it or not, you are intimately involved. I have evidence that Ebola is being deliberately spread by the Physicians' Action Congress. You are their treasurer, and I'm shocked that a man of your reputation could be connected to such a sordid affair."

"You're shocked," countered Dr. Tieman, finally rising to his feet and towering over her. "I'm amazed that you have the nerve to make such irresponsible allegations."

"Save your breath," said Marissa. "It's public knowledge that you are an officer of PAC as well as a limited partner in one of the only labs in the country equipped to handle viruses like Ebola."

"I hope you have plenty of insurance," warned Dr. Tieman, his voice rising. "You'll be hearing from my lawyer."

"Good," said Marissa, ignoring the threat. "Maybe he will persuade you that your best course is to cooperate with the authorities." She stepped back and looked directly up at his face. "Having met you, I cannot believe you approved the idea of spreading a deadly disease. It will be a double tragedy for you to lose everything you've worked for because of someone else's poor judgment. Think about it, Dr. Tieman. You don't have a lot of time."

Pushing through the swinging doors, Marissa left a stunned doctor desperately heading for the phone. She realized she had forgotten to tell Tieman that she was planning to visit the other PAC officers, but she decided it didn't matter. The man was terrified enough.

"There's the girl!" yelled Al, slapping Jake on the shoulder. They were parked across the street from the main entrance to the hospital. George waited behind them in the second car. When Al turned to look at him,

George gave a thumbs-up sign, meaning that he'd also seen Marissa.

"She won't get away today," said Al.

Jake started the car and, as Marissa got into a cab, he pulled out into the street, heading back into town. Al watched as Marissa's cab pulled out behind them, followed neatly by George. Now things were working as they should.

"She must have seen Tieman if she's leaving," said Jake.

"Who cares?" said Al. "We got her now." Then he added, "It would make things easier if she'd go back to her hotel."

Marissa's cab went by them with George in pursuit. Jake began to speed up. Ahead he saw George overtake Marissa. They would continue leapfrogging until Marissa reached her destination.

About fifteen minutes later, Marissa's taxi stopped behind a line of cars waiting to pull up to the Fairmont. "Looks like your prayers have been answered," said Jake, stopping across the street from the hotel.

"I'll handle the car," said Al. "You get your ass in there and find out what room she's in."

Jake got out as Al slid behind the wheel. Dodging the midmorning traffic, Jake reached the front of the hotel before Marissa had even gotten out of her cab. In the lobby, he picked up a newspaper and, folding it commuter style, positioned himself so that he could see everyone coming into the hotel.

Marissa walked directly to the front desk. He quickly moved behind her, expecting her to ask for her room key. But she didn't. Instead she asked to use her safe-deposit box.

While the receptionist opened a gate allowing Marissa into the office behind the front desk, Jake wandered toward the board announcing the various convention meetings. Presently Marissa reappeared, busily closing her shoulder purse. Then, to Jake's consternation, she came directly toward him.

In a frantic moment of confusion, Jake thought she'd recognized him, but she passed right by, heading down a hall lined with gift shops.

Jake took off after her, passing her in a corridor lined with old photos of the San Francisco earthquake. Guessing she was headed to the elevators, he made sure he beat her there, mingling with the crowd already waiting.

An elevator arrived, which Jake boarded before Marissa, making certain there was plenty of room. He stepped in front of the self-service buttons. Holding his newspaper as if he were reading, he watched as Marissa pressed eleven. As more passengers got on, Marissa was pushed farther back into the car.

As the elevator rose, stopping occasionally, Jake continued to keep his nose in the newspaper. When the car stopped at the eleventh floor, he strolled off, still absorbed in his paper, allowing Marissa and another guest to pass him. When she stopped in front of room 1127, Jake kept walking. He didn't turn and go back to the elevators until he'd heard her door close.

Back on the street, Jake crossed over to Al's car.

"Well?" said Al, momentarily worried something had gone wrong.

"Room 1127," said Jake with a self-satisfied smile.

"You'd better be right," said Al, getting out of the car. "Wait here. This shouldn't take long at all." He smiled so broadly that Jake noticed for the first time Al's gums had receded almost to the roots of his front teeth.

Al walked over to George's car and leaned on the window. "I want you to drive around and cover the back entrance. Just in case."

Feeling better than he had in several days, Al crossed the street to the posh, red-and-black lobby.

He went over to the front desk and eyed the mailbox for 1127. There was an extra set of keys, but there wasn't enough of a crowd for him to chance the receptionist's turning them over without asking questions. Instead, he headed for the elevators.

On the eleventh floor, he searched for the housekeeping cart. He found it outside of a suite, with its usual complement of clean sheets, towels and cleaning materials. Taking one of the hand towels, he carefully folded it on the diagonal, creating a stout rope. Gripping an end in each hand, he entered the open suite where the maid presumably was working.

The living room was empty. There was a vacuum cleaner in the middle of the bedroom and a pile of linens on the floor, but he still didn't see anyone. Advancing to the dressing room, he heard running water.

The maid was on her knees in front of the bathtub, scrubbing its interior. A can of Comet was on the floor by her knees.

Without a moment's hesitation, Al stepped behind the woman and, using the folded towel as a garrote, strangled her. She made some muffled noises but they were covered by the sound of the bathwater. Her face turned red, then purple. When Al let up the tension on the ends of the towel, she slumped to the floor like a limp rag doll.

Al found the passkeys in her pocket on a brass ring the size of a bracelet. Back in the hall, he hung a Do Not Disturb sign on the knob and closed the door to the suite. Then he pushed the housekeeping cart out of sight into the stairwell. Flexing his fingers like a pianist preparing for a recital, he started for room 1127.

17

May 24

MARISSA PEELED THE LAST of the breakfast fruit with the wooden-handled paring knife, leaving the knife and rinds on her night table. She was on the phone to Northwest Airlines trying to make a reservation to Minneapolis. She had decided PAC and company would figure she'd probably go to LA next, so Minneapolis seemed as good a bet as any.

The agent finally confirmed her on an afternoon flight. Flopping back on the bed, she began to debate how she should spend the next hour or so, but while she was thinking, exhaustion overtook her and she fell asleep.

She was awakened by a metallic click. It sounded like the door, but she knew she'd left up the Do Not Disturb sign. Then she saw the knob silently begin to turn.

She remembered being caught in the hotel room in Chicago by the man with the vaccination gun. Panic danced through her like an electrical current. Pulling herself together, she reached for the phone.

Before Marissa could lift the receiver, the door burst open, splintering part of the jamb as the screws holding the chain lock plate were yanked out of the molding. A man slammed the door shut then hurled himself onto Marissa. He grabbed her by the neck with both hands and shook her like a mad dog in a frenzy. Then he pulled her ashen face close to his. "Remember me?" he snarled furiously.

Marissa remembered him. It was the blond man with the Julius Caesar haircut.

"You have ten seconds to produce the vaccination gun," hissed Al, loosening the death grip he had on Marissa's throat. "If you don't, I'll snap your neck." To emphasize his point, he gave her head a violent jolt, sending a flash of pain down her spine.

Barely able to breathe, Marissa fruitlessly clawed at the man's powerful wrists. He shook her again, hitting her head against the wall. By reflex Marissa's hands extended behind her to cushion her body.

The lamp fell off the bedside table and crashed to the floor. The room swam as her brain cried for oxygen.

"This is your last chance," shouted Al. "What did you do with that vaccinator?"

Marissa's hand touched the paring knife. Her fingers wrapped around the tiny haft. Holding it in her fist, she hammered it up into the man's abdomen as hard as she could. She had no idea if she'd penetrated anything, but Al stopped speaking in midsentence, let go of Marissa and rocked back on his haunches. His face registered surprise and disbelief. She switched the tiny knife to her right hand, keeping it pointed at Al, who seemed confused when he saw the blood staining his shirt.

She hoped to back up to the door and run, but before she reached it he leaped at her like an enraged animal, sending her racing to the bathroom. It seemed as if only hours before she'd been in the same predicament in Chicago.

Al got his hand around the door before it shut. Marissa hacked blindly, feeling the tip of her knife strike bone. Al screamed and yanked his hand away, leaving a smear of blood on the panel. The door slammed shut, and Marissa hastily locked it.

She was about to dial the bathroom phone when there was a loud crash and the entire bathroom door crashed inward. Al forced Marissa to drop the phone, but she hung on to the knife, still stabbing at him wildly. She hit his abdomen several times, but if it had any effect, it wasn't apparent.

Ignoring the knife, Al grabbed Marissa by her hair and flung her against the sink. She tried to stab him again, but he grabbed her wrist and bashed it against the wall until her grip loosened and the weapon clattered to the floor.

He bent down to pick it up, and as he straightened, Marissa grabbed the phone that was swinging on its cord and hit him as hard as she could with the receiver. For a brief instant, she wasn't sure who was hurt more. The blow had sent a bolt of pain right up to her shoulder.

For a moment Al stood as if he were frozen. Then his blue eyes rolled upward, and he seemed to fall in slow motion into the bathtub, striking his head on the faucets.

As Marissa watched, half expecting Al to get up and come at her again, a beeping noise snapped her into action. She reached over and hung up the receiver. Glancing back into the tub, she was torn between fear and her medical training. The man had a sizable gash over the bridge of his nose, and the front of his shirt was covered with blood stains. But terror won out, and Marissa grabbed her purse and ran from the room. Remembering the man had not been alone in New York, she knew she had to get away from the hotel as soon as possible.

Descending to the ground floor, Marissa avoided the front entrance. Instead, she went down a flight of stairs and followed arrows to a rear exit. Standing just inside the door, she waited until a cable car came into view. Timing her exit to give herself the least exposure, she ran out of the hotel and jumped onto the trolley.

Marissa forced her way through the crowd to the rear. She looked back at the hotel as the car began to move. No one came out.

George blinked in disbelief. It was the girl. Quickly he dialed Jake's car.

"She just came out of the hotel," said George, "and jumped on a cable car."

"Is Al with her?" asked Jake.

"No," said George. "She's by herself. It looked like she was limping a little."

"Something is weird."

"You follow her," said George. "The cable car is just starting. I'll go into the hotel and check on Al."

"Right on," said Jake. He was more than happy to let George deal with Al. When Al found out the girl had flown, he was going to be madder than shit.

Marissa looked back at the hotel for any sign of being followed. No one came out of the door, but as the cable car began to move, she saw a man get out of an auto and run for the hotel's rear entrance. The timing was suggestive, but as the man didn't even look in her direction, she dismissed it as a coincidence. She continued to watch until the cable car turned a corner and she could no longer see the Fairmont. She'd made it.

She relaxed until a loud clang almost made her jump out of her skin. She started for the door before she realized it was just the overhead bell that the conductor rang as he collected fares.

A man got off, and Marissa quickly took his seat. She was shaking and suddenly scared she might have blood stains on her clothes. The last thing she wanted was to call attention to herself.

As her fear abated, she became more aware of the pain where her hip had hit the sink, and her neck was exquisitely tender and probably turning black and blue.

"Fare please," said the conductor.

Without lifting her eyes, Marissa fished around in her purse for some change. That was when she saw the blood caked on the back of her right hand. Quickly, she changed the way she was holding her purse and used her left hand to give the money to the man.

When he moved off, Marissa tried to figure out how they had found her. She'd been so careful . . . Suddenly it dawned on her. They must have been guarding Tieman. It was the only possible explanation.

Her confidence shattered, Marissa began to have second thoughts about having fled the hotel. Perhaps she would have been safer if she had stayed and faced the police. Yet fleeing had become an instinct of late. She felt like a fugitive, and it made her act like one. And to think she'd thought she would be able to outwit her pursuers. Ralph had been right. She never should have gone to New York, let alone San Francisco. He had said she was in serious trouble before she'd visited both cities. Well, it was a lot worse now—for all she knew she'd killed two men. It was all too much. She wasn't going to Minneapolis. She would go home and turn everything that she knew, such as it was, and everything that she suspected, over to the attorney.

The cable car slowed again. Marissa looked around. She was someplace in Chinatown. The car stopped, and just as it was starting again, Marissa stood up and swung off. As she ran to the sidewalk, she saw the conductor shaking his head in disgust. But no one got off after her.

Marissa took a deep breath and rubbed her neck. Glancing around, she was pleased to see that both sides of the street were crowded. There were pushcart vendors, trucks making deliveries and a variety of stores with much of their merchandise displayed on the sidewalk. All the signs were written in Chinese. She felt as if the short cable-car ride had mysteriously transported her to the Orient. Even the smells were different: a mixture of fish and spices.

She passed a Chinese restaurant and, after hesitating a second, went inside. A woman dressed in a Mandarin-collared, red silk dress slit to the knee came out and said the restaurant was not yet open for lunch. "Half hour," she added.

"Would you mind if I used your restroom and your phone?" asked Marissa.

The woman studied Marissa for a moment, decided she meant no harm and led her to the rear of the restaurant. She opened a door and stepped aside.

Marissa was in a small room with a sink on one side and a pay phone on the other. There were two doors in the back with Ladies stenciled on one, and Gents on the other. The walls were covered with years of accumulated graffiti.

Marissa used the phone first. She called the Fairmont and reported to the operator that there was a man in room 1127 who needed an ambulance. The operator told her to hold on, but Marissa hung up. Then she paused, debating whether she should call the police and explain everything to them. No, she thought, it was too complicated. Besides, she'd already fled the scene. It would be better to go back to Atlanta and see the attorney.

Washing her hands, Marissa glanced at herself in the mirror. She was a mess. Taking out her comb, she untangled her hair and braided a few strands to keep it off her face. She'd lost her barrette when the blond man had yanked her by the hair. When she was finished, she straightened her blazer and the collar of her blouse. That was about all she could do.

Jake dialed George's car for the hundredth time. Mostly the phone went unanswered, but occasionally he'd get a recording telling him that the party he was calling was not presently available.

He could not figure out what was going on. Al and George should have been back in the car long ago. Jake had followed the girl, practically running her over when she'd leaped unexpectedly from the cable car, and had watched her go into a restaurant called Peking Cuisine. At least he hadn't lost her.

He scrunched down in the driver's seat. The girl had just come out of the restaurant and was flagging a cab.

An hour later, Jake watched helplessly as Marissa handed over her ticket and boarded a Delta nonstop to Atlanta. He had thought about buying a ticket himself, but scrapped the idea without Al's okay. She'd spent the last half hour closeted in the ladies' room, giving Jake ample time to try the mobile phone at least ten more times, hoping for some instructions. But still no one answered.

As soon as the plane taxied down the runway, Jake hurried back to his car. There was a parking ticket under the windshield wiper, but Jake didn't give a shit. He was just glad the car hadn't been towed away. Climbing in, he thought he'd drive back to the Fairmont and see if he could find the others. Maybe the whole thing had been called off, and he'd find both of them in the bar, laughing their asses off while he ran all over the city.

Back on the freeway, he decided to try calling the other mobile phone one last time. To his astonishment, George answered.

"Where the hell have you been?" Jake demanded. "I've been calling you all goddamn morning."

"There's been a problem," said George, subdued.

"Well, I hope to hell there's been something," said Jake. "The girl is on a plane to Atlanta. I was going crazy. I didn't know what the hell to do."

"Al was knifed, I guess by the girl. He's at San Francisco General, having surgery. I can't get near him."

"Christ!" said Jake incredulously, unable to imagine that the pint-sized broad could have knifed Al and gotten away.

"He's not supposed to be hurt that bad," continued George. "What's worse is that apparently Al wasted a maid. He had the woman's passkeys in his pocket. He's being charged with murder."

"Shit," said Jake. Things were going from bad to worse.

"Where are you now?" asked George.

"Just on the freeway, leaving the airport," said Jake.

"Go back," said George. "Book us on the next flight to Atlanta. I think we owe Al a bit of revenge."

18

May 24

"READING MATERIAL?" asked the smiling cabin attendant.

Marissa nodded. She needed something to keep her from thinking about the horrible scene in the hotel.

"Magazine or newspaper?" asked the attendant.

"Newspaper, I guess," said Marissa.

"*San Francisco Examiner* or *New York Times*?"

Marissa was in no mood to make decisions. "*New York Times*," she said finally.

The big jet leveled off, and the seat-belt sign went out. Marissa glanced through the window at rugged mountains stretching off into dry desert. It was a relief to have gotten onto the plane finally. At the airport, she had been so scared of either being attacked by one of the blond man's friends or being arrested, she had simply hidden in a toilet in the ladies' room.

Unfolding the newspaper, Marissa glanced at the table of contents. Continuing coverage of the Ebola outbreaks in Philadelphia and New York was listed on page 4. Marissa turned to it.

The article reported that the Philadelphia death toll

was up to fifty-eight and New York was at forty-nine, but that many more cases had been reported there. Marissa was not surprised since the index case was an ear, nose and throat specialist. She also noted that the Rosenberg Clinic had already filed for bankruptcy.

On the same page as the Ebola article was a photograph of Dr. Ahmed Fakkry, head of epidemiology for the World Health Organization. The article next to the picture said that he was visiting the CDC to investigate the Ebola outbreaks because World Health was fearful that the virus would soon cross the Atlantic.

Maybe Dr. Fakkry could help her, thought Marissa. Perhaps the lawyer Ralph was lining up for her would be able to arrange for her to speak with him.

Ralph was catching up on his journals when the doorbell rang at 9:30 P.M. Glancing at his watch, he wondered who could possibly be visiting at that hour. He looked out of the glass panel on the side of the door and was shocked to find himself staring directly into Marissa's face.

"Marissa!" he said in disbelief, pulling open the door. Behind her, he could see a yellow cab descending his long, curved driveway.

Marissa saw him hold out his arms and ran into them, bursting into tears.

"I thought you were in California," said Ralph. "Why didn't you call and let me know you were coming? I would have met you at the airport."

Marissa just held onto him, crying. It was so wonderful to feel safe.

"What happened to you?" he asked, but was only greeted by louder sobs.

"At least let's sit down," he said, helping her to the couch. For a few minutes, he just let her cry, patting her gently on the back. "It's okay," he said for lack of anything else. He eyed the phone, willing it to ring. He had to make a call, and at this rate she was never going to let him get up. "Perhaps you'd like something to drink?" he asked. "How about some of that special cognac? Maybe it will make you feel better."

Marissa shook her head.

"Wine? I have a nice bottle of Chardonnay open in the refrigerator." Ralph was running out of ideas.

Marissa just held him tighter, but her sobs were lessening, her breathing becoming more regular.

Five minutes went by. Ralph sighed. "Where is your luggage?"

Marissa didn't answer, but did fish a tissue out of her pocket and wipe her face.

"I've got some cold chicken in the kitchen."

At last Marissa sat up. "Maybe in a little bit. Just stay with me a little longer. I've been so scared."

"Then why didn't you call me from the airport? And what happened to your car? Didn't you leave it there?"

"It's a long story," said Marissa. "But I was afraid that someone might be watching it. I didn't want anybody to know I was back in Atlanta."

Ralph raised his eyebrows. "Does that mean you'd like to spend the night?"

"If you don't mind," said Marissa. "Nothing like inviting myself, but you've been such a good friend."

"Would you like me to drive you over to your house to get some things?" asked Ralph.

"Thanks, but I don't want to show up there for the same reason I was afraid to go to my car. If I were to drive anyplace tonight, I'd run over to the CDC and get a package that I hope Tad put away for me. But to tell you the truth, I think it all can wait until morning. Even that criminal lawyer, who I hope will be able to keep me out of jail."

"Good grief," said Ralph. "I hope you're not serious. Don't you think it's time you told me what's going on?"

Marissa picked up Ralph's hand. "I will. I promise. Let me just calm down a little more. Maybe I should eat something."

"I'll fix you some chicken," he said.

"That's all right. I know where the kitchen is. Maybe I'll just scramble some eggs."

"I'll join you in a minute. I have to make a call."

Marissa dragged herself through the house. In the kitchen, she glanced around at all the appliances and space and thought it was a waste just to be making eggs. But that was what sounded best. She got them out of the refrigerator, along with some bread for toast. Then she realized she hadn't asked Ralph if he wanted some too. She was about to call out but decided he wouldn't hear her.

Putting the eggs down, she went over to the intercom and began pushing the buttons on the console to see if she could figure out how it worked. "Hello, hello," she said as she held down different combinations. Stumbling onto the correct sequence, she suddenly heard Ralph's voice.

"She's not in San Francisco," he was saying. "She's here at my house."

Pause.

"Jackson, I don't know what happened. She's hysterical. All she said was that she has a package waiting for her at the CDC. Listen, I can't talk now. I've got to get back to her."

Pause.

"I'll keep her here, don't worry. But get over here as soon as you can."

Pause.

"No, no one knows she's here. I'm sure of that. 'Bye."

Marissa clutched the counter top, afraid she was going to faint. All this time Ralph—the one person she'd trusted—had been one of "them." And Jackson! It had to be the same Jackson she'd met at Ralph's dinner party. The head of PAC, and he was on his way over. Oh, God!

Knowing Ralph was on his way to the kitchen, Marissa forced herself to go on with her cooking. But when she tried to break an egg on the side of the skillet, she smashed it shell and all into the pan. She had the other egg in her hand when Ralph appeared with some drinks. She broke the second egg a bit more deftly, mixing it all together, including the first egg's shell.

"Smells good," he said brightly. He put down her glass and touched her lightly on the back. Marissa jumped.

"Wow, you really are uptight. How are we going to get you to relax?"

Marissa didn't say anything. Although she was no longer the slightest bit hungry, she went through the motions of cooking the eggs, buttering the toast and putting out jam. Looking at Ralph's expensive silk shirt, the heavy gold cuff links, the tasseled Gucci loafers, everything about him suddenly seemed a ridiculous affectation, as did the whole elaborately furnished house. It all represented the conspicuous consumption of a wealthy doctor, now fearful of the new medical competition, of changing times, of medicine no longer being a seller's market.

Obviously, Ralph was a member of PAC. Of course he was a supporter of Markham. And it was Ralph, not Tad, who had always known where she was. Serving the eggs, Marissa thought that even if she could escape there was no one to go to. She certainly couldn't use a lawyer Ralph recommended. In fact, now that she knew Ralph was implicated, she remembered why the name of the law firm he'd suggested had sounded familiar: Cooper, Hodges, McQuinllin and Hanks had been listed as the service agent of PAC.

Marissa felt trapped. The men pursuing her had powerful connections. She had no idea how deeply they had penetrated the CDC. Certainly the conspiracy involved the congressman who exerted control over the CDC budget.

Marissa's mind reeled. She was terrified no one would believe her, and she was acutely aware that the only piece of hard evidence she had—the vaccination gun—was resting somewhere in the maximum containment lab, to which she knew from painful experience her pursuers had access. The only thing that was crystal clear was that she had to get away from Ralph before Jackson and maybe more thugs arrived.

Picking up her fork, she had a sudden vision of the blond man hurling himself through the bathroom door in

San Francisco. She dropped the fork, again afraid she was about to faint.

Ralph grabbed her elbow and helped her to the kitchen table. He put the food on a plate and placed it in front of her and urged her to eat.

"You were doing so well a minute ago," he said. "You'll feel better if you get something in your stomach." He picked up the fork she'd dropped and tossed it into the sink, then got another from the silver drawer.

Marissa dropped her head into her hands. She had to get herself under control. Valuable time was ticking away.

"Not hungry after all?" asked Ralph.

"Not very," admitted Marissa. The very smell of the eggs was enough to make her sick. She shuddered.

"Maybe you should take a tranquilizer. I've got some upstairs. What do you think?"

"Okay," said Marissa.

"Be right back," said Ralph, squeezing her shoulder.

This was the chance she had prayed for. As soon as he was out of the room, Marissa was on her feet, snatching the phone off its hook. But there was no dial tone. Ralph must have disconnected it somehow! So much for the police. Replacing the phone, she rushed around the kitchen searching for Ralph's car keys. Nothing. Next she tried the adjoining family room. There was a tiny marble urn on the room divider with a few keys, but none for a car. Going back through the kitchen, Marissa went to the small foyer by the back door. There was a cork bulletin board, an antique school desk and an old bureau. There was also a door that led to the bathroom.

Trying the desk first, she lifted its cover and rummaged through its contents. There were some odd-shaped house keys, but that was all. Turning to the small bureau, she began opening drawers, finding a jumble of gloves, scarves and rain gear.

"What do you need?" asked Ralph, suddenly appearing behind her. Guiltily she straightened up, searching for an alibi. Ralph waited, looking at her expectantly. His right hand was closed. His left hand held a glass of water.

"I thought maybe I could find a sweater," said Marissa.

Ralph eyed her curiously. If anything, the house was too warm. After all, it was almost June.

"I'll turn the heat on in the kitchen," he said, guiding her back to her chair. He extended his right hand. "Here, take this." He dropped a capsule into Marissa's palm. It was red and ivory in color.

"Dalmane?" questioned Marissa. "I thought you were getting me a tranquilizer."

"It will relax you *and* give you a good night's sleep," explained Ralph.

Shaking her head and handing the capsule back to Ralph, Marissa said, "I'd prefer a tranquilizer."

"What about Valium?"

"Fine," said Marissa.

As soon as she heard him climbing the back stairs, Marissa ran to the front foyer. There were no keys on the elaborate marble half-table or in the one central drawer. Opening the closet, Marissa rapidly patted jacket pockets. Nothing.

She was back in the kitchen just in time to hear Ralph start down the back stairs.

"There you go," he said, dropping a blue tablet into Marissa's hand.

"What dose is this?"

"Ten milligrams."

"Don't you think that's a little much?"

"You're so upset. It won't affect you as it would normally," said Ralph, handing her a glass of water. She took it from him, then pretended to take the Valium, but dropped it into the pocket of her jacket instead.

"Now let's try the food again," said Ralph.

Marissa forced herself to eat a little as she tried to figure out a way to escape before Jackson arrived. The food tasted awful, and she put down her fork after a few bites.

"Still not hungry?" said Ralph.

Marissa shook her head.

"Well, let's go into the living room."

She was glad to leave the cooking smells, but the moment they were seated, Ralph urged her to have a fresh drink.

"I don't think I should after the Valium."

"A little won't hurt."

"Are you sure you're not trying to get me drunk?" said Marissa. She forced a laugh. "Maybe you'd better let me fix the drinks."

"Fine by me," said Ralph, lifting his feet to the coffee table. "Make mine scotch."

Marissa went directly to the bar and poured Ralph a good four fingers of scotch. Then, checking to see that he was absorbed, she took out the Valium tablet, broke it in half and dropped the pieces into the alcohol. Unfortunately, they did not dissolve. Fishing the pieces out, she pulverized them with the scotch bottle and swept the powder into the drink.

"You need any help?" called Ralph.

"No," she said, pouring a little brandy into her own glass. "Here you go."

Ralph took his drink and settled back on the couch.

Sitting down beside him, Marissa racked her brains to figure out where he might have put his car keys. She wondered what he would say if she suddenly demanded them, but decided it was too great a risk. If he realized she knew about him, he might forcibly restrain her. This way, she still had a chance, if she could just find the keys.

A horrible thought occurred to her: he probably had just put them in his pants pocket. As distasteful as it was, Marissa forced herself to snuggle against him. Provocatively, she placed her hand on his hip. Sure enough, she could feel the keys through the light gabardine. Now, how on earth was she going to get them?

Gritting her teeth, she tilted her face to his, encouraging him to kiss her. As his arms circled her waist, she let her fingers slide into his pocket. Scarcely breathing she felt the edge of the ring and pulled. The keys jangled a little and she began frantically kissing him. Sensing his response she decided she had to take the chance. Please God, please God, she prayed and pulled out the keys and hid them in her own pocket.

Ralph had obviously forgotten Jackson was coming, or he'd decided sex was the best way to keep Marissa quiet. In any case, it was time to stop him.

"Darling," she said. "I hate to do this to you, but that pill is getting to me. I think I'm going to have to go to sleep."

"Just rest here. I'll hold you."

"I'd love to, but then you'd have to carry me upstairs." She pulled herself out of his embrace, and he solicitously helped her up the stairs to the guest bedroom.

"Don't you want me to stay with you?" he asked.

"I'm sorry, Ralph. I'm about to pass out. Just let me sleep." She forced a smile. "We can always continue when the Valium wears off." As if to end any further conversation, she lay on the bed fully clothed.

"Don't you want to borrow pajamas?" he asked hopefully.

"No, no. I can't keep my eyes open."

"Well, call if you need anything. I'll just be downstairs."

The moment he closed the door, she tiptoed over and listened to him go down the front stairs. Then she went to the window and opened it. The balcony outside was just as she remembered. As quietly as possible, she slipped out into the warm spring night. Above was an inverted bowl of stars. The trees were just dark silhouettes. There was no wind. In the distance, a dog barked. Then Marissa heard a car.

Quickly she surveyed her position. She was about fifteen feet above the asphalt drive. There was no possibility of jumping. The balcony was surrounded by a low balustrade, separating it from the sloped roof of the porch. To the left the porch roof abutted the tower and to the right it swept around the corner of the building.

Climbing over the balustrade, Marissa inched her way to the corner. The porch roof ended about twenty feet away. The fire escape descended from the third floor, but it was out of reach. Turning, she started back for the balcony. She was halfway there when the car she'd heard earlier turned into Ralph's drive.

Marissa lay still on the sloped roof. She knew that she was in full view of anybody coming up the driveway if they happened to look up. The car's lights played against the trees, then swept across the front of the house, bathing her in light before it pulled up to the front steps. She heard the doors open and several voices. They were not excited; apparently no one had seen her sprawled on the roof. Ralph answered the door. There was more conversation, and then the voices disappeared inside.

Marissa scampered along the roof and climbed back over the balustrade to the balcony. She ducked into the guest room and eased open the door to the hallway. Stepping into the hall, she could hear Ralph's voice though she could not make out what he was saying. As quietly as possible, she started toward the back stairs.

The light from the vestibule did not penetrate beyond the second turn in the hallway, and Marissa had to make her way by running her hands along the walls. She passed a number of dark bedrooms before she rounded a final corner and saw the kitchen light shining below.

At the head of the stairs, she hesitated. The sounds in the old house were confusing her. She still heard voices, but she also heard footsteps. The problem was, she couldn't tell where they were coming from. At that moment she caught sight of a hand on the newel post below.

Changing direction, Marissa went up the stairs and was halfway to the third floor in seconds. One of the treads squeaked under her foot, and she hesitated, heart pounding, listening to the relentless approach of the figure below. When he reached the second floor and turned down the hall toward the front of the house, she let out her breath.

Marissa continued up the stairs, wincing at every sound. The door to the servants' apartment at the top was closed but not locked.

As quietly as possible, she made her way across the dark living room and into the bedroom that she guessed looked out on the fire escape.

After struggling to raise the window, she climbed out onto the flimsy metal grate. Never fond of heights, it took all her courage to stand upright. Hesitantly, she started down, one step at a time, leading with her right foot. By the time she reached the second story, she heard excited voices inside the house and the sound of doors opening and slamming shut. Lights began going on in the darkened rooms. They had already realized that she had fled.

Forcing herself to hurry, Marissa rounded the second-story platform and was stopped by what seemed to be a large jumble of metal. Feeling with her hands, she realized that the last flight of stairs had been drawn up to protect the house from burglars. Desperately, she tried to figure out how to lower them. There didn't seem to be any release mechanism. Then she noticed a large counterweight behind her.

Gingerly, she put her foot on the first step. There was a loud squeak of metal. Knowing she had no choice, Marissa shifted her full weight to the step. With a nerve-shattering crash, the stairs shot to the ground and she ran down them.

As soon as her feet touched the grass, she ran for the garage, arms swinging wildly. There was no way the men inside the house could not have heard the fire escape's descent. In seconds they would be looking for her.

She ran to a side door to the garage, praying to heaven that it was not locked. It wasn't. As she raced inside, she heard the back door of the house open. Desperately, she stepped into the dark interior, pulling the door shut behind her. Turning, she moved forward, colliding almost immediately with Ralph's 300SDL sedan. Feeling for the car door, she opened it and slipped behind the wheel. She fumbled with the key until it slid into the ignition, and turned it. Several indicator lights flashed on, but the car didn't start. Then she remembered Ralph explaining how you had to wait for the orange light to go out because the engine was a diesel. She switched the ignition back off, then turned the key part way. The orange light went on, and Marissa waited. She heard someone raise the garage door; frantically, she hit the button locking all four doors of the car.

"Come on!" she urged through clenched teeth. The orange light went out. She turned the key, and the car roared to life as she stomped on the gas. There was a series of loud thumps as someone pounded her window. She shifted to reverse and floored the accelerator. There was a second's delay before the big car leaped backward with such force that she was flung against the wheel. She braced herself as the car shot out the door, sending two men diving sideways for safety.

The car careened wildly down the drive. Marissa jammed on the brakes as the car screeched around the front of the house, but it was too late. She rammed Jackson's car with the back of hers. Shifting to forward,

Marissa thought she was free, until one of the men, taking advantage of her momentary halt, flung himself across the hood. Marissa accelerated. The tires spun, but the car did not move. She was caught on the car behind. Putting the Mercedes into reverse, then into drive, she rocked the car as if she were stuck in snow. There was a scraping sound of metal; then she shot forward, dislodging her attacker as she careened down the drive.

"Forget it," said Jake, crawling out from under Jackson's car, wiping grease from his hands. "She busted your radiator," he told the doctor. "There's no coolant, so even if it started, you couldn't drive it."

"Damn," said Jackson, getting out. "That woman lives a charmed life." He looked furiously at Heberling. "This probably wouldn't have happened if I'd come here directly instead of waiting for your goons to get in from the airport."

"Yeah?" said Heberling. "And what would you have done? Reasoned with her? You needed Jake and George."

"You can use my 450 SL," offered Ralph. "But it's only a two-seater."

"She got too big a head start," said George. "We'd never catch her."

"I don't know how she escaped," said Ralph apologetically. "I'd just left her to sleep. She's had ten milligrams of Valium, for Chrissake." He noticed he felt a little dizzy himself.

"Any idea where she might go?" asked Jackson.

"I don't think she'll go to the police," said Ralph. "She's terrified of everyone, especially now. She might try the CDC. She said something about a package being there."

Jackson looked at Heberling. They had the same thought: the vaccination gun.

"We may as well send Jake and George," said Heberling. "We're pretty sure she won't go home, and after what she did to Al, the boys are most eager for revenge."

Fifteen minutes from the house, Marissa began to calm down enough to worry about where she was. She had made so many random turns in case she was being pursued, she had lost all sense of direction. For all she knew, she could have driven in a full circle.

Ahead, she saw street lights and a gas station. Marissa pulled over, lowering her window. A young man came out wearing an Atlanta Braves baseball hat.

"Could you tell me where I am?" asked Marissa.

"This here's a Shell station," said the young man, eyeing the damage to Ralph's car. "Did you know that both your taillights is busted?"

"I'm not surprised," said Marissa. "How about Emory University. Could you tell me how to get there?"

"Lady, you look like you've been in a demolition derby," he said, shaking his head in dismay.

Marissa repeated her question, and finally the man gave her some vague directions.

Ten minutes later Marissa cruised past the CDC. The building seemed quiet and deserted, but she still wasn't sure what she should do or who she could trust. She would have preferred going to a good lawyer, but she had no idea how to choose one. Certainly McQuinllin was out of the question.

The only person she could envision approaching was Dr. Fakkry, from the World Health Organization. He certainly was above the conspiracy, and, conveniently, he was staying at the Peachtree Plaza. The problem was, would he believe her or would he just call Dubchek or someone else at the CDC, putting her back into the hands of her pursuers?

Fear forced her to do what she felt was her only logical choice. She had to get the vaccination gun. It was her only piece of hard evidence. Without it she doubted anyone would take her seriously. She still had Tad's access card, and if he was not involved with PAC, the card might still be usable. Of course there was always the chance that security wouldn't allow her into the building.

Boldly, Marissa turned into the driveway and pulled up just past the entrance to the CDC. She wanted the car handy in case anyone tried to stop her.

Looking in the front door, she saw the guard sitting at the desk, bent over a paperback novel. When he heard her come in, he looked up, his face expressionless.

Rolling her lower lip into her mouth and biting on it, Marissa walked deliberately, trying to hide her fear. She picked up the pen and scrawled her name in the sign-in book. Then she looked up, expecting some comment, but the man just stared impassively.

"What are you reading?" asked Marissa, nerves making her chatter.

"Camus."

Well, she wasn't about to ask if it was *The Plague*. She started for the main elevators, conscious of the man's eyes on her back. She pushed the button to her floor, turned and looked at him. He was still watching her.

The moment the doors shut, he snatched up the phone and dialed. As soon as someone answered, he said, "Dr. Blumenthal just signed in. She went up in the elevator."

"Wonderful, Jerome," said Dubchek. His voice was hoarse, as if he were tired or sick. "We'll be right there. Don't let anyone else in."

"Whatever you say, Dr. Dubchek."

Marissa got off the elevator and stood for a few minutes, watching the floor indicators. Both elevators stayed where they were. The building was silent. Convinced that she wasn't being followed, she went to the stairs and ran down a flight, then out into the catwalk. Inside the virology building, she hurried down the long cluttered hall, rounded the corner and confronted the steel security door. Holding her breath, she inserted Tad's access card and tapped out his number.

There was a pause. For a moment she was afraid an alarm might sound. But all she heard was the sound of the latch releasing. The heavy door opened, and she was inside.

After flipping the circuit breakers, she twisted the wheel on the airtight door, climbed into the first room and, instead of donning a scrub suit, went directly into the next chamber. As she struggled into a plastic suit, she wondered where Tad might have hidden the contaminated vaccination gun.

Dubchek drove recklessly, braking for curves only when absolutely necessary, and running red lights. Two men had joined him; John, in the front seat, braced himself against the door; Mark, in the back, had more trouble avoiding being thrown from side to side. The expressions on all three faces were grim. They were afraid they would be too late.

"There it is," said George, pointing at the sign that said Centers for Disease Control.

"And there's Ralph's car!" he added, pointing at the Mercedes in the semicircular driveway. "Looks like luck is finally on our side." Making up his mind, he pulled into the Sheraton Motor Inn lot across the street.

George drew his S & W .356 Magnum, checking to see that all the chambers were filled. He opened the door and stepped out, holding the gun down along his hip. Light gleamed off the stainless-steel barrel.

"You sure you want to use that cannon?" asked Jake. "It makes so goddamn much noise."

"I wish I had had this thing when she was driving around with you on the hood," George snapped. "Come on!"

Jake shrugged and got out of the car. Patting the small of his back, he felt the butt of his own Beretta automatic. It was a much neater weapon.

Air line in hand, Marissa hastily climbed through the final door to the maximum containment lab. She plugged into the central manifold and looked around. The mess she'd helped create on that other fateful night had all been cleared away, but the memory of that episode flooded back with horrifying clarity. Marissa was shaking. All she wanted was to find her parcel and get the hell out. But that was easier said than done. As in any lab, there was a profusion of places where a package that size could be hidden.

Marissa started on the right, working her way back, opening cabinet doors and pulling out drawers. She got about halfway down the room, when she straightened up. There had to be a better way. At the central island, she went to the containment hood that Tad considered his own. In the cupboards below, she found bottles of reagents, paper towels, plastic garbage bags, boxes of new glassware and an abundance of other supplies. But there was no package resembling hers. She was about to move on when she looked through the glass of the containment hood itself. Behind Tad's equipment, she could just barely make out the dark green of a plastic garbage bag.

Turning on the fan over the hood, Marissa pulled up the glass front. Then, careful not to touch Tad's setup, she lifted out the bag. Inside was the Federal Express package. To be sure, she checked the label. It was addressed to Tad in her handwriting.

Marissa put the package in a new garbage bag, sealing it carefully. Then she put the used bag back inside the containment hood and pulled the glass front into place. At the central manifold, she hurriedly detached her air hose, then headed for the door. It was time to find Dr. Fakkry or someone else in authority she could trust.

Standing under the shower of phenolic disinfectant, Marissa tried to be patient. There was an automated timing device, so she had to wait for the process to finish before she could open the door. Once in the next room, she struggled out of her plastic suit, pulling frantically each time the zipper stuck. When she finally got it off, her street clothes were drenched with sweat.

Dubchek came to a screeching halt directly in front of the CDC entrance. The three men piled out of the car. Jerome was already holding open one of the glass doors.

Dubchek didn't wait to ask questions, certain that the guard would tell them if Marissa had left. He ran into the waiting elevator with the other two men on his heels, and pressed the button for the third floor.

Marissa had just started across the catwalk when the door to the main building opened and three men burst out. Spinning around, she ran back into virology.

"Stop, Marissa," someone yelled. It sounded like Dubchek. Oh, God, was he chasing her too?

She latched the door behind her and looked about for a place to hide. To her right was an elevator, to her left, a stairwell. There was no time to debate.

By the time Dubchek forced open the door, all he could see was the elevator light pointing down. Marissa was already on the lobby level as the three men began pounding down the stairs.

Knowing Dubchek was close behind, Marissa knew she had no time to slow down to avoid alerting the security guard when she'd reached the main building. His head popped up from his book, just in time to catch her streaking past. He stood up but that was all, and she was already gone when he decided that Dr. Dubchek might have wanted her stopped by force.

Outside, she fumbled for the keys to Ralph's car, switching her parcel to her left hand. She heard shouts and then the doors to the CDC crash open. Wrestling the car door open, she started to slide behind the wheel. She was so programmed for flight that it took a minute for her to realize that the passenger seat was occupied. There was also someone in the back. But worse was the sight of an enormous revolver pointing at her.

Marissa tried to reverse her direction, but it was as if

she were caught in a heavy, viscous fluid. Her body wouldn't respond. She saw the gun coming up at her, but she could do nothing. She saw a face in the half-light, and she heard someone start to say "good-bye." But the gun went off with a fearful concussion, and time stopped.

When Marissa regained consciousness, she was lying on something soft. Someone was calling her name. Slowly opening her eyes, she realized that she'd been carried back inside to the couch in the CDC lobby.

Flashing red and blue lights washed the room like a tawdry, punk discotheque. There seemed to be many people coming in and out of the room. It was too confusing. She closed her eyes again and wondered what had happened to the men with the guns.

"Marissa, are you all right?"

Her lids fluttered open, and she saw Dubchek bending over her, his dark eyes almost black with fear.

"Marissa," he said again. "Are you all right? I've been so worried. When you finally made us realize what was going on, we were afraid they'd try to kill you. But you never stayed still long enough for us to find you."

Marissa was still too shocked to speak.

"Please say something," Dubchek pleaded. "Did they hurt you?"

"I thought you were part of it. Part of the conspiracy," was all she could manage to utter.

"I was afraid of that," groaned Dubchek. "Not that I didn't deserve it. I was so busy protecting the CDC, I just dismissed your theories. But believe me, I had nothing to do with any of it."

Marissa reached for his hand. "I guess I never gave you much chance to explain, either. I was so busy breaking all the rules."

An ambulance attendant came up to them. "Does the lady want to go to the hospital?"

"Do you, Marissa?" asked Dubchek.

"I guess so, but I think I'm okay."

As another attendant came up to help lift her onto a stretcher, she said, "When I heard the first bang, I thought I'd been shot."

"No, one of the FBI men I'd alerted shot your would-be killer instead."

Marissa shuddered. Dubchek walked beside the stretcher as they took her to the ambulance. She reached out and took his hand.

Epilogue

MARISSA WAS UNPACKING FROM a two-week vacation, taken at Dr. Carbonara's insistence, when the doorbell rang. She had just returned from Virginia, where her family had done everything they could to spoil her, even giving her a new puppy that she'd immediately named Taffy Two.

As she walked downstairs, she couldn't imagine who might be at the door. She hadn't told anyone the exact date of her return. When she opened the door, she was surprised to see Cyrill Dubchek and a stranger.

"I hope you don't mind our turning up like this, but Dr. Carbonara said you might be home, and Dr. Fakkry from World Health wanted to meet you. This is his last day in America. Tonight he is flying back to Geneva."

The stranger stepped forward and dipped his head. Then he looked directly at Marissa. His eyes reminded her of Dubchek's: dark and liquid.

"I am deeply honored," said Dr. Fakkry, with a crisp, English accent. "I wanted to thank you personally for your brilliant detective work."

"And with no help from us," admitted Dubchek.

"I'm flattered," said Marissa, at a loss for words.

Dubchek cleared his throat. Marissa found his new lack of confidence appealing. When he wasn't making her furious, she could admit that he was actually very handsome.

"We thought you'd like to know what's been happening," he said. "The press has been given as little detail as possible, but even the police agree you are entitled to the truth."

"I'd love to hear everything," said Marissa. "But please come in and sit down. Can I get you something to drink?"

When they were settled, Dr. Fakkry said, "Thanks to you, almost everyone connected to the Ebola conspiracy has been arrested. The man you stabbed in San Francisco implicated Dr. Heberling the minute he recovered from surgery."

"The police think he wanted to be sent to jail so you couldn't find him again," said Dubchek, with a hint of his old sardonic grin.

Marissa shivered, remembering the terrible episode of stabbing the man in the bathroom at the Fairmont. For a moment the image of his ice-blue eyes froze her. Then, pulling herself together, she asked what had happened to Heberling.

"He'll be going before a grand jury on multiple counts of murder with intent," said Dubchek. "The judge refused to set bail, no matter how high, saying that he was as dangerous to society as the Nazi war criminals."

"And the man I hit with the vaccination gun?" Marissa had been afraid to ask this question. She didn't want to be responsible for killing anyone or for spreading Ebola.

"He'll live to stand trial. He did use the serum in time, and it proved effective, but he came down with a severe case of serum sickness. As soon as he's better, he'll also be off to jail."

"What about the other officers of the Physicians' Action Congress?" asked Marissa.

"A number of them have offered to turn state's evidence," said Dubchek. "It's making the investigation inordinately easy. We are beginning to believe that the regular members of the organization thought they were supporting just an ordinary lobbying campaign."

"What about Tieman? He certainly didn't seem the type to be mixed up in such an affair. Or at least his conscience really seemed to bother him."

"His lawyer has been making arrangements for a lighter sentence in return for his cooperation. As for PAC itself, the group's bankrupt. The families of the victims have almost all filed suit. They're also suing the doctors individually. Most of the officers are being prosecuted as criminals. So they should be behind bars a good while, particularly Jackson."

"He and Dr. Heberling would be—I think your word is lynched—if the public got ahold of them," added Dr. Fakkry.

"I guess Ralph will also be sentenced," Marissa said slowly. She was still trying to come to terms with the fact that the man she considered a protector had tried to kill her.

"He was one of the first to cooperate with the prosecution. He'll get some breaks, but I doubt he'll be released for a long time. Aside from his connection with PAC, he is directly linked to the attacks on you."

"I know," Marissa sighed. "So it's really over."

"Thanks to your persistence," said Dubchek. "And the outbreak in New York is definitely under control."

"Thank God," she said.

"So when will you be coming back to the CDC?" asked Dubchek. "We've already gotten you clearance for the maximum containment lab." This time there was no doubt about his grin. "No one relished the thought of your stumbling around in there at night anymore."

Marissa blushed in spite of herself. "I haven't decided yet. I'm actually considering going back into pediatrics."

"Back to Boston?" Dubchek's face fell.

"It will be a loss to the field," said Dr. Fakkry. "You've become an international epidemiological hero."

"I'll give it more thought," promised Marissa. "But even if I do go back to pediatrics, I'm planning to stay in Atlanta." She nuzzled her new puppy. There was a pause, then she added, "But I've one request."

"If we can be of any help . . ." said Dr. Fakkry.

Marissa shook her head. "Only Cyrill can help on this one. Whether I go back to pediatrics or not, I was hoping he'd ask me to dinner again."

Dubchek was taken off guard. Then, laughing at Fakkry's bemused expression, he leaned over and hugged Marissa to his side.

FROM #1 *NEW YORK TIMES* BESTSELLING AUTHOR

ROBIN COOK

CRITICAL

New York City medical examiners Laurie Montgomery and Jack Stapleton return in this stunning new novel from the "master of the medical thriller" (*The New York Times*)—a ripped-from-the-headlines tale of an innovative doctor's dangerous downward spiral.